Gunnison struck one more match and looked closely at the ruined face. Then, fighting off natural reticence to touch the dead body, he explored the jacket pockets.

Everything he found confirmed that the jacket was Kenton's. And the face, impossible to recognize as it was, certainly could have been that of Kenton. The general size of the body, the build and general physical character of it, all also matched Kenton's traits. Even the pistol holstered beneath the coat was Kenton's. Gunnison took it, tucking it under his belt, near his own pistol.

"Oh, Kenton," Gunnison whispered . . .

ST. MARTIN'S PAPERBACKS TITLES BY CAMERON JUDD

SNOW SKY

CORRIGAN

TIMBER CREEK

RENEGADE LAWMEN

THE HANGING AT LEADVILLE

DEVIL WIRE

BRAZOS

FIREFALL

THE UNDERHILL SERIES

THE GLORY RIVER

TEXAS FREEDOM

DEAD MAN'S GOLD

FIREFALL

CAMERON JUDD

St. Martin's Paperbacks

FIREFALL

ISBN: 0-312-97395-0

Printed in the United States of America

St. Martin's Paperbacks edition / March 2000

St. Martin's Paperbacks are published by St. Martin's Press, 175 Fifth Avenue, New York, N.Y. 10010.

10 9 8 7 6 5 4 3 2 1

To Marc Resnick,
with appreciation

CHAPTER ONE

ON AN EVENING IN JUNE OF 1884, IN A SMALL BUT INFAMOUS mining town high in the mountains of the Montana Territory, a ragged and whiskered drunkard named Forrest Peabody staggered toward the welcoming light of an open saloon door.

Peabody's left hand was pressed against the crown of his flop hat, protecting it from loss to a new, brisk wind. His right hand clutched the rope shoulder strap of a satchel he had made from an old feed sack, and carried at all times. In the satchel was his most prized possession: an old copy of the Bible, almost as worn out and rumpled as its owner.

Jed Bloom, a weary miner at the end of a long and unproductive day, sat smoking a meerschaum pipe outside his home, a structure consisting of framing and boards at the bottom and canvas at the top—half-house, half-tent. He eyed Peabody as the latter strode clumsily past.

"Good evening, Parson," Bloom said, with a slight tone of sarcasm. Peabody was usually called "Parson" in the town of Gomorrah. "Right windy weather this evening. The kind of wind that dries things out, and we're dry enough already. But I do believe a storm may blow up before morning . . . Lord willing."

Peabody, who was in a particularly testy mood, stopped and examined Bloom through a bleary, critical eye. "You call me 'Parson,' and you speak of the Lord, but you do both only in mockery," he said. "Always it's this way with you, every time you see me. God will judge you, Jed Bloom. Mark my words. He'll judge you, as He'll soon judge every mocker in this wicked town."

Bloom smiled around his pipestem, puffing smoke. He'd heard this refrain often from Peabody, who always saw divine judgment on its way. "Reckon?"

"You may be assured, sir."

"Now, why do you reckon the Lord would go judging me, a man who on his best day never professed to be no more than a common piece of human flotsam, when He's got such a stronger condemnation he can make in your case?"

"In *my* case? Explain yourself, sir," Peabody demanded sternly.

"Why, it ought to be evident! Here I am, a sinner who pretends to be nothing more than that, and there you are, just as great a sinner, but who claims to be a saint. So which of us is the most deserving of judgment, the man who is honest about what he is, or the one who pretends to be what he is not?"

"We are all sinners. The difference between us is that some of us are saved by God's grace, and others refuse that salvation," Peabody replied. "I don't refuse it."

"Yet you keep on drinking. Doesn't the Bible say that no drunkard will inherit the kingdom of God?" Bloom remembered this bit of information from Sunday meetings from his long-past boyhood.

"My drinking is medicinal, like the wine that Paul himself told Timothy to drink for the sake of his stomach. It is entirely appropriate when done for that purpose, and in moderation," answered Peabody.

Bloom laughed. "Moderation? You call getting skunk-drunk four nights out of five 'moderation'?"

"I do *not* get drunk, sir."

"Why, you're drunk right now! And you'll be drunker soon. It's the same nearly every night."

Peabody's intoxication would be evident to any who saw him, but Peabody had blinded himself to it. In his years of struggling between the faith that called him and the vice that ensnared him, Peabody had become expert in self-deception.

Lifting his thick brows, he said, "Beware, Mr. Bloom. When you mock the servant, you mock the master. And my master is the Almighty God Himself, the maker of the stars and the judge of men." He waved at the darkening sky, marked tonight by an abundance of shooting stars. Only the eastern half of the sky was visible, though; clouds were thickening in the western portion, spreading toward the east like a blanket slowly drawing over the sky.

Bloom shook his head and drew the last puff out of his pipe bowl, then knocked the ashes out on the ground. He was tired and fast losing interest in Peabody. "Sorry if I've offended you, Parson. But take some advice from me, if you would: If you're going to go on harping at people about their own sorry ways, at least show some sign you know how to live the way you ought to yourself. People at least will respect that. Like the preacher McCree, you know. I don't go to his preaching services, don't pretend to follow his religion, but I do respect the man. There's nothing false about him."

Mention of McCree made Peabody bristle. "I think I have the respect of this town as much as Mr. McCree," he said. For Peabody, McCree was always "mister," no ministerial title attached. Peabody, though unordained and unschooled, viewed himself as the only legitimate preacher in Gomorrah, McCree as a pretender to the throne.

"Parson, pardon my free speaking, but you're not respected by nobody. You're held as a laughingstock."

"Why are you saying such hateful things, Mr. Bloom?"

Bloom sighed. "I don't know. It's of no consequence to me, really. Ah, just go on with you. Forget what I said. Have yourself a good evening. I'm going to turn in."

Peabody hitched his satchel strap into a more comfortable position. "I forgive your mockery, Mr. Bloom. You know not what you do. But God may not forgive you! His patience with you and the wickedness in this town is approaching its end!" With a dramatic toss of his head, he headed for the saloon. Peabody always liked to end his conversations with a dramatic flourish.

Bloom refilled the pipe and watched Peabody stagger off, the pouch and the hidden Bible swinging at his side.

"Takes all kinds, I guess," he muttered. He rose slowly and entered his dwelling.

Another shooting star fired north to south across the eastern sky. Off in the west, thunder rumbled and the clouds continued their slow eastward creep.

Peabody had just reached the saloon door when a man came bursting out toward him, moving clumsily sideways with legs and arms flailing as he struggled to keep his balance. He might have succeeded had Peabody not been where he was. The man collided with Peabody. Both of them collapsed, limbs entangling. Peabody dropped his satchel and had the wind knocked out of him as the other man's elbow rammed him hard in the upper belly.

"Damn!" the man bellowed at Peabody. "*You* again! Are you to always be in my way?"

The man was Gibbon Rankin, known to his few friends as Gib and to most others by names that would not be spoken in decent society—not that Gomorrah had enough decent society for it to matter.

A burly saloonkeeper named Decker Smith, who had just evicted Rankin forcibly from his establishment, threw out a deck of cards after him. They scattered and rained down around Rankin and Peabody.

"There's your marked deck, Mr. Gib Rankin, and if you know what's good for you, you'll bring it into my place of business no more! I'll not have cheating within my walls."

Peabody found his breath again. "Get off me!" he gasped at Rankin.

Rankin was already struggling to disengage himself. He pushed up and away from Peabody, dusting himself off like he'd been fouled by touching the man.

It wasn't the first time the pair had literally run into one another in almost this same manner. A week before, Peabody had stumbled around a corner and right into Rankin. Both had managed to keep their footing that time, but Rankin had given Peabody a cursing, and Peabody had given Rankin a sermon in turn.

Peabody got up and shook his clothing back into place. He picked up his dropped Bible pouch, brushed it off, and slung it over his shoulder. Like an offended king, he stepped toward the saloon door, ready to enter.

The saloonkeeper, along with a crowd of patrons who'd gathered in the doorway behind him, craning their necks to look out, blocked him. "And where do you think you're going, Parson?" Decker Smith asked.

Peabody, puzzled, stepped back. "Inside. I'm feeling poorly. I need a tonic."

"No. No more 'tonic' for you here. New rules in this house: no more cheating gamblers, and no more drinking preachers, especially those who run up tabs they can't pay. Spelled out clearly, that means no more of you, Gib Rankin, and no more of you, Parson."

The rabble behind Decker Smith raised a cheer at his words. Most of them despised Rankin and Peabody equally. Besides, a good confrontation was always entertaining to watch in any situation.

"Throw 'em out of town!" someone called. "Send both of 'em down the mountain!"

Similar cries arose, and out of the saloon the half-drunk miners spilled out the doorway past Smith. They encircled

Peabody and Rankin. Both had been burrs under the saddles of most men of Gomorrah, in their distinctive ways. Rankin, the gambler, had cheated more than a few men, and Peabody, the preacher, had thrown unwanted, hypocritical sermons into too many faces, too many times.

Rankin idly picked at a tooth with the nail of his little finger and tried to look above it all. Parson Peabody, not as suave, glared around at the encircling men, disbelieving, and quite offended that he, a man of God, would be treated so shabbily.

"Let's take them out and beat the hell out of both of them!" suggested one of the drunker miners. "And go fetch Rankin's partners—we'll beat the hell out of them, too!"

This suggestion caught fire quickly. Several men advanced threateningly, eager for violence.

Parson Peabody stumbled back, lips moving without words, face going white.

"Hold! Hold on here!" a voice with a noticeable Scottish lilt called from outside the circle and back on the street.

Every man turned to look.

A gray-haired man, clad in gray, pushed through and stood between Rankin and Peabody, hands lifted. This was James McCree, Scotsman and clergyman of a far more conventional variety than was Forrest Peabody. He was a minister assigned to preach the gospel to a raucous mining town—not a position designed to gain him many friends in Gomorrah. But he'd proven himself a strong and good man, and therefore enjoyed influence and respect even among the rowdy and profane element that had given the town its wicked reputation, and its name. But he was everything that "Parson" Forrest Peabody was not and secretly wanted to be, and therefore Peabody despised him.

"Reverend, this is none of your concern," Decker Smith said.

"It's my concern indeed when I hear men talking, and

seemingly quite seriously, about hauling men away to 'beat the hell' out of them," McCree replied. "What's going on here?"

"I'll tell you, sir!" one man said, stepping up to face McCree. "What's going on is that we're all damned tired of Rankin and his marked decks and his bottom-dealing! And we're tired as well of being harped upon by this whiskey-guzzling scripture-spouter, too!" He waved contemptuously at Peabody. "The idea has come up to run these scoundrels out of town, and I, for one, favor the notion strongly."

The crowd, growing as the hubbub attracted attention, rumbled its approval, and surged toward Rankin, Peabody, and McCree.

Rankin's hand crept toward the inside of his coat and the hidden pistol he always carried. But he didn't dare actually produce it among a group of hostile men, some of whom also carried hidden pistols, and so he wound up frozen in a Napoleonic pose that only made him look all the more haughty.

McCree lifted his hands again. "Hold! Hold! If we're to throw out these scoundrels, let's at least do it in the right fashion."

Decker Smith, after a moment of stunned silence, said, "You *agree* to running these two out of town, Reverend?"

"Of course I do. Why shouldn't I? Rankin and his partners have lowered the moral climate of this place since they arrived—and lowering the moral climate of Gomorrah is no small achievement. And Peabody there, poor fellow, does nothing but make a mockery out of a faith that I take seriously. I'd be glad to see them go. But I want no talk of beating! Let's do this as civilized men."

For once, the Reverend McCree had the full attention of the hard-drinking miners of Gomorrah: a state of affairs he'd never really expected to see. But it didn't last long.

"Look there!" one of the crowd yelled, pointing.

"There's Rankin's *compadres* right yonder!"

Thomas Shafter and Otto Dorner, perpetual companions of Rankin and of his moral ilk, were walking cautiously toward the crowd, curious about what was happening. With them was a woman, usually seen at Rankin's side instead of theirs.

She had been beautiful once; shadows of it remained even yet, particularly in those rare moments when she smiled. Her age was hard to determine, but she'd left her girlhood behind long ago. She'd come to town with Rankin, Shafter, and Dorner, but had seemed attached to Rankin in particular. Seldom speaking and with dark, often-averted eyes that suggested mystery, she was an object of curiosity in Gomorrah. Because of her dark hair and complexion, she was sometimes called "the Gypsy" by the miners. Rankin himself called her "Princess," and most assumed she was his lover, maybe even his wife.

The three newcomers were quickly swept in by the miners; they, and Rankin, were pushed into the center of the circle.

"Tar and feather them all!" one man suggested. "Ride them on a rail out of town!"

"No need for tar and feathers," Reverend McCree said. "We're civilized men here. We'll send them out of town, never to return. That's good enough."

Peabody threw back his head. "Am I to understand you want to run me out of this town . . . with *them*?" He gestured at Rankin and companions.

"I'm glad you comprehend our position with such clarity of mind, Parson Peabody," McCree said, smiling.

Peabody snorted. "And you claim to be a representative of the Most High! If you were what you pretend to be, you'd recognize a fellow man of the Lord!"

"And if you were what you claim, you'd not live the life of a common drunkard," McCree replied. Then, to the group around him, he said, “In the name of God and common decency, men, let’s send these scoundrels on their way! But do show the woman the respect due her sex.”

With a roar of agreement, the drunken raff of Gomorrah, led by, of all things, a minister, grasped their victims, and in one great group, herded them toward the road that led down the mountain and out of town.

CHAPTER TWO

PARSON PEABODY WAS LIVID. HE'D NEVER FELT SO INSULTED, so misused.

The worst was not the eviction itself. Peabody knew that prophets were often excluded and persecuted. The worst was that these men seemed to view him as on a level no higher than Rankin and his partners, who were human vermin if ever Peabody had seen them. It was insulting, very nearly blasphemous. But for now he held his peace, determined to follow the biblical example and be led away with a quiet dignity, like a sheep to slaughter.

With McCree at their head, the gang of miners prodded their victims out of town and down the long road that led to the ridge-and-valley region below, filled with ranches, then eventually on to Fort Brandon, a military outpost some miles away.

Rankin was clearly infuriated by this ouster, his usual bland dignity losing hold. "This is outrageous!" he bellowed. "I can't leave Gomorrah now—I'm awaiting an important meeting!"

"I don't think anyone is listening to you, Mr. Rankin," McCree said.

"But I'm to meet a very important journalist soon! Brady Kenton himself!" Rankin went on. "Damnation, man, it's taken me a long time and lot of effort to arrange this meeting, and now I'm to be deprived of it! Look, I can prove what I say is true—I have a wire from him, right here in my pocket!"

"No one is interested," McCree said.

"This is outrageous! Utterly unfair!"

"It's a difficult life we all must lead," McCree said.

"Damn you, psalm-singer, you don't understand the problem you're creating for me! If I miss this meeting, then I may lose my chance to—"

Peabody tripped and fell with a loud grunt, drawing all attention away from Rankin.

McCree reached down and offered Peabody a hand.

Peabody, overcome by temper, refused it and rose by himself. He faced the group, and in the dimming light of dusk, leveled his finger at them and all but shouted into their faces.

"In the name of God, I shake the dust of your wicked town from my feet! In the name of God, I declare to you that the Lord is not mocked, and will not forgive this sin against his servant!"

McCree said, "Oh, Peabody, do be quiet. Don't embarrass yourself!"

Peabody was like a man transformed. He turned and aimed his finger into McCree's face. "You, you false prophet, you mocker of the true speaker of God's voice, you jealous liar, you Pharisee . . . all that awaits you is the fire of God's judgment. This night you will be destroyed! This night your soul will be required of you!"

McCree, despite his utter disbelief in anything Peabody had to say, was nevertheless somewhat taken aback by this unexpectedly venemous outburst. Peabody spoke so intensely that his words carried a surprising sense of weight.

"This is nonsense," muttered Rankin.

Peabody wasn't finished. He looked around the group as a whole, swinging that trembling finger.

"This night the fire of God will fall! Like the Gomorrah

of old, this town will burn with a fire like that of hell itself! If you are wise, you will flee . . . you will flee now!"

Now McCree grew angry. It was an affront to all decency that such a worm as Peabody should actually pretend to prophesy in the name of God.

"Hush this chatter, Peabody! Away with you!" McCree said, his Scottish accent intensifying in his anger. "All of you, get away from this town! Don't return!"

"Flee!" Peabody shouted. "Flee from the wrath of God!"

Rankin rolled his eyes. "God help us," he muttered.

Peabody seemed to shrink all at once, as if all his energy had just drained from him. "Yes," he said, suddenly no longer wrought-up. "God help us indeed."

The sky gave forth an appropriately thunderous rumble.

Rankin said, "Well, if we're to go, let's go." To his partners he whispered, "And let's see if we can't leave this drunken babbler behind."

They set off down the road, into the gathering darkness.

Peabody stayed put. He seemed deflated and tired.

"You must go, too," McCree said quietly to him.

Peabody, no longer argumentative, began to stagger off down the road after Rankin and his companions.

"Don't come back!" McCree called after him.

Peabody's form vanished in the dark. McCree, feeling somber, and the rough group behind him—oddly sober all at once—stared after Peabody before turning and walking slowly back up into Gomorrah.

"We did a good thing then, running them off," one of them said.

"We did," Reverend McCree said. "I really do think so. Don't you all agree?"

Nobody had anything more to say.

Since boyhood, Peabody had never liked the dark. It was part of the reason that saloons had always held such an appeal for him: they were lighted refuges, places of safety and enclosure when the world was dark.

Now only the darkness enclosed him, and it was growing darker by the moment. The clouds had spread over almost all of the sky by now. There was an electric feeling in the air, the rumbling of thunder. Back in Gomorrah there was light, warmth, liquor . . . but Peabody couldn't return to it.

Strangely, though, he wasn't sure he really wanted to go back. He'd actually managed to frighten himself with that little outburst of his. He'd been angry when he spoke, and he was able to admit, at least to himself in this dark isolation, that when his emotions were aroused he was capable of spouting all sorts of nonsense, spiced up with religious-sounding words.

His prophecy of the destruction of Gomorrah wasn't the first one of its sort he'd voiced in dire circumstances. He'd once declared in a moment of public rage that the city of Denver would be washed away by a flood. Everyone had laughed, Denver had of course survived, and he'd made himself look like a fool.

Now he'd done it again. Fire from heaven! Why had he said such a thing?

Feeling weary and lonely and desirous of liquor, he wondered how far ahead Rankin and his companions were. As much as he despised Rankin, just now the company of anyone at all would be pleasant. The dark mountain road was fearsome, rousing in him boyish kinds of passing-the-graveyard terrors, making the wind whisper threats and danger in his ears. And he knew Rankin sometimes carried a flask.

"Mr. Rankin?" he called to the darkness ahead. "It's Peabody . . . can you hear me?"

No one replied to him.

He walked forward, moving faster. "Mr. Rankin! It's me, Peabody! I'd like to ask if you'd let me walk with you, at least as far as the first town! I'll be no bother! I'll keep my mouth shut, I promise!"

He was sure they were close enough to hear him, but they refused to answer.

"Please, Mr. Rankin! There's sometimes highwaymen along these roads. I'm frightened, having to walk alone."

Rankin's voice came back through the darkness. "Let Jesus walk with you, then. I got no desire for your company."

It was at that moment that the sky burst into something like brilliant flame, streaking from west to east, illuminating the entire bank of storm clouds very eerily, brighter than any lightning ever could. It happened with no warning signs at all.

Peabody dropped to his knees.

The flare in the sky revealed to him Rankin and his companions, far ahead, looking back in his direction. They were ducking, lifting their hands to cover their heads, hiding from that burst of light that was nearly as bright as noonday despite the clouds.

A hot, downdraft wind struck Peabody. Back up the mountain, Gomorrah exploded in fire.

Peabody didn't see the actual moment of destruction. He was turned the wrong direction for that. But he felt it.

The ground shook; a wind of nearly tornadic force bent trees toward the ground as if they were sticks. A brilliant orange-yellow light from the ignited mountaintop illuminated the forest. A wall of heated air struck Peabody, knocking him forward, rolling him down the trail toward Rankin and his companions.

By the time he reached the place they had been, they were no longer there. The same searing swell had caught them, too, only half a moment after Peabody, and pushed them away before it like bits of driftwood on the crest of a wave.

Peabody struck a boulder and stopped, stunned, as the wind swept over him, so hot he feared his skin would blister.

He groaned and rolled, looking back toward Gomorrah.

"Almighty God, save me!" he prayed, awed and terrified.

Rubble began to rain down around Peabody. Twigs, sticks, evergreen boughs severed as if by a large bomb, even fragments of flaming lumber and other bits and pieces of Gomorrah, all of them flaming, peppered all around him and on him, burning him, setting blazes on the forest floor.

Peabody could scarcely breathe; the air had suddenly grown too hot.

"Lord have mercy on me, a sinner . . . Lord have mercy on me, a sinner . . ."

He turned his back to Gomorrah and pulled himself into a fetal position, lying up against the boulder with his face buried in his arms. He continued to pray fervently as Gomorrah burned behind him.

CHAPTER THREE

BELOW, GIB RANKIN, STUNNED AND COVERED WITH DIRT AND ash, rose up on his forearms and stared up the mountain at the flames engulfing Gomorrah and much of the mountainside around and below it. For half a minute he simply gazed, then said, aloud, "How did he know? How could he have possibly known?"

He heard a feminine moan behind him. Twisting his head, he saw Princess rising, as stunned and bewildered as he, shaking her head as if to clear her vision, and digging grit from her ears.

"What was it?" she said. "What just happened?"

"Fire," Rankin said. "A fire just came down from the sky."

"The sky?"

"That's right. Fire from heaven."

She hesitated, then said, "So he was right? That crazy preacher really *knew*?"

"So it would seem."

"He really is a prophet, then?"

"Maybe. Or maybe it's for him like it is for me at the faro table: you get lucky sometimes."

Rankin stared deeply into the boiling flames up at Gomorrah. The town was burning fiercely. The forest was ablaze, too, but because most of the trees had been knocked flat as they ignited, their flames burned low to the ground.

The few trees that did remain standing flared magnificently, like great torches.

Thomas Shafter appeared from behind, staggering out of the darkness into the light of the burning trees all around. He was stunned, filthy, his face blackened, maybe outright burned. "Otto's dead," he said. "He's lying over there, dead. Big old tree blew over right on him. He's dead. Dead!"

"Sorry to hear it," Rankin said. "I rather liked old Otto." His distracted, unemotional tone of voice betrayed just how shallow his affection for Otto Dorner really had been.

"What the hell happened up there, Gib?"

"The fire of God fell," Princess said. "That drunk preacher said the fire of God would fall, and it did."

"I'll be damned!"

Rankin shook his head. "Nope. Not yet you're not. We're still alive. And maybe Peabody is living, too. I heard him call right before the fire came." He looked at the sky, and listened as he heard a very distant roll of thunder. "Hear that? Storm building up. That should put out the worst of the fire. Maybe the Lord's smiting Gomorrah with one hand and soothing it with the other. Come on . . . let's go see if we can find Peabody."

"Hell with him!" Shafter said. "Why do you care about him?"

"I'm just a naturally tender-hearted soul," Rankin replied. He brushed himself off and headed back up the mountain, toward the flaming town.

A huge bolt of lightning flashed nearby and thunder exploded loudly, startling all of them. Rankin quickly noted to himself, though, that the lightning bolt, as powerful as it was, seemed pitiful compared to what had happened above Gomorrah. Clearly whatever had struck before had been something much more powerful than lightning.

Rankin walked fast, Princess and Shafter following because it was always their way to follow him.

* * *

They found Peabody still huddled against the boulder, hiding his face. "I'll never drink anymore, Lord," he was saying. "I'll never taste another drop."

Rankin knelt beside Peabody and pulled a flask from beneath his coat. "Here you go, preacher. Something to make you feel better."

Peabody looked at the flask glinting in the light of the fire, licked his lips once, and reached out for it. He turned it up. His Adam's apple bobbed up and down.

Rankin took the flask away and repocketed it. "Glad to find you alive, Parson. Or maybe we ought to call you 'Prophet' now. Because it sure happened just like you said it would."

"I didn't know," Peabody said. "I swear, I didn't know. I was just talking when I said all that. I didn't know the fire would really fall!"

"Why, sure you knew!" Rankin said. "You said it would happen, and it did. Likelihood is, you *caused* it to happen, Parson."

"I didn't cause it! I didn't!"

"Well, something, or somebody, sure did. And I didn't hear anybody else making predictions. You've got the power to tell what's coming, Parson. A gift from God, for you to use."

"I don't want that gift! I don't! Can I have another drink?"

"Surely."

When Rankin pocketed the flask again, he said, "Parson Peabody, I want to follow you."

"What?"

"I want to follow you. Be around you. Help you with your work. Be sort of a disciple for you."

"A disciple . . ."

"You've got the gift, Prophet. Whether you want it or not. It's something you ought to use."

"But I didn't do nothing! I didn't!"

Rankin put his face close to Peabody's. The reflected firelight gave his eyes a piercing glitter. "There are those in Gomorrah, if any are left alive, who would be hard-pressed to believe that. They'll believe in you. So will plenty of others who hear about this."

"Do you think they all died up there?"

"Let's go up and see."

They proceeded up to the edge of the flaming town. By now they could see that there were indeed survivors. They staggered through the desolated streets like damned souls in some medieval saint's fevered fantasy of eternal suffering.

Many more people had not survived. Burned bodies lay all about—smoking, blackened husks that had been living people minutes before.

Rankin made a face of disgust as he eyed the corpses. It looked as if the dead had been nearly incinerated in a virtual flash.

He felt something that wasn't common for him: a sense of quick panic, a feeling that he was contacting something here big and incomprehensible, maybe dangerous . . .

What if Parson Peabody really *had* somehow foreseen this? Could a divine hand truly have smitten this town, just like its biblical namesake had been smitten centuries before?

Whoa, Gibbon Rankin. Get control of yourself, friend. Don't start thinking that way. Whatever caused this, it's probably nothing you can control. Maybe nothing you can even understand . . . but even if you can't understand it, that doesn't mean it's nothing you can't use.

Peabody looked around, eyes wide, taking each step with the care of a man walking among upturned nails. Nearly every building was aflame. The ground itself was hot beneath his feet, like hell was trying to break through from below.

He saw the burning remnants of the dwelling of Jed Bloom. The canvas top was burned fully away, the timber portion smoldering. Drawn to it, he looked over the wall, then felt weak and disgusted as a lightning flash combined with the light of the burning town itself to reveal to him what remained of Bloom. He turned and lurched away, wishing he hadn't looked.

His own words came back to him: *God will judge you, Jed Bloom . . . He'll judge you, as He'll soon judge every mocker in this wicked town.*

"I'm sorry, Mr. Bloom," he said. "I didn't know it would really come true."

Princess, tears streaming down her face, was staying close to Rankin. The bodies appalled her, as did even the living people, all of whom were terrified, most of whom were at least to some measure burned.

She pleaded with Rankin, whose sweaty, ash-dusted face glowed and glistened in the light of the many fires all around. "Take me away from here, please, Gib! This is a terrible place!"

Rankin's own thoughts were elsewhere, as his answer revealed. "I'll bet you that when that fire fell, they could see it for miles and miles. I'll bet you they could see it all the way to Fort Brandon."

"Please!" she begged. "I don't want to be here. Let's go away from here!"

"Word's going to spread fast about this," Rankin said. "Look . . . people are fleeing the town already. They'll talk about this. This thing's going to become known across the country."

"Gib, please!"

"Hush, woman. There's still things to be done here."

Peabody had moved far away from Bloom's burning dwelling. He walked slowly, looking around at the flames, stepping aside when hurt survivors tottered by, and recoiling from the dead he found at his feet.

A hand gripped his elbow tightly. He turned and saw McCree, burned terribly, face already peeling. "You *are* surely a prophet!" McCree said in the tone of a man delirious from pain. "Forgive me . . . forgive me for not having recognized you for what you are!"

McCree's face was awful to see. As he spoke, his burned lips kept trying to stick together, fluid oozing from the deep and terrible cracks in them that the heat had caused. Peabody, full of both horror and pity, could hardly bear to look at him. He'd always despised and envied McCree. Now he only felt the deepest pity for him, and oddly responsible for the man's pathetic condition.

"I was just talking, that's all. Just talking! I didn't have nothing to do with this!"

"You are a prophet . . . of the Most High God."

"I'm a drunk. That's all. That's all I've ever been. Just a drunk. You know that! You've always said it yourself!"

Lightning crackled and the wind rose. It would be raining soon, drenching the flaming town and quelling the forest fire before it could spread to the dry mountains around.

"A prophet . . ." McCree looked around; other Gomorrah survivors who had been among the group that threw out Rankin and company, and who had therefore heard Peabody's prophecy, were beginning to notice Peabody. They circled around him just they had encircled him earlier at the saloon door. Now, though, they looked at him with awe and fear instead of disgust.

"A prophet . . . of the Most High," McCree said. Then he shuddered, collapsed, and died at Peabody's feet.

Peabody, overwhelmed and scared, burst through the surrounding circle, ran off alone, and was sick on the ground.

When he straightened, he saw Rankin walking toward him. "I don't want to be here," Peabody said to the gambler. "I don't like this place now."

Rankin said not a word, but got down on his knees and knelt before Peabody, bowing his head. "I repent," Rankin said, loudly, so all would hear. "I've been a sinful man, and you have spoken the word of God. I turn away from my wicked life and recognize you for what you are: a man of God."

Others drew near the gambler, watching what he was doing. Then, one by one, they knelt beside him, paying homage to the prophet.

CHAPTER FOUR

"WATCH OUT, YOU YOUNG FOOL!"

The shout, delivered in a coarse and unpleasant voice, was all but lost in the clatter of wagon wheels. Alex Gunnison scrambled out of the way of the speeding wagon just in time, fell at the edge of the boardwalk, dropped his carpetbag, and twisted his head in time to see his wife's precious letter, in which he'd been engrossed for the fifteenth time that day, fall under the wheels. It was smeared into the moist dirt street by the front wagon wheel and shredded by the rear one.

The driver, a freighter who'd just unloaded his wagonload and was speeding off with utter unconcern for public safety, hollered some foul words across his shoulder at Gunnison and was gone in a great rumble.

Gunnison stood, slipped in a previously unnoticed heap of fresh horse dung, and promptly fell again, across his own well-stuffed carpetbag.

He reddened as onlookers on the boardwalk laughed.

Hard-hearted town, he thought. *First they try to run you down in the street, then laugh at you for surviving.*

He stood, successfully this time, and looked at the ruined letter with a sad sigh. A thought that was becoming more frequent passed through his mind again: *The life I lead is not one for a married man.*

He retrieved the tattered letter, not because it was in any shape to keep, but because he didn't want some stranger picking up its fragments and reading the intimacies his beloved wife, far away in St. Louis, had written to him.

Picking up his carpetbag and hat, he strode on toward the railroad station. Turning a corner, he passed a church just as the doors opened and a crowd surged out, all smiles and cheerfulness. A moment later, through their midst, a bride and groom emerged. Gunnison paused to watch the celebration, and smiled as the bride paused to kiss a man, evidently her father, on his whiskered cheek.

Gunnison began to feel even more dejected. He longed to see his own wife. He sadly fingered the ruined letter in his pocket.

What kind of profession was this traveling journalist business, anyway? For the sake of *Gunnison's Illustrated American*, America's most popular national magazine—the creation and namesake of publishing magnate J.B. Gunnison, Alex Gunnison's own father—Alex Gunnison was spending more days of his precious young manhood away from his beloved wife than with her. Their most frequent contact was through letters and wires.

At the time of his own wedding, the plan had been for him to give up his life as assistant and professional shadow for the famous, eccentric Brady Kenton, America's best-known writer/illustrator and the single greatest asset of the *Illustrated American.*

It hadn't worked out that way. Gunnison was nearly five years into his marriage, and still traveling the country with Kenton, doing his best to keep up with him, and when possible, to keep him out of trouble. Both jobs were difficult at best.

He should never have let Kenton talk him into staying on this long. It was all Kenton's fault—Kenton and his blasted persuasiveness.

Making Gunnison's life all the harder was Kenton's tendency to wander off by himself, leaving Gunnison alone and clueless to try to figure out where he had gone, and why. It was no way for a man to treat a partner. Yet it was so much a part of the life routine of Brady Kenton that Gunnison had come to expect it.

Its familiarity made it no less annoying, though. At times like this, abandoned by the man who was supposed to be his professional partner and tutor, Gunnison could very nearly hate Brady Kenton. How many elaborate showers of abuse had he rehearsed, honed, polished, to heap upon the man when next he saw him? But he knew he wouldn't. As always, when he saw Kenton next, he'd be glad to see him. Anger would give way to relief, and they'd go on as before, through the same familiar, obnoxious cycle.

Mere days ago, he had been with Kenton in eastern Montana, working on what was to Gunnison a rather boring story about ranching, when Kenton had vanished. He'd received a batch of mail forwarded to him from the *Illustrated American* home office. Kenton went through it, turned brooding and moody and incommunicative all at once—a mood that alternated, oddly, with barely restrained bursts of excitement. Kenton had studied one letter intently, over and over, and jotted down notes on every available scrap of paper. He drank a little too much, too, as he sometimes did in times of depression or excitement.

Then, before Gunnison knew it, Kenton was gone.

Once Gunnison realized that Kenton had abandoned him yet again, he began the search-and-follow process that had led him this far. Some of Kenton's left-behind scribbled notes gave him the lead he needed. Gunnison had taken the train west.

As best Gunnison could ascertain from the notes, Kenton was headed for the mountains and the mining town of Gomorrah, southwest of where Gunnison was now, to meet a man who had written to him, promising some valuable information.

What that information purported to concern astonished Gunnison so much, though, he could hardly believe he was rightly interpreting the notes.

"Well, well! It's Alex Gunnison himself! I do believe my eyes haven't deceived me!"

The voice from behind, unexpected and instantly identifiable by its slightly high pitch and subtle Irish accent, made Gunnison cringe. He turned reflexively, too quickly to hide his expression of surprise.

The sight of Paul Callon's grinning face, ruddy and broad, topped with curling dark hair and framed by thick sideburns, greeted him. Callon advanced, hand outthrust, small eyes moving quickly, sizing up and evaluating Alex Gunnison from head to toe.

Gunnison knew what Callon was doing: He was examining him for any possible clues about why he might be here in Greer City—a map or train ticket sticking out of a pocket, perhaps, clothing freshly rumpled in the back to indicate recent long travel on train or stage, the amount and type of dirt on his shoes, and so on.

Callon fancied himself an expert in observation and deduction. He overrated his detective skills, but as a journalist for the *National Observor and Gallery*, a publication that fought hard for market inroads against the *Illustrated American,* was a talented and formidable competitor. He was an excellent writer, one of the nation's most skilled illustrators, and a work-alone reporter with the aggressiveness of a rabid dog. Everyone associated with the *Illustrated American,* including Gunnison, wished he'd find a new line of work.

Nevertheless, there were professional courtesies to maintain, civilized men and all that sort of thing. Gunnison put out his own hand. "Paul, good to see you," he lied with a smile.

"Ah, yes. Always a pleasure when our paths cross," Callon lied right back, pumping Gunnison's hand with vigor. "But I must say I'm not surprised to see you. You're on your way to Gomorrah, no doubt."

Gunnison was surprised. "Well . . . yes. I am. Are you?"

"Oh, certainly. Astonishing, isn't it? Have you any theories about how to explain it?"

"Explain it?"

"Yes. What do you think it is? What caused it?"

"Caused it . . ."

Callon laughed. "Are you going to repeat everything I say, Alex?"

"No. No . . . I'm sorry." He surrendered. Time to confess. "Paul, I'm afraid I have no idea what you're talking about."

Callon cocked a brow. "Then why are you going to Gomorrah?"

"To find Brady Kenton. I think he's already gone there."

Callon's face fell. "Kenton is in Gomorrah?"

"I have reason to think so."

"Blast it all! I'd hoped I could, at the least, be among the first journalists there."

"Paul, obviously something has happened at Gomorrah that I don't know about."

Callon seemed stunned to hear Gunnison say this. "You mean you actually haven't heard about the Gomorrah incident?"

"No, I admit I haven't."

"Well, surely Kenton has—why else would he have gone there?"

"Personal reasons, I think."

Callon looked condescendingly smug. "And he didn't take you with him. He's abandoned you like this before, hasn't he?"

There was no point in trying to cover up what was, unfortunately, a well-known truth within Gunnison's professional circles. "Yes. Several places. Dodge, Leadville . . ."

Callon suddenly grew serious. "Alex, how long has Kenton been in Gomorrah?"

"I don't really know. He could have been there a couple of days, I suppose. Why?"

Callon blanched. "Oh, my. Competitor though he may be, I'm not happy to hear that. I hope he's all right."

Gunnison stepped forward and grabbed Callon by the collar. "What do you mean, 'all right'? Why shouldn't he be? Exactly what happened at Gomorrah?"

Callon, stunned by Gunnison's aggressiveness, said, "There was a fire. A very big one . . . many people killed. If Kenton was there . . ."

"A fire?" Gunnison let go of Callon. "Is that all? Well, I would think Kenton would certainly have every chance of holding his own in a fire."

"This was no ordinary fire. It was more an explosion. Very big. Very."

"What kind of explosion?"

"That's the very question I hope to answer. It's the one I assumed you were going to Gomorrah to answer yourself."

"A bomb of some sort, you think?"

"From the sound of what I've heard, it would have to be one very big bomb."

"Where did you hear about this?"

"Rumors, really. Second-hand talk. But I know for a fact that there have been people who have come out of Gomorrah, telling a whale of a story. They say that fire fell from the sky, burned the town, killed most of the residents, and exploded all across the mountaintop night before last."

"Fire from the sky?" Gunnison laughed heartily.

Callon glared at him. "You think it's just a wild story. Maybe it is. But the rumors are persistent. I think there's something to it. It's at least worth investigating."

"Pardon me if I find the notion of fire from above a little hard to swallow."

"Then don't go to Gomorrah. Leave the story to me."

"I'm going to Gomorrah, but I'm not chasing some sort of absurd story. I need to find Kenton. I hope there's a train line leading to Gomorrah. I was on my way to the station to find out."

"I'm ahead of you on that one. I'm afraid there is no rail line up Gomorrah Mountain."

Gunnison sighed. Bad news. "A stagecoach, then?"

"Cheer up. There's no rail line up the mountain, but there is a new spur line that goes to the base of it."

"Good." Gunnison put on a false smile. "So I suppose you and I are going to be traveling partners for a spell."

"So it appears." Callon smiled right back, just as fulsomely.

CHAPTER FIVE

THE *ILLUSTRATED AMERICAN*, COMPARED TO THE *NATIONAL Observor and Gallery*, was by far the better and more established publication, and Callon and Gunnison both knew it. But one advantage the *National Observor and Gallery* did possess: an exceptionally fine print quality, which resulted in a publication filled with wonderfully detailed, crisp illustrations, the best of them created by Callon himself.

As he sat beside Gunnison in the rocking and rumbling train car, Callon flipped through a recent edition of the *Observor*, pointing out the wonderful clarity of the pictures and the best stories, and making sure to mention those that the *Observor* had published but the *Illustrated American* had missed.

"Paul, the *Illustrated American* is not some small-town newspaper, trying to publish every item of news before the paper across the street gets it," Gunnison said defensively. "The *Illustrated American* is a reader's magazine, intended not so much to break out new information for the first time as to explore it and expound upon it for the benefit of the discerning reader who wants more than superficial information." The line wasn't really Gunnison's; he'd heard Kenton use it many times.

"Nonsense," Callon replied. "You and I know full well that the *Illustrated American* has always prided itself on beating out its competition. And it's done well at it so far.

But now that *we're* in the business"—he rattled the tabloid-sized newspaper in his hand—"it's going to be increasingly difficult for the *Illustrated American* to retain that distinction." He grinned that familiar, smug grin that always made Gunnison want to backhand him. "You know, had I not been so sure when I saw you that you already knew about the fire-fall at Gomorrah, I'd not have mentioned the matter to you. And the *Illustrated American* probably would have missed the story altogether."

"Not with Kenton already there. If there's a story to be had, he's probably already got it written and ready to wire in, and illustrations already in the mail."

Callon said, "I almost hope you're right, believe it or not. I want Kenton to be alive and well. As much as I compete with the man professionally, I do like him. I don't want harm to come to him."

"You really *believe* this fire-from-heaven story, don't you?"

"I believe *something* happened. Rumors usually have some sort of basis."

"Well, whatever happened, you can be sure Kenton's not harmed. Brady Kenton has survived more dangers and adventures already than most men encounter in several life-times. He's told me stories from his war years that would send ice down your spine."

"He was a spy for the Union, right?"

"You could call him that. I do know he was involved in very covert, behind-the-scenes intelligence, sabotage, and so on."

"He reported directly to Lincoln himself, I've heard."

"At times."

"Remarkable man, Brady Kenton."

"Indeed he is."

Callon paused, thinking. "I'm not wanting to be pessimistic or morbid here, but as famous as Kenton is, it would be big news in itself if something did happen to him."

This was fully true. Kenton was indeed one of the most famous traveling journalists in the nation. His picture ran in every edition of the *Illustrated American*, and people everywhere knew his name, face, and work. Within the past couple of years, the *Illustrated American* had begun publishing in book form collections of Kenton's best-known stories from its pages; the three volumes published so far, in dime-novel-style paper binding, had become big sellers and revenue-generators. Kenton was constantly being asked to sign copies everywhere he went.

If Kenton were killed or put out of action, there would indeed be intense interest, and grief, all across the nation. But hearing Paul Callon point out this fact greatly irked Gunnison.

"Paul, I worry for you. First you swallow some wild tale of fire falling from heaven. Now you've got Kenton dead and gone and are already writing his obituary."

"I seem to be annoying you every time I open my mouth," said Callon.

"I just want to find Kenton, that's all. Not talk about a lot of absurdities."

Callon pulled a cheap saloon-counter cigar from his pocket and began to study it. He didn't light it, just turned it in his fingers. For a few minutes there was no conversation. Then Callon chuckled. "You know, this firefall tale . . . one of the oddest parts of it all is that there was supposedly a man in the town, some sort of backwoods-preacher type, who predicted that it all would happen. Wrath of God, you know. Just like the Gomorrah in the Bible."

"So now we've got a mining-town prophet in the picture, too?"

"It's just part of the rumors."

"Most likely this 'prophet' had something to do with the explosion itself. Gomorrah is a mining town . . . that means there would be access to explosives. Maybe this fellow made his prediction, then fulfilled it," Gunnison suggested.

"No. No. What was described to me couldn't have been achieved that way, I don't think."

"Have you considered that your information might be faulty? If there's anything to this story at all, I suspect you'll find it's just another mining-town fire, maybe with some explosives in the mix."

"We'll see." With those words, Callon put his cigar back into his pocket and turned his face to the window to watch the increasingly rugged landscape pass by outside.

The grade was steeper now, the train slowing, straining a little as it began to climb.

They stood, with their baggage and gear, on the roofless porch of the tiny train station at the northern base of Gomorrah Mountain and watched the train chug away.

The stationmaster was a thin man with spectacles, thinning hair, eyeshades, and an armband. He was alone in the station house except for one other occupant, an ancient Indian with a square face, hooded eyes, and a broad-brimmed hat.

The Indian wore his hair in long braids behind his ears and smoked a homemade pipe made of old buffalo bone. He eyed the fold-up drawing tables and other journalistic trappings of the two newcomers as he sent thick clouds of smoke out around his expressionless face. His skin was like an expanse of very old, soft leather.

"Good day, sir," Callon said to the stationmaster. "Pleasant day."

"Uh-huh."

"I'm in need of information: How's the best way for a man to get to Gomorrah?"

The stationmaster, a very thin man with a nervous manner, glared through his glasses at Callon. "Don't know if I can answer that question."

"Why's that?"

"Well . . . I ain't really sure there's a Gomorrah left to be got to."

Callon glanced at Gunnison, a told-you-so look. "Yes. That's why we're here. We're journalists, come to write about the fire."

Speak for yourself, Gunnison thought. *I'm chasing Kenton, not a story.*

"Journalists, huh?" said the stationmaster, obviously not impressed.

"That's right. I'm Paul Callon, *National Observor and Gallery*. My companion here is Alex Gunnison, *Gunnison's Illustrated American*." Callon hesitated, then added, "He's the partner of Brady Kenton."

Gunnison was privately amused by this addendum, which amounted to a subtle admission by Callon that Kenton was king when it came to travel journalism. The names of Paul Callon and Alex Gunnison would be recognized by few, but Brady Kenton's name was one to open doors all across the nation. No other traveling writer had generated such a level of celebrity.

At mention of The Name, the stationmaster's demeanor changed. "Kenton, you say? Truly?"

"Yes."

"Odd you should mention him. I think he was here himself, right before the big fire. It looked like him, anyway." He reached beneath the counter and pulled out a copy of an old edition of the *Illustrated American*, and tapped his finger on the prominent woodcut illustration of Kenton's handsome and rugged face. "He looked just like this—I commented on it to several who were here at the time. But he wouldn't own up to being Kenton. Called himself Mr. Houser."

This was confirming news to Gunnison. Houser was one of several aliases Kenton was known to use at one of those rare moments he didn't crave recognition. "I think it *was* Kenton you saw. Have you seen him since?" Gunnison asked.

"No, I ain't."

"Then he's probably still at Gomorrah."

The stationmaster looked somber. "Maybe you should hope he ain't."

Callon asked, "And what did happen at Gomorrah?"

"I couldn't say. Nothing like I've ever seen before. I could see the light of it all the way from my house, which stands back behind the station here." He hesitated, then said, "It was like the mountain exploded."

Volcanic activity, then, Gunnison thought.

"Tell us more," said Callon.

"That's all there is to tell. There was an explosion, a fire, God only knows why or how, and by morning there were folks coming back down from there as fast as they could, saying a bunch of folks had died. Most of them I saw were scorched pretty bad. A couple of them swore that some man in the town had predicted it right before it happened, right before he himself left town. Said it was the fire of God falling on Gomorrah to punish it for its sins."

Callon gave Gunnison a triumphant look. His "absurd story," as Gunnison had termed it, evidently might not be so absurd after all.

The stationmaster went on, "Those people didn't linger long to tell stories. Some waited to catch the next train. A lot just took off walking or riding. Anything to get away as fast as they could. Scared folks. Mighty scared. And then the army came in and nobody that I know of has come down the mountain since."

"Army?"

"Yes. From Fort Brandon, on the far side of Gomorrah Mountain from here. The man who told me about it said he barely made it away before they came in and closed up the town tight as a drum."

"They've sealed off the town?" said Callon.

"That's right. Hey, you ain't planning to quote me in no story, are you?"

"Do you want to be quoted?"

"Oh, no. I got no desire to get my name brought into whatever happened up on that mountain. No, sir, not me."

Gunnison, grudgingly, was beginning to see that there might be something to Callon's wild rumors after all. He asked, "Think the soldiers will let us into Gomorrah?"

"The question might really be: If they do, will they let you out again?"

"How far did the fire burn down the mountain?"

"I ain't been up there; I don't really know. There was a hard storm after the fire. I'm told it put out most of the blaze before it could spread very far."

Callon asked, "Have you seen any other journalists hereabouts that you know of, other than Brady Kenton?"

"No, I ain't."

"Good. How can we get transport up to Gomorrah?"

"There's no real stage line. Just some folks who run supply wagons, and also haul people for a fee." He nodded significantly toward the old Indian in the corner.

"Ah, yes. Thank you, sir," Callon turned and approached the Indian. Smiling down on him, he raised his hand, palm outturned, and said, "How."

Gunnison cringed.

"Howdya-do," the Indian replied, gazing at Callon with those tired-looking eyes of his.

"Have you a wagon in which two well-paying professional journalists might catch a ride to Gomorrah?"

The Indian slowly shook his head.

Callon looked irritably back at the stationmaster. "I thought you said this old man could help us!"

"It's his son who's got the wagon, not him."

"Ah!" Callon grinned at the Indian again. "Well then, old Tecumseh, where might we find your son?"

"I would fetch him for you . . . if only I wasn't so weak from hunger. I have no money to buy food."

Callon sighed and pulled money from his pocket. "Here you go, then. Maybe this will give you some strength."

The old man bit each coin, one by one, before pocketing them. He rose slowly. "I'll go find him," he said. He walked in a stooped posture out of the station.

"Weak from hunger, my eye! Looks well-fed to me," Callon said. "Blasted red-skinned opportunist, if you ask me. Did you see how he took advantage of the situation to get money out of me?"

Gunnison wasn't interested. He stared out the window, looking at the near end of the rugged road that led toward Gomorrah.

He hoped that if Kenton was up there, he was all right.

CHAPTER SIX

THE INDIAN'S SON LOOKED ALMOST AS OLD AS HIS FATHER. But he moved much more quickly and was even more adept than the old man at gouging for gratuities. Gunnison was just cold-hearted enough to let Callon pick up almost all of these.

The wagon was a rattletrap pulled by an ancient but strong draft horse. The rear of the wagon had been outfitted with a removable benchlike seat. Gunnison admired the genius of the contraption, which allowed the wagon to be used alternatively for hauling people and hauling ore or freight. But he wished the designer—probably the wagon driver himself—had figured out a way to incorporate some springs to make the jolts a little easier on the human tailbone.

Callon sat leaning forward so he could fire questions at the driver, whose responses were lean at best.

"Have you been to Gomorrah since the fire?"

"No."

"Close, then?"

"Close."

"What did you see?"

"Ashes. Trees down. Smoke rising. Some fire, even after the rain. But not much."

"Trees down, you say. Like something had knocked them down?"

"Yes."

"What do you think it was?"

A shrug.

"Have you ever heard of any such a thing before?"

"Yes."

"Really? Tell me about it."

"Old stories. My father's father told them. There was a town of the Crows. An enemy cursed the town. One day the sky grew brighter than the sun, and suddenly the town was gone. There was fire, and trees knocked down. Many dead. Worse than Gomorrah."

"When did this happen?"

"Long ago. Generations ago."

"What did your grandfather think caused it?"

"The curse of the enemy."

"Oh, I see." Callon looked around at Gunnison, and whispered far too loudly: "Typical Indian superstition. Probably nothing to it. These people believe that when you have a stomach ache, you've got a snake or a fish or an insect or something swimming around in your entrails. Very primitive minds. It's no wonder they're being swallowed up in the progress of history."

Gunnison said, "I've been thinking about what that stationmaster said about the soldiers sealing off the town. Maybe what's happened to Kenton is that he entered the town, but now the soldiers won't let him leave."

"If they've got Kenton, then that means he can't have sent out his story," Callon said, speaking more to himself than Gunnison.

"Always competing, aren't you, Paul?" Gunnison said. "Do you think that right now I care about this story? I just want to find Kenton and make sure he's not been hurt."

"Fine," Callon said. "Then I'll write the story as an exclusive. The *Illustrated American* can miss it altogether."

"The point is, Paul, I care more about Kenton's welfare than about any story."

"Good for you."

The driver spoke. "We are being watched."

"What?" Callon asked.

"To the north, men in the woods. Two of them. One in black, the other in a gray coat with the sleeves cut away."

"Amazing, the observant powers of Indians," Callon said to Gunnison. He was scanning the woods, looking hard and not being at all subtle about it. "But I think he's wrong. I don't see anything."

"I do," Gunnison replied. "I see them." He leaned up and asked the driver, "Do you know who they are?"

"I think they are from the place where the Rebels are," he replied.

"I don't know what you mean."

"There is a place, two mountain ridges beyond Gomorrah, where there are men living who fought against the United States in the war, and who still have not made their peace with it."

"I'll be!" Callon exclaimed. "An enclave of Rebs, still unreconstructed after all this time?"

The Indian shrugged, perhaps not quite following Callon's terminology. "Confederate Ridge," he said. "So they call it."

"Why do you think they're watching us?" Gunnison asked.

"I don't know," the driver replied.

The wagon rolled on, climbing more slowly as the elevation increased. Gunnison sniffed the air.

"Smell that?" he asked Callon. "Charred timber. Scorched ground."

"Yes," Callon replied. "Look over there, through the trees."

Gunnison did, and for the first time realized that something significant, something far bigger and more powerful than he had heretofore imagined, had indeed happened at the top of Gomorrah Mountain.

Before him was an expanse of mountain ridge, quite black, and virtually stripped of standing timber. Trees that had stood there before now lay on the ridge, burned black. They had all fallen in the same direction, tops turned down the slope, clearly pushed down by a powerful force that had struck them from the direction of Gomorrah.

Gunnison gaped in awe, too stunned to speak. Callon muttered an oath of astonishment under his breath.

The wagon stopped. "I can go no farther," the driver said. "I don't like soldiers."

Gunnison paid the driver and thanked him. Callon, who'd been financially drained from tip-giving, didn't volunteer to contribute to the fare. They dismounted the wagon, gathering their bags and gear.

The driver turned the wagon and began rolling down the mountain again, leaving Gunnison and Callon alone with their baggage.

"Did you really see a couple of old Rebels watching us along the way?" Callon asked.

"I saw men. I don't know if they were old Rebels."

Callon looked thoughtful. "A town burns mysteriously after God only knows what explodes with enough heat and force to knock down trees and incinerate much of a mountaintop . . . the army comes in, seals off the town . . . and nearby there happens to be an enclave of unreconstructed Rebels who hide and watch newcomers along the roadway. Surely there has to be a connection?"

Gunnison said, "What are you driving at?"

"Maybe these Rebs are onto something new. Some kind of extremely powerful explosive. And if they're still bitter over the late war, and if they're of a subversive and retaliatory mentality . . ."

"No. It doesn't make sense. You don't develop massively powerful new explosives living in some remote mountain outpost."

Callon shrugged. "I'm just trying to contrive a few theories."

Gunnison eyed the baggage sitting on the ground. There wasn't much of it; as men who traveled constantly as part of their profession, both he and Callon had learned to carry as little as possible. But even what they had was cumbersome under the circumstances.

"You know, we'll never be able to move around with all that gear," Gunnison said. "I suggest we find a safe place to hide most of it, and carry only what we can't do without."

Callon was agreeable to this. They carried their baggage off the road and found a small knoll, pockmarked with caverns too little for human accommodation but just the right size for stashing away a few goods.

They removed from their bags a few essential items and placed these in small satchels—custom-designed for traveling illustrator/writers by none other than Brady Kenton himself some years back and therefore known in the business as "Kenton packs." Kenton had made a fine sideline income from royalties paid on the satchels by the company that made them.

"What now?" Gunnison asked. "On to Gomorrah?"

"Yes . . . but not along the road."

"I agree," Gunnison said.

"First, though, I wouldn't mind a closer look at that fallen timber."

Again, Gunnison agreed. Though his goal was to find Kenton, his journalistic instincts were also at work, and he was curious about whatever mysterious force had wreaked such destruction hereabouts.

The two journalists were careful to make sure there were no obvious observers in the vicinity before they moved out into the expanse of fallen and burned timber.

Ash and grit crunched beneath their feet. Hardly a leaf, hardly an evergreen needle, had not been burned away by the fire. The only greenery that remained was on the bottom side of the fallen trees.

Many trees had been uprooted, but most had been snapped off near their bases or about halfway up.

"What would do this?" Callon asked. "How . . . and why?"

Gunnison replied, "Assuming we're dealing with some natural event here, however unusual, there may not be any 'why' to it. It may just be something that simply happened."

"A natural event," Callon repeated. He paused, cleared his throat. "Gunnison, do you think there's any chance that . . . well . . ."

Gunnison anticipated him. "A supernatural event?" he said. "Is that what you're asking?"

"Uh . . . yes."

Callon's question seemed so sincere that Gunnison resisted the temptation to poke fun at it. As he so often did, he pulled from memory something he'd heard Kenton expound upon at some time past. "What is 'supernatural,' after all?" Gunnison said. "We live in a world about which we know very little, no matter how wise we may think we are. There may be parts of reality that we seldom see, but which are real nonetheless. Maybe reality has layers . . . worlds upon worlds, stacked one upon another, one sometimes bleeding over into another, on some rare occasion, so that an event in one layer causes a seemingly unexplainable effect in another. Maybe what we tend to call 'supernatural' is really nothing more than the parts of nature we haven't yet come to understand. So who can say what the limits of explanation are for something like this?"

Callon laughed. "Well, aren't *you* quite the little philosopher! Where'd you pick all *that* up, Socrates?"

Gunnison was about to fire an insult back at Callon, but something intervened to distract him.

Off in the distance, down below the mountain at the train station, a train whistle sounded.

"Hear that?" Gunnison asked.

"Yes. What of it?"

"Another train coming in, but there's none scheduled today. I looked at the tables myself back in Greer City and at the train station below the mountain as well."

"A special train run, then. It has to be."

"Why, I wonder?"

"I don't know. I have a gut feeling it probably has something to do with all this." Callon waved at the charred wasteland around them.

Gunnison scratched his chin. "Perhaps it's best for us not to even consider entering the town at all until we've had a chance to do some unobserved reconnoitering."

"Why? We'll never find answers creeping around in the outer shadows," Callon said.

"And I'll never find Kenton if I'm a detainee of the military inside a burned-out town."

"Unless Kenton is a detainee there, too."

"Yes, but I don't know that he is. But if I can just watch the town for a time, I might be able to spot him." He turned. "Come on, Paul. Let's go."

"Where?"

"To find a good vantage point to observe the town of Gomorrah. And maybe to see whoever, or whatever, might come up the mountain from the train station."

CHAPTER SEVEN

AN HOUR LATER, IN THE DIMMING LIGHT OF DUSK, GUNNISON and Callon lay on their bellies, hidden in tangled, burned timber, and studied what remained of the town of Gomorrah.

"Astonishing!" Callon said. "Not one completely undamaged building, and many gone altogether! What kind of explosive could do such a thing?"

"A very, very powerful one . . . if it *was* an explosive," Gunnison said.

"Surely it was. Why else would *they* be here?"

Callon pointed at soldiers who patrolled in the dirt streets and around the perimeter of the town. The military presence here was dominant. The images were reminiscent of a war that both the observing journalists had been too young to take part in—images of a town destroyed, then occupied by soldiers wearing blue.

"I'd considered the possibility of volcanic activity, but I don't see any of the usual signs that go with it," Gunnison said. "Maybe it was some sort of unusual volcanic burst. Or a venting of gasses out of the mountain."

Callon shook his head. "A town explodes, a mountaintop is charred black, and the army shows up and seals the place off. What does that imply? To me it implies a military kind of concern, a security concern. They've got some specific sort of suspicions about this, I'll bet you."

"Maybe it's simpler than that, Paul. Maybe they came because they *don't* know what happened, not because they do. Maybe they came just to help out the survivors."

"What survivors? I've seen nothing so far but soldiers."

Gunnison shrugged. "So maybe all the civilians have left or been moved out of town. Or maybe they're being held inside some of those tents, or in some of those buildings still standing."

"Or maybe they all died in the explosion and fire."

Gunnison didn't like to think about that possibility. *Kenton, where are you?*

Callon read his thoughts. "Don't assume the worst, Alex. He's a tough bird, Kenton is."

"I know."

"I wouldn't be surprised if he's already come here and gone back. He might be looking for *you* somewhere else right now, Alex."

Gunnison nodded.

"Or maybe he's . . ."

Gunnison raised his hand abruptly, interrupting. "Listen!" he said. "Do you hear that?"

Callon had heard it too. Over on the road that led from the railhead to Gomorrah, there was motion and noise. Gunnison and Callon dropped low amid the blackened timber.

There was just enough visibility to see that the travelers on the road were more soldiers, about a dozen of them, moving toward the edge of the town. A delegation of other soldiers advanced from within the town to meet them. By the light of torches there were salutes, words exchanged, but nothing audible reached the two unseen watchers.

Callon pulled from his pocket a small collapsible spyglass. He put it to his eye and studied two men who were speaking to one another beneath a flaring torch. Gunnison wished he'd brought a spyglass, too.

"Astonishing!" Callon exclaimed abruptly, under his breath.

"What is it?"

"One of those men over there is none other than the infamous Colonel J.B. Ottinger!"

"Ottinger?"

"That's right. Old Ottinger himself, mangled face, blind eye, and all! I thought he was in Texas."

Gunnison scanned the dustier corners of his mind and pulled something from one of them. "You know, I recall that the *Illustrated American* carried some mention, a few months back, that Ottinger was leaving Texas for the Montana Territory. Fort Brandon, as a matter of fact."

"He did this by choice or necessity?"

"Choice, I think."

"But isn't Fort Brandon considered one of the least desirable stations out of all the frontier forts?"

"So I've always heard. He must have had some unobvious motivation, I suppose."

"Fort Brandon is the closest military installation to where we are right now . . . right?"

"Close enough that you could probably see the Gomorrah fire from it."

Callon put the spyglass back to his eye and quietly studied the scene.

"Do you recognize anyone else?" Gunnison asked.

"No. There's a civilian there, though. I assume he's a civilian, anyway. He's not in uniform."

"Kenton?" Gunnison said eagerly.

"No, afraid not. I think it must be whoever came in on the train. A lot of baggage . . . some of his gear looks like things a surveyor might carry. Or a mining engineer."

"I want to get closer," Gunnison said, jealous because he had no spyglass of his own. He rose and moved forward, as quietly as he could. Even so, a charred stick snapped loudly underfoot.

Callon scolded him in a sharp whisper: "Gunnison, be careful!"

"I'm always careful," Gunnison grouchily replied. He went on, but more slowly yet, Callon now rising to creep along behind him. It was quite dark now; there was little chance they'd be seen from the town.

Gunnison stopped abruptly only a few paces on.

"What is it?" asked Callon.

"That smell . . ."

Callon's nose caught it, too, the wind having shifted slightly. "Have mercy!" he exclaimed. "What is it? A dead horse?"

With a hand across his mouth and nose, Gunnison explored around a bit. He'd gone only a few more yards, Callon trailing some distance behind, when he stopped again, looking down.

"Not a horse. A man," he said.

Callon came to his side. He looked down, then reflexively pulled back in disgust.

"Can we can risk a match?" Gunnison said. "Low to the ground, hidden by the timber?"

"I suppose so . . . not that I'm really eager to see him," Callon said. His voice was that of a man fighting nausea. "I can tell you from smell alone that there's no chance we'll find him alive."

"Still . . ." Gunnison knelt, carefully, and struck a match. He held it out, cupping it, letting its feeble light play over what lay on the ground. It blew out quickly in the wind, but in its brief moment revealed clearly the blackened remnants of a human face, looking up, mouth open, the one remaining eye half-closed, the skin charred and ugly, the stench of burned flesh, now decomposing, rising from it.

The face was unrecognizable, half of it burned away, the rest black from fire and decay.

"Horrible!" Callon said. "Truly horrible!"

"Poor fellow," Gunnison said. "Whoever he was."

Callon's professional curiosity—and a desire to not appear less steel-willed and tough than Gunnison—overcame his rather weak stomach, and he came forward again, bravely close to the corpse, examining it with his hand clamped over his mouth and up against his nostrils.

"Alex . . . light another match," he said, his hand muffling his voice.

"Why?"

"Just do it!"

A new flare revealed again the hideous countenance. The flame held longer this time.

"Lower it . . ."

Gunnison did so. The faint light played down the body, and just before it went out, glittered on something pinned on the remnants of the coat.

Gunnison fumbled for another match, but his hands had begun to tremble badly.

"Here . . . let me," Callon said.

He took the matches, struck one, and held it low.

Glittering back at them was a Masonic pin, stuck on the lapel of the coat. It looked familiar . . . but there were many such pins in existence. The match went out, to be replaced by another.

Gunnison controlled his trembling sufficiently to remove the pin from the lapel. He freed it as this match, too, blew out.

He turned it over and waited for Callon to strike another match. This time the light revealed the unsoiled rear of the pin, and on it, engraved initials: B.K.

It was Brady Kenton's pin.

"Kenton?" Callon asked, barely even a whisper.

Gunnison, stunned and horrified, nodded. This was precisely what he'd feared . . . but he hadn't *really* thought it would be Kenton. It seemed too unlikely.

Callon exhaled slowly, then said, "I can't believe it. I truly can't believe it."

Those words were the last spoken for a time. Gunnison was too jolted to weep, but the feelings inside him were the most painful he'd experienced in years. Callon crouched beside him, watching, uncomfortable, and completely unable, for once, to find words.

Gunnison spoke at last, obviously struggling not to cry. "He must have been out here, almost to town, when the explosion happened."

"I'm so sorry, Alex. Truly sorry."

"This pin . . . funny about it. Kenton wasn't even a Mason. It was given to him by his wife . . . her father had worn it. When he died, she wanted Kenton to have it, in her father's memory. She had his initials engraved on the back."

"This is a tragic news." Callon paused, then expressed a newly risen realization: "But it is news, nonetheless."

Gunnison looked up at him, though by now the darkness was heavy enough that he could barely see his outline. He fought back an extreme annoyance. How dare Callon treat this with such a cold and impersonal professionalism! "Yes, Paul. I know. I also know that it's only appropriate that this information be published first in the *Illustrated American*. It's how Kenton would want it."

"I know. And I agree. When will you wire in the news?"

"I can't think about that now. I can't even believe he's gone, much less tell the world about it. I want to be absolutely sure first."

"What more evidence do you demand? Who else would be wearing Kenton's pin?"

"I have to *know*, Paul."

Gunnison struck one more match and looked closely at the ruined face. Then, fighting off natural reticence to touch the dead body, he explored the jacket pockets.

Everything he found confirmed that the jacket was Kenton's. And the face, impossible to recognize as it was, certainly could have been that of Kenton. The general size of the body, the build and general physical character of it, all also matched Kenton's traits. Even the pistol holstered beneath the coat was Kenton's. Gunnison took it, tucking it under his belt, near his own pistol.

"Oh, Kenton," Gunnison whispered.

"He died doing what he wanted to do. He was here pursuing a story," Callon said, searching for some kind of comfort, feeble as it might be.

"No," Gunnison said. "He was here on the trail of a ghost . . . one he hoped would end up to not be a ghost at all."

"What ghost?"

"Victoria Kenton. His wife."

"But his wife is dead. For many years."

"So everyone believes. So Kenton himself believed, or tried to make himself believe, for most of the time I've known him. But ever since he and I found Briggs Garrett still alive in Leadville, back in 'seventy-nine,* he felt compelled to investigate the accident that took Victoria from him. I mean, if Briggs Garrett could still be alive, when everyone was sure he'd died years before, then maybe Victoria was alive, too. Anything seemed possible."

"How did Victoria die—if she did?"

"A railway accident. But her body was never identified. There was a terrible fire, you see. They could never even accurately number the victims."

"But that's hardly grounds for assuming someone survived."

**The Hanging at Leadville*

"I know. But Kenton was always a hopeful man. After Leadville, he became obsessed with Victoria's death. He studied that accident in morbid detail, and the more he did so, the more he began to persuade himself she truly might have survived. He even started talking about it to me, and Kenton was never one to discuss deeply personal matters. Then, about a year ago, it all intensified. Kenton told me he thought he had found actual, positive *evidence* she had lived through that accident."

"What kind of evidence?"

"He never told me. And then, all at once . . . well, he just closed the door again, so to speak. Would tell me nothing more. It all became completely private to him again. I suspect his 'evidence' hadn't panned out like he'd hoped. But I do know he hadn't given up looking for her. The hope that Victoria is still alive has been the driving force of his life for the past few years. Frankly, his search wasn't as big a secret as he believed. Many people knew."

Callon himself could have confirmed this. Brady Kenton's search for his wife after years of believing her dead had become well-known among the circles of traveling journalists. Callon had simply not let on to Gunnison that he knew, because he wanted to see if Gunnison might tell him something he hadn't yet heard.

Some who knew of Kenton's quest thought his obsession and unwillingness to yield up hope was vaguely pathetic. Others—Callon included—found it touching, romantically tragic. Callon's soul had a romantic facet that he hid from the world like an ugly wart.

"Did Kenton believe he could actually find his wife in Gomorrah?" Callon asked.

"I suspect not, though I can't be sure. But the notes he left behind seemed to me to imply he was coming here to meet someone who had important information about Victoria."

"I wonder who?"

"The name 'Rankin' was written down several times."

"Rankin. I'll keep the name in mind, in case I find him in the town."

"So you are going into Gomorrah after all?"

"Yes. I think I will. Can't learn much out here, after all."

Gunnison knew what was happening. The chemistry of the situation had changed now that Kenton had been found dead. This tragedy had charged the atmosphere unpleasantly, and Callon was ready to flee it. He was obviously one of those types who shunned grief and the grieving. Gunnison understood; he was sometimes that way himself.

Gunnison didn't care that Callon wanted to abandon him. He wanted only to be alone with his sorrow just now.

"No word from you, in print, of Kenton's passing, Paul, all right?" Gunnison reminded the man. "The *Illustrated American* is the appropriate publication to give this news to the world. *Not* the *Observor*. Are we agreed?"

"You have my word, Alex." Callon reached over and patted Gunnison's shoulder. "I'm truly sorry. Kenton was a great reporter, a master illustrator, a pioneer of his craft. I admired him deeply."

"He was worthy of admiration." *Please, Paul. Just hurry up and go away!*

"Well . . . goodbye. Wish me luck in Gomorrah."

Callon moved off into the darkness and left Gunnison alone with the burned and moldering body, hidden now in the darkness near his feet.

CHAPTER EIGHT

THE NEXT SEVERAL LONELY HOURS WERE AMONG THE MOST sorrowful of Gunnison's life.

The occupied town of Gomorrah quieted, the streets emptying except for a few patrolling guards. Gunnison remained where he was, initially obsessed with the notion that he had to do something appropriate for the remains of Brady Kenton . . . find some way to have the body removed from this place, treated with dignity, taken away for proper ceremony and burial. He quickly realized, though, that he could do nothing alone. He had no way to deal with a moldering corpse. For now, Kenton would have to lie where he was. Maybe the soldiers would eventually find him, and give him some sort of appropriate burial.

For the sake of his nose, Gunnison moved far away from the body. For the sake of his mental state, he forced his thoughts to the situation at hand.

What would Brady Kenton himself have done in this kind of circumstance?

The question was easy to answer. As fascinated as Kenton would have been by the mystery of Gomorrah's destruction, nothing would have diverted him from his quest to find Rankin, and maybe Victoria.

So Gunnison would carry on the quest in his place. He'd remain here long enough to determine if Rankin was still alive and in Gomorrah, or if he was one of those who had survived and fled. Whatever it took, he'd find the man if he was alive to be found.

Sleepless, brooding hours passed. Instinct told Gunnison that dawn would break before long. He realized how weary he was. Quietly he slipped away, moving around the perimeter of the town, looking for some place he might rest. He found an old shed back in a stand of charred trees, and lay down inside it.

Just before he fell asleep he heard a shout in the town. He moved to the doorway and looked out, watching a pair of guards running in answer to the alarm.

"Caught you already, did they, Paul Callon?" he said aloud, quietly. "I'm surprised it took even this long."

He'd have found it amusing if amusement was a feeling he was capable of feeling just now.

He lay down and closed his eyes.

Daylight spilling into the cabin awakened Gunnison from a hard sleep. Where was he? Why was he sleeping on the ground? Where was Kenton?

Memory suddenly clarified, and Gunnison felt a wave of grief.

Kenton . . . dead. The shock became new to him again, and Alex Gunnison began his day with tears.

He didn't cry long, though. Kenton wouldn't favor that kind of thing. Gunnison pulled himself together, ate breakfast from the supply of food he'd brought in his satchel, and checked his pistols. He was glad to have the weapons; they made him feel safer. Kenton had taught him that the best use for a weapon wasn't for fighting, but as a tool by which a man could avoid a fight. "Always best to negotiate for yourself from a position of maximum strength," Kenton would say. "The man with a gun has a voice that can say 'no' very loudly."

Gunnison placed Kenton's old pistol in his satchel and

stashed the satchel in a corner under dried evergreen needles that had blown in through the open door, and which had provided his natural mattress the night before. He retained in his pockets a notepad, pencils, a small sketch pad, a bit of trail food, and some extra bullets for the pistol holstered under his jacket.

He looked over the town from the vantage point of the shadowed shed doorway. Guards patrolled as before, and there was still no sign of civilian activity.

Though he'd decided not to pursue the mystery of the firefall, he couldn't keep from speculating.

What could have caused such a massive and unusual explosion? And why would the military find it of such interest?

Gunnison had never been a military man himself, but Kenton had, and had taught his young partner much about the military mindset. Kenton knew whereof he spoke, having been a special agent for the United States government during the Civil War, working in intelligence and espionage right in the heart of the Confederacy. He'd been an "officially unofficial" agent, Kenton had told Gunnison, meaning he'd been indeed an authorized representative of the United States, but one who would have been completely disavowed by the U.S. government had he been captured.

Not part of the normal military hierarchy, Kenton had enjoyed a vital but dangerous near-total freedom in his wartime spying days. He'd worked himself deeply into the heart of many a dangerous scenario on behalf of his government, and had never revealed the secrets he'd uncovered except to those to whom he directly answered . . . sometimes to the President himself.

It was an unlikely background, in one way, for a man destined to become a journalist, for the instincts of the intelligence agent and the journalist often run counter to one another, Kenton had sometimes pointed out. Both seek facts, but one wishes to possess and guard them in secret, the other to reveal them to the world. If Kenton had experienced any difficulty in making the transition from one mindset to the other, though, it had never shown.

Gunnison left the shed and moved farther back into the woods. He headed for an area where a full stand of trees had managed to survive the explosion and fire and stood like lone survivors of a massacre. Among them, and in the snarled wood at their base, he could hide quite well, and also gain a better general vantage point on the town, and particularly upon a row of army tents set up along one side of a street. He heard something behind him. Turning, looking beyond the stand that hid him, he saw only the blackened terrain, fallen trees . . .

No! There, moving across the landscape in a manner and posture that indicated they were trying to be as covert as possible, he saw the same two men that the Indian wagoner had pointed out the day before. Gunnison ducked, intrigued and concerned. Had they seen him? Were they trying to remain unseen by him, or by the soldiers in the town?

One of the men pulled out a spyglass, extended it, put it to his eye. Gunnison was relieved to see the man wasn't looking back at him, but far past him to the right, into the ruined town. So it was the soldiers who held the interest of these men, not Alex Gunnison.

Gunnison stayed where he was for a long time, watching the town and at times the two spies in the woods.

For a long time, though, nothing happened. The two supposed Rebels in the burned-out woods behind him eventually vanished. The guards in Gomorrah changed shifts.

Gunnison took notes, sketched, and fought mounting boredom. He was beginning to think he'd have no choice but to do what Callon had, and walk right into the town, if he wanted to learn anything worth knowing.

Then, finally, something worthy of note occurred.

The civilian who had come in on the special train emerged from a tent, and with him a small guard of soldiers.

Gunnison sketched rapidly, making an almost photographic rendering of the scene before him. This would not be his final sketch, only the basis for it. Here and there he put odd scribbles and letters and notes—codes that Kenton had taught him, quick ways to tell himself, later on, that at this point there should be an evergreen tree, or a spot of sunlight, or an expanse of shadow. It was an efficient and workable shorthand that Kenton had developed, and it had always given him a time advantage over his competitors, who usually tried to draw their final renderings directly on the scene—an inefficient process often doomed to utter failure when the scene changed before they had a chance to finish their work. Kenton's system was better.

The unidentified civilian's posture and general bearing made Gunnison believe the man wasn't entirely comfortable here. Gunnison tried to sketch him, but was too far away for the man's features to be discernible.

Colonel Ottinger emerged from a tent and approached the civilian. Hands were shaken, and a conversation ensued. A minute later the man was ushered into the tent with Ottinger's hand resting on his shoulder, Ottinger himself leaning in close and talking intently.

Gunnison pondered again Ottinger's presence here, and mentally reviewed what little he knew of the controversial colonel with the spotted past.

Ottinger, once considered a handsome man, was still imposing despite being disfigured on the right side of his face and blind in the right eye—a disfigurement dating from a certain infamous series of wartime events. Even more disfigured by those same events, though, was the man's military and moral reputation.

A "close-quarter battle," Ottinger had always referred to

the Virginia bloodletting that had made his name infamous to so many. Others used a stronger word: massacre.

Under Ottinger's command, Union soldiers had wiped out, cruelly, a band of Confederate sympathizers who just happened to be civilian, and not a few of whom happened to be children and women. Several blacks had also been killed for reasons no one had quite understood.

Kenton, who had encountered Ottinger a time or two during his own covert wartime career, had loathed the man even though they served the same flag. Kenton saw Ottinger as a wartime opportunist who used his military position for personal gain, and often for personal vengeance, even at the cost of his own men's lives.

After Kenton began writing and illustrating for *Gunnison's Illustrated American*, he took up the cause of exposing Ottinger's crime in an article that helped make Kenton famous, and very nearly made Ottinger infamous. Kenton pointed to evidence that the massacre itself had been carried out not for valid military reasons, but because Ottinger had things to hide, personal sins, and certain people had to die to ensure that hiding took place.

The Virginia massacre, Kenton had told Gunnison, had involved cruelty equal to or worse than the well-known Carolina massacre carried out during the Revolutionary War by the hated Bannistre Tarleton. Kenton had said he believed Ottinger should have stood trial for wartime crimes, and would have done so had not he been owed several large favors by men in positions of high authority. In what Kenton saw as one of the great failures of military and national justice, Ottinger escaped all prosecution for his crimes.

So, despite his transgressions and these many years after the war, Ottinger remained an active, if aging, colonel, serving the latter half of his career in the West, mostly in Texas.

But now, abruptly, in the Montana Territory. Why? Gunnison wondered what could motivate an aging man to uproot from his familiar life and move so far, to Fort Brandon of all places.

One thing was growing clear to Gunnison: He wasn't going to find the answer by mere observance. Somewhere along the line, he was going to have to talk to someone.

CHAPTER NINE

SOLDIERS BROUGHT OUT SOME OF THE UNUSUAL-LOOKING baggage that had accompanied the unidentified civilian, and began to unpack it. Gunnison wished again that he had a spyglass.

With straining eyes he watched with great interest the unveiling of what he thought at first was some sort of surveying equipment, but which at second glance seemed to be something not quite that, though similar. Scientific gear of some sort, he could see . . . and suddenly a possible explanation for the presence of this anomalous civilian figure in a militarily dominated setting began to dawn on Gunnison.

This fellow was surely some sort of scientist, brought in to determine what had happened here! If so, that would tend to validate the presumption that the destruction of Gomorrah had come as the result of some sort of natural event.

Two soldiers, plus the civilian, loaded themselves down with the equipment in addition to their weapons. A couple of other soldiers followed, armed with carbines.

Gunnison sketched furiously, then froze—the presumed scientist and soldiers were walking directly toward the place he hid!

Gunnison readied himself to be discovered. They would spot him, raise a yell, and he'd be hauled in . . .

He reached under his jacket and touched the cold butt of the pistol. But he moved his hand away again, ashamed of himself for even having the thought. These were men who, like him, were doing what they were supposed to do. They were not enemies. If he was caught, he was caught, and would just make the best of it.

The men veered off before reaching the stand of trees, though, and trudged across the burned landscape and toward the south. Gunnison was not seen.

He gave them a good head start, then carefully followed them, making sure to remain out of sight of anyone in the town.

He found the presumed scientist at work with the instruments. Some of the soldiers aided him, clumsy at the unfamiliar tasks, while others stood guard. Gunnison found a hiding spot that gave him a good view of the work going on and also a line of sight into the town. His observations erased any question he might have had that the man was anything other than a scientist of some kind.

Gunnison sketched the scientist and his assistants. Eventually they moved away, going across a hill and almost out of sight.

Before Gunnison could follow, new activity began back in the town. The door to one of the few remaining original buildings, a damaged store building, was opened, and people emerged. Civilians!

So Gomorrah wasn't emptied of all its original residents after all. They were simply being held out of sight.

They filed out of the building, one by one, moving slowly, looking like refugees. They were dirty, wearing ash-blackened clothing. Several limped, and a few had burns and bandages. One man's hairless head was discolored from scorching. The people walked out into the street and formed a line outside a tent whose rear faced the place Gunnison hid.

There were only a few women. They were allowed to enter the tent one at a time in advance of the men. When they came out again, the men were sent in.

Gunnison realized that these people were being allowed to pay a visit to a latrine, which the tent covered. It had probably been dug by the soldiers after they encamped in the town.

Gunnison was struck by how much this all looked like a captors-and-prisoners scenario. Someone stumbling upon this scene without any advance knowledge of what had happened here would come away with the impression that he was seeing a town that had been bombed and burned into submission and overrun by a force of uniformed military invaders, its surviving population captured.

Gunnison's attention was suddenly diverted: the rear canvas wall of the latrine tent had moved. A man inside had just rolled out underneath it, and lay there hugged up against the tent for a few moments, hidden from the soldiers but fully visible to Gunnison. A few moments later, he rolled again, three full turns away from the tent, rose, and dodged behind a heap of charred firewood. There he crouched, peeping up over the top of the pile, and then he moved again, circling around behind the remnants of a shed, then over to a still-intact cabin, and behind it toward the very stand of trees in which Gunnison hid.

Gunnison crouched lower. The man dodged into the grove, dropped to his belly . . . and saw Gunnison. He gaped in surprise, scared and wild-looking, and began to rise to run away.

With motions, Gunnison indicated he should remain where he was, and tried to convey that he, too, was hiding. The man, though looking suspicious, seemed to understand, nodded, and did not run.

Eyeing one another occasionally, he and Gunnison quietly watched as the people finished their latrine shifts and were herded, like weary cattle, back to the building from which they'd come.

Gunnison crept over and put out his hand.

"My name's Gunnison, Alex Gunnison," he said. "I'm a journalist, from *Gunnison's Illustrated American*."

The man's eyes showed his recognition of the famous publication's name. Gunnison received the inevitable, familiar follow-up question: "Gunnison, you say? Is it your magazine, then?"

"My father's," Gunnison replied. "I just work for him."

"I see," the man replied. He was a big fellow, middle-aged, burly, broad-faced, and nearly hairless. The left side of his face was darker than the right and mildly blistered. This indicated to Gunnison that this man had been here when the fire occurred, but hadn't been directly exposed to the full fury of it. Lucky for him. "My name's Decker Smith," the man went on.

They shook hands, and Smith asked, "You ain't the journalist I'd have expected to see. A man here name of Gib Rankin had swore Brady Kenton himself was coming to talk to him."

Gunnison said, "Brady Kenton did come. It's only too bad he came when he did . . . I found his body myself, on the far edge of town, badly burned."

Decker Smith let out a long, slow breath. "So he was too close when hell fell on Gomorrah."

"Yes."

"Mighty sorry to hear that. Mighty sorry."

"I need to understand what happened to him, Mr. Smith. I need to know what happened on this mountain, and what's happening now in this town. And most of all, I want to know about Rankin."

"And I'm glad to tell you, young man. But let's you and me get away from here, eh? Find us a place a little farther away from our soldier friends and damned old Colonel Ottinger." He spat the name like it was a bad-tasting bug that had flown into his mouth.

"Fine . . . but tell me first: Was there another man, named Paul Callon, dark-haired, slender, about my age, also a journalist, maybe caught sneaking around town . . ."

"There was such a fellow, yes. Didn't hear his name and didn't know he was a journalist. They've got him under guard, away from everybody else."

Gunnison and Smith slipped away, using the terrain and natural cover—what was left of it—to keep themselves hidden.

Seated on a fallen log just past the point where the outermost flames of the Gomorrah Mountain fire had been rained out, Decker Smith stared at the clouds thickening in the sky and told the note-scribbling Gunnison his story.

"I'm a saloonkeeper in Gomorrah . . . or was. My place is gone now. I've thrived there, though. The miners from these parts love their liquor.

"The best way to tell this tale, I suppose, is to begin with Rankin, and Parson Peabody. Rankin first.

"Rankin's a gambler and a general cheat. As deft a man at bottom-dealing and such as ever I seen. The man would sit down at the gambling table, fumble around, drop the cards, act like he'd hardly ever held a deck before, just to draw in the gullible . . . but on the street one time, I watched him once doing card tricks for a couple of children who'd passed through with their folks. Amazing, what that man could do. He could handle the cards, make the deck seem to vanish and come back again, pull cards out of the air, out of the children's pockets and hair . . . a regular conjurer, Rankin was. After that I watched him close whenever he commenced to gamble in my place, knowing he was surely cheating, which is something I won't stand for in my own saloon."

Gunnison asked, "Was Rankin a permanent resident of Gomorrah?"

"No. Came here maybe a month ago, just him and a couple of cronies, and a woman he calls Princess. I don't know if that's her real name."

"Tell me all you can about Princess," said Gunnison.

"I'd put her in her forties. A woman who's lived a difficult life . . . but still with some of the bloom on the rose. Dark hair, thick. And the prettiest eyes maybe I've ever seen. And she's no soiled dove, even though she keeps company with a rough kind of man. I can always tell your soiled doves . . . there's something that gets into the eyes of a bad woman, a kind of a flinty hardness that Princess ain't got. When we ran her out of town with Rankin, I was wishing she could have stayed behind. She deserved better company than that sorry rodent."

Gunnison felt the skin on the back of his neck tighten as if in a cold wind as a new possibility rose to mind. Might Kenton have been coming here not for mere information about his wife, but for Victoria herself? Might Princess actually *be* Victoria? It was a tenuous stretch, but possibile.

"So Rankin and Princess were run out of town before the fire?"

"Yep. Plus a couple of Rankin's companions. And Parson Peabody."

"Tell me about Peabody."

Smith arched his brows. "I'm not sure what to tell you. I'm not as religious a man as I should be, and I've never put stock in your mystical-spookish types . . . but the parson, he seemed to *know*."

"About the coming fire?"

"Yes. Yet he's no more than a common drunk who fancies himself a saint and a preacher. Totes a Bible around in a satchel, throws sermons at every sinner he meets, drinks like the devil himself. I always thought him a pest and a hypocrite . . . but now I'm wondering if maybe the parson proved himself to be something a lot more than any of us thought."

Gunnison asked, "How does Parson Peabody fit in with Rankin?"

"He didn't, not until now."

"I'm confused."

"T'other night, about dusk, there sits Gib Rankin in my saloon, dealing cards, gambling, going through his fumbling act, all the while cheating three new miners out of their day's earnings because they hadn't been in town long enough to know better about him. Finally I had enough and told him to get out of my place.

"Old Rankin puts on a show of being truly hurt that I'd been so unkind to him. I got unkinder yet and took him by scruff and belt and heaved him right out the door. Meanwhile he's protesting that he's got legitimate business in town, waiting for Brady Kenton to come meet him and talk about something important. Nobody really took Rankin seriously about that—I figured it was just one more of his lies being told for some self-serving reason.

"Anyway, here's Rankin. He's been thrown out of the saloon, and the idea comes up that while we're at it maybe we ought to just run him and his friends all the way out of town and be done with them for good. The preacher McCree—he was a real preacher, not like Parson Peabody—shows up and goes along with the notion of throwing them out of town, for he had no use for them any more than I did.

"Meanwhile, Parson Peabody has stumbled into the middle of all this, and everybody figures, why not just throw him out, too, while we're cleaning house? The parson was harmless, but just so aggravating, you see. I swear, the man could have made Job shoot himself. So we herded them all, Princess included, to the edge of town and told them to head down the mountain and not come back."

"And that was all there was to it?"

"Not quite. Something odd happened right then with the parson. He got mad, and started in to talking about the coming wrath of God, about to fall on the town and all of us in it . . . fire from heaven, he said. Fire from heaven."

"And then it happened," said Gunnison.

"Not right away. But a little later, yes, it happened."

"Tell me about it."

"Maybe I'll let you tell me. You tell me what it would be if hell itself exploded in the sky above you and rained down all around. Tell me what it's like when buildings burn like matchsticks, and the air gets too hot to breathe, and the trees are pushed down like sticks . . . people dying all around, screaming, burning, others killed too fast even to scream. God. God, it was awful." He closed his eyes, squeezing them so tightly shut that the slits of them disappeared in the creases of his weathered face. Gunnison wondered if the man was about to weep in front of him.

CHAPTER TEN

GUNNISON GAVE HIM A MOMENT OR TWO TO COLLECT HIMSELF, then asked, "Where were you when it happened?"

"In my saloon. The building shook, the roof split apart, half of it gone before you could say billy-hi, and all above you a sky full of light and fire and heat like you never felt. I dove down under a table, and that probably saved me. But the building was ablaze right off. That's the kind of heat we're talking about.

"I ran outside, looking for safety. There was none. It was hell out there, people crumpled down like wilted flowers, dead and dying. I saw the Reverend McCree beating flames on himself, trying to put himself out. Old Jed Bloom, who lived in a tent-roof house not far from my saloon, died on his bed, that canvas roof burned away like it was a piece of paper you'd roll yourself a smoke in. I never seen such a thing, and hope I never do again."

"How did you survive once you were outside?"

"There's a water trough on the street. I throwed myself into it. The water heated like it was in a pot on a fire, heated fast, but by the time I came out of it, the flash of heat was past."

"How many died?"

"I don't know. You never could say how many people were in this town. It was always changing. But I can tell you there's no more than twenty still left in the town, not counting the soldiers there now. Most others who survived left town right after it happened, right through the burning woods. The rest, dead. All those who are left alive now are them who were lucky enough, like me, to have been indoors when it happened, in places with thick enough roofs and walls to knock off the worst of the heat."

"So . . . what do you think it was?"

"I'll answer you by telling you this: When the call came for Parson Peabody to be given his due offering, he got everything I had in my pocket. What fell on us was the fire of God, and Parson Peabody knew it was coming. So when they said pay, I paid."

"I thought you said Peabody was already gone when the fire came."

"He was. But after it happened, him, Rankin, Princess, and one of Rankin's friends, name of Thomas Shafter, came back into town. The other man who'd gone down with them wasn't with them when they came back. I suppose he died, or ran off. But the Parson was certainly alive, and Rankin himself was a convert to the Parson. Right in front of everybody Rankin dropped to his knees before Parson Peabody, calling him a prophet and repenting for his sins. And most of us still here, who knew about the prophecy he'd made, knelt right beside him. That man knew the fire was going to fall, Mr. Gunnison. I can't explain it, but he *knew*."

"It was surely coincidence, Mr. Smith."

Smith firmly shook his hairless head. "You'd not say it if you'd been here. If you'd heard that prophecy and seen how exact it came out, you'd have believed, too. And you'd have paid your offering."

"Who asked for the offering? Parson Peabody?"

"Not directly. Rankin asked it on his behalf."

Gunnison frowned. "Did the money go to Peabody after it was collected?"

"I didn't watch what they did with it. I didn't care. I just wanted Peabody to go away, and not make it happen again."

"You believed the parson actually *caused* the fire to come down?"

"I considered it a possibility. At that point, I could have believed anything."

"But to think something like this could have been *caused* by nothing but a common drunkard seems . . . well, unlikely at best."

For the first time, Smith seemed offended. "Listen to me, young man: you weren't here. You didn't see the sky explode. You didn't see people's clothes burning off them while they screamed and ran. You didn't see Parson Peabody's face as he predicted it all, like something had just overcome him all at once, some kind of power, or spirit, or something. You can't judge what happened, nor what anyone here thought about it. I know what I saw, and I can't explain it."

"I'm sorry. I didn't intend to—"

"I mean, after what I seen, anything seemed possible. Anything! If you'd been here, you might have believed that the parson was a true prophet, too."

"Yes. I'm sorry. I really wasn't trying to—"

Smith tiraded on. "Sure, it seems impossible to you that the parson caused it. But hell, the whole thing is impossible anyway! The sky doesn't catch fire at night. Hell doesn't fall from heaven. Trees don't get knocked flat as matchsticks for no reason. But look around you. *It happened!* So sometimes the impossible is possible after all."

"Obviously so. I apologize for offending you. And I hope you'll let me ask you another question."

Smith's anger was mostly vented away now. "Go ahead, then."

"Where are Parson Peabody and the ones with him now?"

"Gone. Rankin, Princess, and Shafter with him. They got out well before Ottinger and his soldiers came in from Fort Brandon."

"They'd seen the firefall from there?"

"You could see the thing for miles and miles, I'm sure."

"Why did they come?"

"I assumed they'd come to investigate it, and to give aid and support to those who were left. Maybe that really was the idea to start with. Now I believe Ottinger has another motive in mind. The sorry old murderer."

"Why do you despise him?"

"My two brothers were among those his men massacred in Virginia."

"I'm sorry."

"There was division in my family during the war, you see. My brothers wore the gray, me the blue. But I lost a lot of my respect for the Union cause after what Ottinger did."

"There's plenty besides you who feel the same," Gunnison said. "Brady Kenton himself despised the man like he was the devil."

"I think he *is* the devil," Smith said, and spat on the ashy ground.

Gunnison asked, "Who is the civilian they brought in on the train with all the scientific instruments?"

"A mining geologist, I think."

"A geologist? So they think this was a volcano or something?"

"Nobody thinks that. This geologist just happened to be the only kind of scientist they could round up on short notice. They grabbed the first one they could find and brought him in to figure out what happened here. But not *really* to figure it out. This soldier told me that the Colonel already has made up his mind about what happened, and just wants this man to back up his story for him—to say that whatever happened, happened because of something some person done."

"How does Ottinger plan to explain it?"

"A bomb. Can you believe that? He plans to claim that a

bomb did all this!" Decker Smith made a circular motion with his hand, indicating the surrounding landscape.

"Nobody who has seen this level of destruction could believe it was a bomb," Gunnison said. "These trees, all blown down in the same direction, burned on one side . . . anyone who sees them will know it was no bomb."

"Ah, yes," Smith said. "But what's been partly burned can be set afire again and burned completely. That's Ottinger's plan. He's going to rekindle the forest fire, destroy all these trees so you can't tell any more how strong the explosion was. Then, with this geologist backing him up with an official report saying it was no volcano or nothing like that, he can claim that somebody set off explosives in Gomorrah, caught the town on fire, and that the fire then spread into the woods."

"So Ottinger doesn't really *believe* it was a bomb . . . he just plans to make that the official explanation?"

"That's the long and short of it."

Gunnison asked, "But what about the people who witnessed what *really* happened, and who have already gotten away to tell the tale? Or, for that matter, the survivors he's still holding? Once they're let go, they'd contradict such an explanation."

"No big problem. Ottinger will just contradict them right back. He'll say they exaggerated what they saw, or misunderstood it. And let's face it: Most people will never see this mountain for themselves, and these trees fallen out like they are. Once they're burned up and the evidence gone, Ottinger can pretty much pass off whatever story he wants to to explain this fire."

"How do you know all this?"

"Like I told you: talkative soldiers. One in particular. Young private with a loose tongue and a mistrust of Ottinger."

"I guess the real question is, what's Ottinger's motive for

telling such a big lie, and going to such trouble to cover the truth?"

"I'm surprised you even have to ask. Can't you figure it out for yourself?"

Gunnison gazed blankly at Decker Smith, wondering what he'd missed. "I admit that I can't."

"Ain't you ever heard of Confederate Ridge, young man?"

"You mean that place somewhere nearby with the old rebels in it?"

"Not just any old rebels, son. Pernell Jones's old rebels, these are."

"Pernell Jones . . . wait a minute. I remember that name. A Confederate irregular out of Virginia, a raider . . ."

"And the very man who maimed and blinded Colonel Ottinger with a shotgun blast. You ought to know all about it, if you're really Brady Kenton's partner. It was Kenton who told the world the truth about the Ottinger massacre, right in the pages of the *Illustrated American*. Showed Ottinger for the murderer he is. I'm surprised the man was able to keep up a military career at all after what Kenton wrote."

"I do remember. He wrote that long before I ever started working with him. My father keeps a copy of that story on his office wall, hanging in a big frame."

"Therein lies Ottinger's motive for all of this, young man. He plans to blame Jones and his men for setting the blasts and fires that destroyed Gomorrah and killed all these people. He'll then have grounds for taking his soldiers in to overrun Confederate Ridge—and I'll bet you anything you want that Pernell Jones will be killed during the raid. Probably by Ottinger himself. The old bastard had carried a bitter grudge against Jones ever since the war. Everybody knows it. They say that's why Ottinger came up here from Texas after his wife died. He knew about Confederate Ridge, and wanted to come up near so he could settle his old score with Jones once and for all."

"One loose-tongued private told you all this?"

"Him and a few others. A lot of it I'd already heard. There's been a lot of talk about Ottinger drifting up from Fort Brandon ever since he got there."

"How long will Ottinger keep the survivors confined?" he asked.

"My suspicion is that they'll send them away soon to Fort Brandon, and there try to convince them that what they remember they don't remember right, and what they saw was just a bomb of some kind. Ottinger's already started that process, as a matter of fact. He spoke to the group of us several times, dropping the idea, very lightly, that when you see something bad happen, what is seen is sometimes blown out of proportion by your mind. And he talked a lot about Jones and his Rebs. That confirmed to me that he really does plan to lay the blame for this at Jones's feet. Now, Mr. Gunnison, I must say good-bye. I'm moving on down the mountain, and I ain't looking back. God has smit this place, and I want no more to do with it."

"Mr. Smith, can I quote what you've told me?"

"If you keep my name out of it."

"I will."

"I'm mighty sorry that Brady Kenton is dead. I'll miss his work."

"So will I," Gunnison replied. "And I'll miss the man himself far more. Tell me one thing before you go: Which way did Rankin leave? Toward the railhead, or the Fort Brandon Road?"

"The latter. But exactly where he was going, I can't say. Now, good-bye. I've got to get away before them soldiers take a head count and come looking for me."

CHAPTER ELEVEN

DECKER SMITH SLIPPED AWAY WITHOUT ANOTHER WORD. GUNNISON watched him for a while, sneaking, dodging, working his way across the burned terrain and down the mountain. Before long he was out of sight.

Gunnison mulled over what he'd heard, wondering how much of Decker Smith's information he could trust. The parts about Ottinger's plans and vengeful motivations sounded terribly speculative. He soon realized, though, that none of it really mattered beyond the crucial information he'd picked up about Rankin and the woman called Princess: They were alive, and no longer in Gomorrah.

Returning to the little shed that was his hiding place, he ate, rested a few moments, then left. He returned to the place where he and Paul Callon had hidden the bulk of their luggage, and from it added to his supplies. Most of it he would abandon, because he was on foot and probably would be for a long time to come.

The only aspect of leaving here that bothered him was abandoning Kenton's body. It wasn't right, leaving him there on the ground, like a dead dog. Maybe, if they really did set the trees afire again, like Decker Smith predicted, they'd find Kenton's body and give it a proper burial. Or maybe the flames would simply cremate him. There was at least some dignity in that . . . wasn't there?

He looked at Gomorrah, the town he'd never even fully entered, for one last time. "Paul, good luck with your story," he said. "I'll look forward to reading it."

Alex Gunnison turned his back on Gomorrah and headed west, hoping that, somehow, he could find the trail of Rankin and his companions.

Gunnison was long gone by the time darkness fell, and so did not see the man who strode in through the night from the burned-out woodlands toward Gomorrah. This was a man in pain, joints aching, head throbbing. He did not understand why the landscape around him was burned and the trees gone. He could not comprehend why there were reddened blisters on his face, why even part of his hair was singed away. He could remember no fire, for he had been unconscious until only a couple of hours before.

The last thing Brady Kenton could remember was traveling up the lonely road toward Gomorrah, eager to meet the man named Rankin who had contacted him, dropping tantalizing hints about Victoria being alive. And then . . . he wasn't sure after that.

A robbery, he thought. He seemed to remember that. A man rising from the brush, catching him by surprise. Striking him on the head, hard. He remembered falling, weak and helpless. Feeling his coat stripped from him, his possessions taken. He remembered the man's laugh as he put on the coat. "Fine fit!" he'd declared. "Just like it was made for me!" He vaguely remembered seeing the man picking at the Masonic pin on the lapel.

Then he'd passed out. And everything had been black, for a long time.

He stopped, staring into the town of Gomorrah, more confused than ever. The town wasn't as it should be . . . it was substantially . . . *gone*.

He stood still for a full minute, trying to figure out what had happened. Nothing made sense.

At last he saw a man walking through the dark streets of the town. A soldier? Why would a soldier be here?

It didn't matter, though. He was thirsty, hurting, hungry. He needed help.

He walked slowly toward the ruined town, trying to call out to the soldier. At first he could not find his voice, but at last it came. The soldier stopped, turned, half-raised his rifle, but lowered it again and advanced.

Kenton was deeply relieved. He speeded up, trying to close the gap between himself and the approaching soldier, but he was weak, and dizzy, and fell.

The soldier came on, calling now for help.

Kenton was too dazed to really take in what happened over the next hour or so. He heard words spoken at him, saw faces before him. One of them appeared to be that of Colonel J.B. Ottinger—a human devil if ever there was one! He assumed he was hallucinating, but just in case, mumbled out his name as Grant Houser, one of his several aliases.

He was in Gomorrah, but in what building he didn't know.

Oh, no. He was hallucinating again. The face of that rather obnoxious young journalist from the *Observor,* Paul Callon, was floating around in space above him.

First he'd hallucinated that human devil Ottinger, now an irritating competitor. Why did his illusions have to be so unpleasant?

"Hello, Kenton," Callon's face said. "Glad to see you coming around at last. Glad to see you alive at all, for that matter."

Good Lord . . . the illusion talked! Or maybe it wasn't an illusion at all.

"You look like someone has run you through a wringer," Callon went on. "Several times. I didn't recognize you at first. Of course, I wasn't expecting to see you at all. Last time I saw you, you were a charred corpse."

Charred corpse? Ah, yes, this was definitely a hallucination. The Callon-shaped thing was babbling nonsense.

"I wonder if Ottinger recognized you? You really don't look yourself at all," said the Callon phantom.

Kenton licked his very dry lips. "That isn't really you, is it, Callon?"

"One and the same." Callon reached down and touched his shoulder. A flesh-and-blood touch. No hallucination after all!

"Thunderation, Callon! I didn't expect to see you here . . . wherever 'here' is." Kenton licked his lips again and tried in vain to swallow. "Water . . . is there water?"

"Got a whole bucket of it over here. Hang on."

Callon vanished, then returned with an overflowing dipper in his hands. He knelt beside Kenton's bunk and helped him get himself upright to take a swallow. When that water passed his lips and flooded down his throat, cool and refreshing, it was on the whole one of the finest experiences of Brady Kenton's life.

"Thank you, Paul."

Callon laid the dipper aside. "Better lie down again, Kenton."

"No . . . no, I want to sit up." Kenton rubbed his temples gently, eyes closed.

"I must say you've recovered quite nicely from your recent death," Callon said.

"What are you talking about?"

"Gunnison and I found a body outside town. Burned to a crisp, wearing your coat, bearing your pistol. We were sure it was you."

"Gunnison is here?"

"Not right here precisely. I left him out in the forest outside town."

"He believes I'm dead?"

"He may have already so informed the *Illustrated American*."

"Thunderation!"

"For what it's worth, he was very grief-stricken when we found your corpse."

"Obviously it wasn't my corpse, Paul." Kenton twisted his neck, wincing. "If it was wearing my coat, it had to be the highwayman who attacked me while I was coming up to Gomorrah. He took my pistol, too." He looked at Callon suddenly. "Burned to a crisp, you say?"

"That's right. Just like the town itself, and much of the mountaintop. You're a bit on the charred side yourself. I suppose you must have been lying senseless out in the woods when the firefall came. By the way, I found an old coat in that wardrobe yonder that looks like it would fit you. You're welcome to it—the original owner is probably dead and gone."

"Thank you. What was that you said about a firefall? What's a firefall?"

"Well, you've just asked the question of the hour. Something very strange happened on this mountain, Kenton. An explosion that killed much of the population and spread fire through the town and the woods. And now the army has come in, from Fort Brandon, and taken the town over."

"Fort Brandon?" Kenton frowned. "Thunderation . . . then that *was* Ottinger I saw!"

"That's right. He's here. The man in charge."

"I wonder if he knew me?"

"Hard to say. Like I said, you don't look yourself right now."

"I told him my name was Houser."

"Good thing. I doubt that Ottinger has any affection for Brady Kenton."

"No. Not at all." Kenton paused, then said, "He even hired a man to kill me once, after I exposed him in the *Illustrated American*."

"*What?*"

"The effort failed, obviously. It was never repeated. I just let it go."

"Colonel J.B. Ottinger actually tried to have you *assassinated?*"

"Yes. I've never mentioned it to anyone. Not even Alex. For heaven's sake, don't you dare spread the story."

"The man must be insane!"

"Mad with vengefulness. Willing to do anything to even a score, and unwilling ever to drop a grudge. Other than that, as sane as you or I. But evil. Very evil."

"What will you do, Kenton? You're in his hands now."

"Where are we?"

"Locked up in this cabin. One of the few structures to make it through the firefall mostly unscathed. I've been here since early yesterday morning. They caught me sneaking about."

"What's become of Gunnison?"

"I wish I knew. He may still be hiding out in the woods. I wish I'd stayed out there with him . . . I'm achieving nothing locked up in here."

"Paul, I was to meet a man here, named Rankin. A very important meeting, for personal reasons. Do you know if he survived this great fire?"

Though Gunnison had told Callon the reason Kenton had come to meet Rankin, Callon thought it prudent not to reveal to Kenton that he knew something so personal. "I don't know. I don't know much of anything. How can I, locked up here?"

"Why did they put you here?"

"Because they determined that I was a journalist, and Ottinger has no use for journalists."

Kenton pondered deeply. "I wonder if the fact they've put me in here with you indicates that I've been recognized as a journalist, too?"

"Maybe. Or maybe it's just the most convenient place to lock up stragglers who stray into this burned-out town."

Kenton sniffed and frowned. "What is that horrific stench?"

"That's one question I can answer: It's the dead, my friend. The dead of Gomorrah. Lined up in rows in a tent not far from this cabin. Growing quite ripe by now. There's a little hole through the wall over there; I look through it to see what's going on outside. I saw soldiers with shovels a few minutes ago. A burial detail, I suppose. It's about time. They've been photographing the bodies."

"Callon, I don't understand this 'firefall' business."

"Something happened here, Kenton. Something very strange and lethal."

Callon outlined the story, giving every detail he could. He told as well of how Gunnison came to enter the picture, his finding of Kenton's stray notes, his learning of Kenton's planned meeting with the man Rankin. Callon did not, however, give any indication that Gunnison had told him about Kenton's search for his lost wife. This, he knew, was too delicate a topic to be brought up with Brady Kenton. He also made no mention of the Confederate Ridge Rebels, though this was merely an oversight in his haste to tell the tale.

Kenton listened with fascination, and Callon observed an interesting phenomenon: As the details of a tantalizing, unusual tale were fed to him, Kenton's color and vigor visibly returned. He even stood and began pacing back and forth, unable to hide his mounting fascination.

But his first comment when Callon was done let the latter

know that part of Kenton's energy also stemmed from worry.

"I wonder how I can find out if Rankin survived? And anyone who might have been with him?"

"I don't know, Kenton. But I think your biggest worry has to be your own safety. If Ottinger actually tried to have you killed once before, and if he realizes that he has you literally in his clutches . . ."

"I know, I know. But don't worry about it. I'll find a way to handle Ottinger."

"You have an abundance of confidence, Kenton."

"I always have."

"I think you should try to find some way out of here."

"Sounds like a certain way to get shot at."

"But if he recognizes you . . ."

"I've told them my name is Houser. I'll stick with that story."

"You really should get away."

"Not until I know beyond a doubt that Rankin isn't here among the survivors."

"The numerical odds are against it. There are more dead than alive. There were a few who survived who got away from Gomorrah before the army sealed the town off."

Kenton's stomach growled loudly. "I'm starving. I hope they bring some food soon. They have been feeding you, haven't they?"

"Yes. But not nearly enough."

CHAPTER TWELVE

THEY DID BRING FOOD, ABOUT AN HOUR LATER. BEFORE THAT, though, an army doctor showed up to examine the newly arrived "Houser."

The doctor was young, uniformed, and seemed substantially disinterested in Kenton except as one more medical specimen. But he did a sufficiently decent job of examination, and seemed content that Kenton, a stranger to him, was headed for a fast and thorough recovery.

"A lot had it worse than you," he said in a weary tone. "We've got several people with much worse burns; we'll be moving them out by wagon later today, taking them to the Fort Brandon infirmary, where I can better treat their injuries."

"Are any in danger of their lives?"

"Those injured *that* severely have already died, I'm sorry to say. I expect recovery for all who are left alive at this point."

"Do I need to go to Fort Brandon, too?"

"Not for medical treatment. But as I understand it, all civilians are to be taken to Fort Brandon."

"Why?"

"Look, I'm a physician. I've said more than I should already."

"Can I leave here?"

"Not up to me."

"Doctor, what caused the fire?"

"The incident is under scientific investigation. It appears at this point that the event resulted from the explosion of a man-made incendiary device, and was complicated by the resultant spread of fire through the town and the woods around. This is what Colonel Ottinger says."

"An 'incendiary device,' you say. A bomb, in other words."

"That's right."

"Quite a large bomb, to do what this one did."

"I'm unqualified to comment, Mister . . ."

"Houser. Grant Houser."

"Houser. All right." The doctor closed his medical bag. "Bombs are out of my sphere. I'm merely repeating what I've been told."

"By Colonel Ottinger?"

"You ask a lot of questions, Mr. Houser. I thought it was this one here who's the nosy journalist." He thumbed toward Callon.

"I've always been overly curious," Kenton said.

Callon spoke up. "There's a compound of former Rebels not too far from here. I know, because I've seen two of them with my own eyes. Is it the army's position that these Rebels are behind this blast?"

"I'm not authorized to speak to that matter and have said too much already," the doctor said. "Good day to you both." He went to the door, rapped for exit, and was let out by the guard, who shut and locked the door again.

Kenton said, "You should have let me ask the questions. He'd never have answered you, knowing you're a reporter, but he thinks of me as a private citizen. He might have told me."

Callon answered, a bit smugly, "Yes . . . but you didn't know to ask the question. I forgot to mention the old Rebel compound when I was briefing you earlier."

"You didn't need to. I'm fully aware of Confederate Ridge."

Callon gritted his teeth. Blast Kenton! Was the man on top of every situation?

"Well . . . do you know a pair of Confederate Ridge Rebels watched Gunnison and me when we first came up to Gomorrah?"

"It's not surprising. I'm sure they're as curious about the destruction of the mountaintop as anyone else, especially considering they live not far away. And if they know that Ottinger is there, they have all the more cause for concern. Confederate Ridge is the home of the old renegade rider Pernell Jones, you know. He's the man whose shotgun blast mangled Ottinger's face."

Callon could hardly believe it. Kenton had only regained consciousness a short while ago, and already he knew more about the situation than did Callon himself.

The young journalist, with effort, swallowed down his sizeable load of pride.

"Kenton, listen to me. I know we're competitors, but maybe it's time to put that aside. Together we could tell this story like neither one of us can do alone. Let's work together. Be partners."

"I have a partner already, Paul."

"Yes. But he's not here, and I am. I can join with you, help you ferret out this story—if you'll let me. We can publish in both the *Observor* and the *Illustrated American*. Simultaneously, joint credit, everything right down the middle."

"What makes you think I'm working on this story at all, Paul? It's interesting, certainly, but I've got other, more personal concerns."

"This Rankin fellow."

"Yes."

In a burst of mean-spiritedness and frustration, Callon

almost threw into Kenton's face what Gunnison had told him. But he held back, and instead asked, "What is it you want from this Rankin?"

Kenton's eyes actually misted. "Information. Very important, and very personal."

Callon let out a long, slow breath. "All right. I'll ask no more. But I will make a request. If you're not going to try to write the Gomorrah story yourself, at least can you try to help me gather some facts? They may let you leave this place. They may put you with the survivors of the firefall, maybe even take you to Fort Brandon like the doctor was talking about. Me, they're just going to keep locked up."

Kenton went back to the bunk he'd been lying on before. He sat down. "Patience, Paul Callon. Patience. They'll surely not keep you locked up here forever."

"You won't help me?"

"If I can, I will. But you have to know that my chief interest isn't in this story, Paul. Normally it would be, but this is not a normal situation for me. And, you must remember . . . you are, after all, a competitor."

"Damn it, Kenton! I'll not have you leave me high and dry! You *will* help me, or I'll make sure myself that Ottinger knows who you really are!"

Kenton stared at Callon. "You wouldn't do such a thing, Paul."

"I would! I will!"

"Then you are not the man I've taken you to be."

"Can't you see how important this story is, Kenton? Can't you see what it would do for my professional reputation? It's obvious, yet here you sit, wrapped up in yourself, caught up in some fool's quest for a wife who died years ago—"

Callon cut off, realizing what he'd just said.

Kenton blanched slightly. He stared numbly at Callon for several moments, silent.

"So you know," he said, softly.

Callon slumped into the nearest chair. "Dear Lord, what a fool I am. And what foolish things I've been saying. I'm sorry."

"How did you know?"

"Gunnison told me. But only after he believed you were dead."

"I see."

"I'm sorry. I didn't intend to let you know that I knew. I understand that it's deeply personal."

"It is."

For a while, neither man conversed further.

"Kenton," Callon said after a time, "I really wouldn't reveal you to Ottinger."

"I know."

"I don't know why I said such a thing."

"Because you were angry. Because you find me unprofessional, being distracted by a personal concern and ignoring what admittedly is a very big and unusual story. And I suppose I *am* being unprofessional. But this is my wife I'm hoping to find, Paul. My wife."

Callon said, "Could she really be alive, Kenton?"

"I don't know. I hope so . . . I pray so."

"This Rankin fellow has information about her?"

"So he wrote to me. He implied that . . . he might even have Victoria herself."

"Amazing . . ."

"Yes. And maybe nothing but a falsehood. My fear now, of course, is that he really did have her, and that both of them were here when this mysterious explosion occurred . . ."

"Take it one step at a time, Kenton. Right now you have no facts upon which to make judgments."

"You're right, of course." Kenton lay down.

"Kenton, are you going to go to sleep on me and leave me without company again?"

"I might. I've been through the wringer, like you said. I need rest."

"Rest? After how long you've been lying out in the woods? It's bad enough in here even *with* someone to talk to. It's worse when there's no one. I wish you'd stay awake."

It was no use to plead. Brady Kenton drew in a deep breath, closed his eyes, and within moments began the steady, slow respiration of sleep.

He didn't sleep long. A private bearing a platter of food showed up. One plate for Callon, another for "Houser."

Kenton awakened fast, accepted the meal gratefully and fell to at once. The private stood watching him for a few moments, saying nothing, then left.

"I don't like the way that soldier stared at you, Kenton," Callon said. "I think he recognized you."

"Hmm?"

"I think he knew you."

"Really?" Kenton said, taking another bite. "I didn't notice."

He spoke in an idle way, but Callon could tell Kenton was concerned.

CHAPTER THIRTEEN

AN HOUR LATER, THE DOOR RATTLED AND OPENED AGAIN. A young soldier entered, trying to look authoritative and tough, but actually looking only like most western soldiers Kenton had seen: a boy struggling hard to make the best of a life he'd hoped would be adventurous but which had proved mostly to just be boring and disheartening. "Mr. Houser, sir," he barked.

Kenton, blinking, sat up, feeling very groggy. "What is it?"

"The Colonel wishes to speak with you, sir. Right away. Are you strong enough to walk?"

"I don't know that he is," Callon said quickly, standing from his chair in the corner. With nothing to do, he'd fallen asleep as well. "Maybe I should go in his place."

"Nonsense," Kenton said, swinging around his legs and standing. He brushed his hair back with his hands and tried to make his rumpled and ruined clothing look as good as possible. "I'll gladly see the Colonel." Kenton glanced at Callon. "I'd consider it an honor to meet so famous a man."

As he followed the soldier across the charred town, Kenton saw other soldiers at work, digging a massive trench. He'd seen mass graves during the war and knew what they were doing. With the smell of death strong across the town, he hoped they would finish with all haste.

Other soldiers were in the woods, chopping down the

remnants of trees, stacking them as if for great bonfires. Others dealt with trees that had already fallen, shoving and heaving them about to make contact with one another.

"They're going to set fires?" Kenton asked the soldier.

"I'm not at liberty to answer your questions, sir," the soldier said. "That's up to the Colonel."

When they reached Ottinger's tent, the Colonel's voice could be heard from inside, speaking rather loudly. The soldier rapped gently on one of the tent supports. "Sir!"

Ottinger appeared at the flap doorway, caught sight of Kenton, and eyed him up and down. Ottinger's dead right eye gleamed like a marble, unmoving. He looked back at the soldier. "Stay with him—I'll be only a moment. Bring him a stool to sit on."

A camp stool was provided for Kenton, who sat near the tent, looking around the town, giving every appearance of a man distracted by all he saw. In fact he was listening to the voices inside Ottinger's tent.

"So there's simply no way this event can be accounted for in volcanic terms," Ottinger was saying.

"No, sir, certainly not. That was never really a possibility. Vulcanism makes quite distinctive displays, none of them evident here."

"Without a volcanic origin, then, we're left with human agency as the only possible cause of this," Ottinger said.

"No, sir, not entirely. There are other possibilities, but they are well outside my field of expertise. I'm a mining geologist, not qualified to speculate outside my own field."

"Then I suggest you don't attempt to do so. You've ruled out volcanic activity, and have no credentials to suggest other possible causes. Does that sum it up accurately?"

"Well, I suppose it does . . . but, sir, everything I've seen indicates to me that what caused this fire was massive, tremendously powerful, and exploded in the sky high above the town. The direction of the fallen trees is sufficient to prove that. I suggest that you consult with a qualified astronomer. And also, sir, I hope you'll desist from your plans to reburn the fallen trees. You'll wipe out much important evidence if you do."

"I'll keep your recommendations in mind. But what I really need from you now is a report indicating that you've ruled out a volcanic explanation for this fire. I want no speculation about other causes. None. Do you understand me? Good. And of course, I'll arrange very adequate compensation to be made to you for the time you've given to the aid of the United States government."

The geologist, hesitating a moment, said, "Colonel Ottinger, sir, was I brought here to give you an honest view of what probably caused this event? Or simply to—"

Ottinger cut him off. "You were brought here, sir, to rule out the possibility of a volcanic explanation. And you've done so. And you need concern yourself no further with this. Simply write your report. Keep it brief. You may go, Mr. Johnston."

Kenton watched as the geologist exited the tent and walked rapidly across the charred ground toward his own quarters. He pushed his way into his tent with a big sweep of his arm. This was clearly an angry and frustrated man.

Ottinger reappeared at the entrance of his own tent. He examined Kenton coldly with his one good eye. "Mr. Houser, do come in, sir."

Kenton stood and followed Ottinger back inside.

Ottinger waved Kenton to a seat, and said nothing for about a minute as he busied about with a pipe and tobacco, loading it carefully and firing up the bowl with great concentration. He drew and puffed, filling the tent with the aromatic smoke of an expensive tobacco blend.

"Beg pardon," Ottinger said abruptly. "Would you care for a pipe or a cigar, Mr. Houser?"

"No, sir, not at the moment, thank you, sir," Kenton

replied. "Though I wouldn't mind at all having one to enjoy later."

Ottinger blew smoke out his nose as he removed a cigar from a box on a nearby folding table that was evidently serving as his desk. He handed it to Kenton, who accepted with many thanks.

Ottinger perched himself on a stool and examined Kenton closely through the smoke of his pipe. "You look quite familiar, Mr. Houser."

"Beg your pardon, sir?"

Ottinger's brows knitted together in concentration. "I question whether you're name is really Houser."

"Of course it is, sir."

A little smile flickered across Ottinger's face. "What's your trade, Mr. Houser?"

"I've mostly farmed, sir. In Illinois, before I came out west. I tried my hand at storekeeping in Kansas for a few years, near Wichita."

"What brought you to Gomorrah?"

"I was thinking of opening a store here. I wanted to look the town over and see if I thought it would thrive here."

"And where were you when this town caught afire?"

"Outside of town, unconscious in the woods. I was attacked and robbed on my way into town."

"What bad luck."

"I've had my share. First that, and then the town burned up."

"You and I, we know one another. There's no point in this foolish pretense."

"Well, of course I know who you are, Colonel. You're a famous man. But me, I'm not anybody."

"Oh, you're definitely somebody, Mr. Kenton. You're a man of very great power, in fact. The power of the printed word . . . of your printed lies. I've been the subject of some of your most venomous lies yet. I find it interesting that now, as we meet face to face, you lack even the courage to admit who you are."

Kenton bristled, but hid it. He'd not let Ottinger lure him like some bait-hungry fish. Yet it was hard to bear such an insult from this man, of all men.

Just remember, he told himself, *he just insulted Brady Kenton. And that's not you. While you're here, you're Grant Houser.*

"Colonel, sir, you've obviously mistaken me for someone else."

"I didn't recognize you right away. You're burned and bruised. The private who brought you your meal was the one who drew my attention to you. He was in Leadville some years ago, and saw you there. When he told me our new foundling was Brady Kenton . . . well, that was a surprise indeed. Couldn't quite believe it. But damned if he wasn't right. I've never seen you face-to-face until now, Mr. Kenton, but that likeness of you on your publication is quite good."

Kenton forced a laugh. "It's Brady Kenton you think I am? I'll be! I've had people tell me I looked a little like him, but nobody ever thought I *was* him before! Wait until I tell my wife!" Kenton paused, then couldn't resist adding, "I'll take it as a compliment. Kenton is a mighty good writer. At least I think so . . . you talk like you don't like him much."

"I despise Brady Kenton, sir. He's libeled me far too deeply, and I have no use whatever for him." Ottinger stared hard into Kenton's face and came a few inches closer. "But, you know, that's a situation that could change. For once in my life, I might actually have some good use for Brady Kenton. Something that would benefit him as well as me. Something that could close old wounds."

Ottinger was obviously attempting to pique Kenton's curiosity, and it was working. But Kenton wouldn't change course now.

Kenton did his best to look rather simple and befuddled. "Well . . . I wish Kenton was here to help you out, then."

Ottinger's narrowed left eye remained fixed on Kenton's face; the dead right one, as always, was lusterless and unmoving. "Very well, Mr. *Houser*. Too bad, in a way. I'm positioned to hand Brady Kenton the greatest story of his career."

"What's that, sir?"

"An explanation of what happened to cause this unusual fire. But it's of no concern to you, of course."

"Well . . . I'm as curious about it as anybody else."

Ottinger smiled and shook his head. "Perhaps, if you should happen to see Brady Kenton . . . or decide to be honest about who we both know you are . . . then perhaps we can find grounds to put old animosities aside."

Kenton stared at him. There were many things that cried out to be said, but which the circumstances would not allow. The pretense had to go on.

Kenton smiled brightly and snapped his fingers. "Well, I just had an idea, sir! I'm no reporter myself, but there's a man I been locked up in that cabin with who is. He writes for that other publication, you know . . . the one that's not as good as Kenton's—the *Observor*. That's it! Maybe *he* can write your story for you."

"Maybe he can. He's no Kenton . . . but I suppose he'll have to do, hmmm?"

Kenton smiled brightly. "I'm glad you like my idea, sir."

Ottinger glared at him, making no effort to hide his hatred.

"Can I ask you for a favor, sir?" Kenton asked.

"What's that, Mr. *Houser*?" Again the mocking emphasis on the false name.

"I would like to ask if I might be allowed to not be locked up in that cabin anymore. I'd like to go be with the other civilians." Only by joining the company of the survivors of Gomorrah, Kenton knew, could he determine if Rankin was still alive in this town.

Ottinger wasn't biting. "You'll stay right where I've had you. Where we can keep an eye on you." Ottinger called out, "Sergeant! Please come escort Mr. Houser back to his cabin!" He turned back to Kenton and looked at him closely. "We've played a foolish game here, Kenton. An exercise in futile dodgemanship. But don't think it will do you any good. I have you now."

"I wish I could persuade you that I ain't Brady Kenton, sir."

"Get on with you. Get out. Kenton, you have a chance to reconsider . . . a limited chance. When I send for your cabin companion, like I sent for you, you'll know my patience has been exhausted and your chance has passed." He smiled darkly. "That would be too bad. If only you would cooperate with me, Kenton, and write the story I'm prepared to give you . . . if you would only present to the world a different vision of Colonel J.B. Ottinger than the false one you contrived so many years ago . . . if you would do that, sir, I can assure you that your life will be much longer, and happier, than otherwise."

Kenton was angered by these words, but hid that emotion and did his best to look like the easily confused, somewhat bumbling would-be merchant he was presenting "Grant Houser" to be. "Are you saying you'd hurt Brady Kenton, Colonel?"

"I'm trying to tell Brady Kenton that I'm a man who has reached a stage of life when an evening of the balance has become important. There are old scores that have waited a long time to be settled. I'm growing older. I don't intend for my life to end with the balances still tilted. I am a man who pays my debts. And paying time has come."

"Houser" frowned in apparent confusion at the Colonel, then brightened, sighed, and shrugged. "You're a hard man to understand, Colonel," Kenton said. "But I'm honored to have got to visit with you. I can't wait to tell Mrs. Houser I got to meet so famous a military man."

Ottinger spun on his heel and with a grunt of disgust all but shoved Kenton out of the tent and into the custody of the waiting sergeant.

Kenton walked with his escort back toward the cabin, chatting, keeping in character as Grant Houser, jabbering about the pleasure of having gotten to personally talk to a well-known man.

The stench of bodily decay was blessedly declining now. Soldiers with kerchiefs tied around their mouths and noses were covering the burned and rotting dead in the trench grave, and a fresh breeze was clearing the air at last.

CHAPTER FOURTEEN

CALLON CAME TO HIS FEET AS THE DOOR WAS OPENED. KENTON entered, then sank onto his bunk and lay back. He'd been exhausted by the tense gamesmanship with Ottinger. Every injury he'd suffered when attacked by that doomed highwayman now hurt twice as much as before.

"Well? What happened?" Callon asked when the door was locked again.

"Colonel Ottinger has this loco notion that my name's not Grant Houser. He seems to believe I'm Brady Kenton."

"Ah. Recognized. You're lucky he didn't kill you."

"I kept up the pretense of being Houser," Kenton said, speaking with eyes closed. "But he's not buying that bill of goods."

"What did Ottinger want with you?"

"He wants to use me. He wants me to write a version of the Gomorrah story as he wants it told. And to, in effect, recant my earlier story about him in the process."

"How does he want the Gomorrah story told?"

"He didn't say. But I do know he's intent on attributing the incident to a human cause. If I had to take a guess, I'd say the human he'll blame is Pernell Jones, and anyone else at Confederate Ridge. He talked about how he's entered a period of settling old scores. Jones, the man who maimed him, is one of those he feels he owes vengeance to, I'm sure."

"Did you accept his bargain?"

"Of course not. I couldn't, if I was to continue to be Grant Houser. I made the suggestion that perhaps he should ask you instead. I hope that was not a mistake—I don't want to drag you into a dangerous situation."

Callon certainly didn't seem worried. He did a brief little jig of happiness. "Yes, indeed! Thank you, Kenton. I'd hoped something like that would happen!"

Kenton said to Callon, "Just remember: Ottinger isn't interested in presenting the truth. He's just wants a willing journalist to use as a tool for his own ends."

"No need to worry, Kenton. I'll lie for no one in print. That's an absolute. But I'd welcome the chance to interview the Colonel . . . then, of course, publish whatever is the *real* truth. Did he truly want to give me his version of the story?"

"He wants to get his version out so it will be believed."

"Good. Good." Callon paced back and forth very rapidly.

"Callon, sit down. You're making me nervous."

"I can't sit down. I've been locked up in here too long. I wonder when he'll send for me?"

Kenton decided not to mention that the moment Ottinger did so would be the same moment Kenton himself would lose his last chance to change his mind. At that moment, he was sure, he would be in danger of his life. He said only, "Be careful of him, Callon. Ottinger is a dangerous man, in many ways. And he'll place you in a dilemma: cooperate with him and destroy your professional ethics, or decline to help him and be in danger of your life. It truly could be that serious for you, and for me."

"You've already refused to cooperate."

"Yes."

"So you've chosen to put yourself at personal risk."

"That's right."

Callon was thoughtful a couple of moments, then put on

a brave face. "I can do no less. And don't worry about me. I can take care of myself."

"Just don't underestimate Ottinger."

"I won't."

Callon stood by the window, peeping out through a crack.

"Kenton, wake up."

Kenton stirred and mumbled.

"Kenton, wake up. Come here."

Kenton sat up, winced, and rubbed his face.

"Kenton, they're leaving!"

"Who?"

"The people—the survivors. They're herding them out like cattle."

Kenton rose and went to Callon, who stepped aside and let him have a look out the hole. The people of Gomorrah were indeed being moved out, soldiers guarding them. They filed toward wagons parked where the Fort Brandon Road met the edge of town.

"Do you think they'll come get us, too?" Callon asked.

"I don't know," Kenton said.

"If they don't . . . would that be a good or a bad thing?"

"I don't know that, either."

Kenton watched the people mounting the wagons. A pitiful lot indeed, burned and limping and bedraggled. He wondered if one of the number was Rankin.

He looked among the number for a woman that might resemble Victoria as she would be at this age. He saw no one.

The soldiers did not come to get them. The wagons loaded and moved out.

At dusk, two soldiers came for Callon. "The Colonel wants to talk to you, friend."

Callon gave Kenton a tight, nervous grin. "Wish me luck, Mr. Houser. And fortitude."

Kenton nodded.

This was it. Kenton knew the deadline for his cooperation had passed. He was now expendable.

The soldiers closed and barred the cabin door again.

Kenton went to the shuttered window and through a crevice watched Callon being led to the Colonel's quarters. He knew the great pressure that would be brought to bear against Callon over the next little while. He hoped Callon would keep his head and his temper.

Out in the woods, soldiers were lighting fires, burning the fallen trees.

He had to get out of here. And away from Gomorrah and Ottinger's reach. A man who would actually seek to manipulate and reshape the evidence of a natural disaster so he could blame it on an old enemy was a dangerous man indeed.

Kenton watched the woods grow bright with flame, the soldiers busy and preoccupied with maintaining and controlling the blaze.

He noticed that, for the moment, no one was directly guarding his cabin. Probably all the soldiers were needed for fire-control duty.

He began exploring the cabin, examining the corners, the windows, the barred door, even the place where the roof met the walls. At last his attention settled on the fireplace.

Kenton went to it, knelt, and examined it closely. It was rough, made of stones and crude, sandy mortar. Probably not a particularly strong mortar, either. He scratched at it with a fingernail, then found an iron poker and went at it with that. The results were satisfying, mortar falling away in big chunks, one of the stones gradually loosening.

He worked hard and fast, but carefully, trying to minimize noise in case a guard returned.

Colonel Ottinger seemed to be in a calm and reflective mood. He walked slowly through the smoky dusk, hands clasped behind his back, brows lowered, words softly spoken and carefully chosen. His posture, expression, and tone created the impression of Ottinger as a man in control, a man devoted to truth and duty, a man speaking to Callon as one ready to be his friend and confidant.

Underneath Ottinger's cool veneer, though, Callon detected turbulence and heat. This was a tense and angry man.

"I'll not seek to persuade you that I'm generally a friend of journalists," Ottinger was saying as he and Callon walked side-by-side through the ash-colored avenues of the ruined mining town, which was weirdly lighted now by the flames of the rekindled forest. "I've been ill-used by a certain journalist in the past, and have no love for your trade. I tell you this because I'm not a man who wishes for either of us to have any misunderstandings as regards the grounds on which we stand, one to another."

"I understand, sir," Callon said. "I'm aware that, in print, you've been a . . . controversial figure." Callon, too, was choosing his words carefully, which didn't come naturally for him. He tended to speak frankly, even rudely, particularly when he knew he was being toyed with, lied to, or manipulated.

"Controversial. Yes. I'll accept that designation," Ottinger said. "A man who is firm and decisive, a man who acts upon his best instincts and highest motivations, often stirs controversy. Such has been my situation all my life. But I've been misunderstood and misinterpreted through the years. The wartime incident that rendered me so controversial is one that has never been rightly understood by the public at large. But I, sir, am not a self-serving instigator of some needless massacre, as I was characterized in print. I am a devoted servant of my nation and my President, and of the great moral order of this universe." He paused, then said, "Write that down, if you would. 'I am a servant of my nation, my President, and the great—"

"Yes, yes, I've got it," Callon said, scribbling on his notepad. Ottinger had only moments ago returned to Callon the pad and pencils that had been confiscated when he was captured by the soldiers.

Ottinger glared angrily after Callon cut him off. Callon noticed and took warning. *Careful there, Paul,* he counseled himself. *This is a volatile man. Don't let his cloying ways make you lose your temper here. Play along with him for now.*

Callon read the quote back to the Colonel, just to look cooperative. Ottinger now looked pleased.

"Yes, right. Now, as I was saying, though I've got not much favor to grant to the journalistic trade, I do believe your presence here can be useful. Clearly a terrible event has happened in this town, and it's important that the people of this nation understand precisely what caused it."

"A natural event of some kind, sir?" Callon asked.

"It might appear so. But no, this event, I'm afraid, was caused by human agency."

Callon scribbled and nodded. Ottinger was saying the things Kenton had predicted.

"The town of Gomorrah was destroyed by deliberately set explosives that were put in place, no doubt over a period of several days, by men of the lowest character and with the greatest hostility toward this nation and its people," Ottinger said.

Callon stopped writing. "You mean to say that all this destruction was deliberately done?"

"Precisely. The fire, of course, spread naturally after it began, but the initial cause was a planned, carefully designed detonation."

"Brought about by whom?"

"Write this down: Done by a band of insurgents who,

after all these years, bear the deepest of resentments stemming from the late war of Southern rebellion. Former Confederates are whom I'm talking about, sir. Men who have failed to put the past behind them and still plot and connive toward the harming of this nation and its people."

Callon frowned. "Who are these 'insurgents,' precisely?"

"All of their individual identities I don't know. I do have cause to believe they are led by a former Rebel irregular and murdering bushwhacker whose identity I will not yet reveal."

"You wouldn't be talking about the purported compound of unreconstructed Rebels that is supposedly somewhere in these mountains around us, are you?" Callon asked. "The so-called Confederate Ridge compound?"

Ottinger seemed surprised that Callon was ahead of him. The man clearly wanted to lead in this little dance, not follow.

"I suspect we're thinking of the same people, yes," Ottinger said.

"But I don't understand," Callon said. "What would be the point of such an act? What would these old Rebels hope to gain by destroying a mining town?"

Ottinger's jaw clenched again; his one good eye bulged angrily and his brow furrowed. He put out a gloved fist and shook it. "Symbolism, young man! Symbolism! These damned unreconstructeds are not rational men. They are men of emotion and anger, men who are utterly unwilling to admit their defeat even after nearly two decades, yet also utterly unable to do anything substantive about their frustrations. Therefore they choose to act in a symbolic fashion. Having hidden in these mountains, hating the very nation that harbors them, they now see the tendrils of that growing nation reaching toward them. The railroad, the telegraph wire, the roadway, the cattle trail, the mining town. They see the mighty United States expanding, growing stronger and larger while they grow weaker, and their frustrations boil and fester all the worse because of it. Thus they reach out and strike, in an almost childish manner, through the planned destruction of a town."

CHAPTER FIFTEEN

CALLON WASN'T WRITING NOW. HE FROWNED AND PACED BACK and forth before the Colonel, thinking. He shook his head. "I'm sorry, sir, but it makes no sense to me."

Ottinger's jaw did its little clench again.

Callon went on despite an inner voice that urged him not to. "There's something far too unlikely in it all. Why, after all these years, would a band of former Rebels go to such trouble, all for mere symbolism? Why would they pick a two-bit mining town, known mostly for its sinful ways, as a point of attack? They could better make their point by destroying a railroad, or even sneaking these explosives of theirs under the walls of Fort Brandon itself and setting them off there.

"And about these explosives . . . do you really ask me to believe, and ask my readers to believe in turn, that anyone at all, particularly a band of stubborn old Rebels, would possess enough explosive power to do *this*?" Callon waved his hand, indicating the destroyed town, the ruined forest.

Ottinger was not a man accustomed to being questioned, particularly by an upstart young civilian journalist. He scowled fiercely at Callon, and spoke in a colder, even more formal tone of voice. "What you see around you, sir, was not solely the result of the initial blasts. Those explosions were carried out in such a way as to cause extremely severe and fast-moving fires, which spread through this tinderbox town and into the woods around them. The forest damage you see resulted from the fire, not the explosions."

"Colonel, those trees didn't burn down; they were *knocked* down, by an incredible explosive force. They didn't burn very thoroughly, and mostly on one side, the side facing Gomorrah. They all fell in the same direction. This was no common forest fire, sir."

"How dare you argue with me! I am in command here!"

Callon was doing the very thing he'd promised himself he wouldn't do—losing his temper—but he couldn't stop himself. Nothing roused his ire more than perceiving that he, as a journalist, was being used and lied to. "You may be in command of your soldiers, sir, but I'm a private citizen. A civilian. And I work for the *Observor,* not for you, and not for the United States Army. And I'm not a fool. I can see clearly what you're up to here."

Ottinger stared at him. "And tell me, then, what it is I'm up to."

Ottinger did an odd thing then: without giving Callon a chance to answer, he turned and walked away, toward the woods, heading for a portion not at the moment being burned. It was darker there, more remote from the town.

Callon hesitated, then followed. "I'll tell you what you're up to, sir. You know as well as I do that what happened here was something very strange, something unusual, something maybe we cannot yet explain. Whatever it was, though, it certainly wasn't the work of some gaggle of old Confederates, and you know it.

"But you also know that this event provides you opportunity. You can use this incident to cast blame on these old Rebels, and have a pretext to move against them, arrest them, whatever. So you keep the people of Gomorrah, who know what *really* happened here, under your control as long as possible, to keep them quiet. You reburn the forest because you know that anyone who sees the pattern in which these trees fell, and the pattern by which they originally burned, will know that this was caused by an explosion much stronger than any human being could bring about. And you seek to use me, and my publication, to further your lie before the nation. Because once you get the false version in print, you've won the day. Most people will never travel up to this mountaintop to see the evidence of the kind of blast that really occurred. And with the fallen trees all burned to ashes, there would be little evidence left to see, anyway. Everyone would simply accept the official story. Any eyewitness or survivor who tells a different story would simply be labeled an exaggerator and dismissed."

Ottinger faced Callon. "Tell me, then, what *did* happen here, if you consider my version so faulty. And don't speak of volcanic activity. I've had this site studied by a trained geologist, and *that* theory has already been ruled out."

"I don't believe this was caused by volcanic activity," Callon said. "To be honest, I can't guess exactly what caused it . . . but I think something fell from the sky, and exploded above the town."

Ottinger laughed. "Fell from the sky? What? Fire and brimstone from heaven?"

"Maybe not fire and brimstone. I'm no scientist, but I know there are objects out there, moving through the heavens, sometimes falling toward earth. Maybe it was something like that. I've heard that such things can happen."

"Well, it didn't happen here. This was the work of insurgents, and that, young man, is what you will report."

"The *Observor* is not under the control of you or the United States government, Colonel. In this nation the press enjoys freedom from such control."

Ottinger pushed himself into Callon's face, waving his fist. "Damn you! Can't you see what I'm doing for you? I'm offering you an exclusive privilege, to report first-hand the way this town was attacked and destroyed, and the response to that attack! Are you going to turn your back on this?"

Ottinger again made his odd move, and turned away before Callon could respond. He walked two dozen more paces into the woods, crossing a small ridge and actually going completely out of Callon's sight.

Callon hesitated, very unsure about all this now. The thought of turning and running came to mind. But perhaps Ottinger wanted him to do just that. He might even have unseen guards about, ready to shoot him down if he tried it.

Another thing as well kept him from running. He heard something, off in the woods. Movement, as if someone were out there, watching, listening. Perhaps just an animal, perhaps a man . . . if the latter, a man probably close enough to have heard much of the conversation so far.

"Alex?" Callon whispered. "Alex Gunnison, is that you?"

No one answered.

Callon followed Ottinger over the ridge. It was much darker here; Callon could barely make out the Colonel's form in the blackness. "Colonel, what 'response' are you talking about?"

"Do you agree to write the story? If you will, I'll tell you."

"I'll write the story . . . but I'll not have its terms dictated."

"If you write anything at all, young man, it will *indeed* be on my terms, and I'll not allow a word to be sent out by you, in any form, without my prior approval."

"I'll not allow a prior restraint on any story I write, Colonel Ottinger."

Ottinger shook his head. "You're as big a fool as Kenton. He turned me down as well."

"It's only because Kenton follows the ethics of a professional, and will not compromise it."

Ottinger smiled triumphantly. "Ah-ha! So it *is* Kenton! I knew it!"

Callon's heart sank. With no intention to do so, he'd just confirmed Brady Kenton's identity. Ottinger had outfoxed him.

Callon strode toward Ottinger, made bold by anger. "Don't you dare harm him! Don't even think of it!"

Ottinger laughed. "Harm him? Why would I do that? What do you think I am?"

Callon stammered a moment, then said, "I know you and Kenton have a bad history between you. I know you're a man prone to vengeance."

"Do you think so? Why? You don't know me at all, Mr. Callon. All you know of me is what you've read, printed by liars like Brady Kenton. He's probably been telling you more lies there in that cabin. I'm not the wicked creature Kenton says I am, Mr. Callon. And he's not the great warrior for truth he claims to be."

Callon wondered if it was too late to backstep somehow. He'd at least try. "Listen, Colonel, I don't personally know Brady Kenton. Never met the man. I can't say for certain that Mr. Houser is really him. He just bears a resemblance, that's all."

"You needn't try to change your story now, young man. I didn't really need your confirmation in any case. That is indeed Brady Kenton in that cabin. One of my soldiers who saw him in the town of Leadville has already confirmed his identity to me. But enough of that: the question between us is whether you are willing to write the story here in the way I wish. I take it that the answer, at this point, is no."

"Sir, I can't and won't write a story I know to be a contrived lie."

Callon expected Ottinger to explode, but instead he spoke more softly. "I'm not a man without means. I can certainly make it worth your while to reconsider."

Callon gaped. "You're offering me a bribe?"

Ottinger, nearly invisible in the darkness, reached beneath his coat.

Callon exclaimed, "You *are* offering me a bribe!" He laughed in astonishment. "Now that, sir, is a story I am willing to write. Colonel J.B. Ottinger himself, trying to pay a journalist to manipulate the facts for him!"

"Are you trying to threaten me, Mr. Callon?"

"I'm not willing to prostitute my profession, sir, for a handful of cash."

"I'm very sorry to hear that," Ottinger said. "I've given you every opportunity to make wise choices, but you've failed to do so. Now you have become a problem to me. I can't have you, or Kenton, engaged in trying to further muddy my name before the public."

"I can't compromise with you, Colonel," Callon said. "I intend to write and publish a story, but it will be a story telling the truth."

Ottinger replied, "I'm very sorry you've chosen to attack me."

"I haven't attacked you."

"Yes, you have. You lured me this far, out of sight of witnesses, and attempted to physically harm me. Therefore I have no choice but to defend myself."

Callon stepped back, wary. "What are you talking about?"

Ottinger pulled a pistol from under his coat, leveled it, and shot Callon through the heart.

CHAPTER SIXTEEN

BRADY KENTON WAS LABORING HARD, BUT PAUSED WHEN HE heard the distant crack of a gunshot. He wondered who had fired it, why, and at what.

Spurred by concern, he began working harder, faster, pulling away stones and mortar from the fireplace and gradually opening a hole between the imprisoning room and the dark world outside.

He prayed that no one would detect what he was doing before he could get out, and that once free, he could somehow manage to get out of town without gaining attention from the military guards.

Gomorrah was no longer a place he wanted to be. Ottinger, he was convinced, could be an authentic danger. And the people of Gomorrah, the group he hoped included Rankin, were no longer here. He had to follow them.

It troubled him, however, to think of abandoning young Callon here. His suggestion to Ottinger that he give his story to Callon had been ill-advised and irresponsible, he now believed, a bad call made under pressure.

Yet he couldn't remain here. If he did, Ottinger would probably arrange for him to die in some convenient "accidental" fashion.

He'd have to hope that Callon was mature enough and clever enough to deal rightly with his own situation.

He tugged at another stone, but it held fast. Blast it all!

The mortar was proving more difficult to chip away the deeper he dug into it, and the hole he was making was still not nearly large enough to accommodate him.

Ottinger stared down at the corpse of Callon and sighed. Too bad. He'd not really wanted to harm this fellow. If only the young fool simply had cooperated!

He scuffed about with his boot toe until he found a heavy wooden stick. This he picked up and placed into the hand of Callon.

There would be no questions raised about what had happened. His own soldiers, having heard the shot, were probably charging through the woods toward him even at this moment. He'd simply tell them that Callon had attacked him with the stick, and he'd been forced to shoot him.

Yes, he could hear them approaching now . . . but no. There was indeed noise in the charred woods, but from the wrong direction.

Someone was out there, nearby. Close enough, from the sound of it, that he might have witnessed the shooting of Callon.

"Who's there?" Ottinger demanded, facing the darkness, still brandishing his pistol. "Show yourself! I order you under authority of the United States Army!"

He heard movement, going the other direction. Someone scrambling away.

Ottinger swore and raised the revolver, ready to fire into the darkness. But it was useless; whoever it was, was gone.

Ottinger panicked. Who might be roaming about in the dark? Why? He knew that his soldiers had lost one of the townsfolk, some saloonkeeper who apparently slipped out the back of the latrine and ran away. Maybe it was he. Or perhaps it was simply some newcomer, or another cursed journalist, who had sneaked up the mountain undetected. It could even be some spy or scout out of Confederate Ridge.

Behind him, Ottinger heard soldiers coming, calling, scrambling up the far side of the ridge. They'd cross over and reach him in a moment. He could send them chasing after whoever he'd heard in the darkness . . . but what if they caught the unknown party, and the party told what he'd just seen? He could deny it, of course, but didn't want to be placed in a position in which he had to.

He turned, pistol in hand, to await his soldiers.

Kenton, sweating and sore, gave another tug at a stubborn chimney stone. It moved slightly in his hands, the mortar around it finally cracking. He pushed hard, then pulled back, and it gave way with even more gratifying results than he'd anticipated.

The stone fell inside the hearth, and several others crumbled down of their own accord. Kenton looked out through a gaping opening. It was now big enough that he believed he had a good chance of squeezing through.

He could see to the edge of town through the hole. There were no soldiers between him and the woods just now, but the woods were filled with huge bonfires of fallen trees, and some of the undergrowth that had survived the initial Gomorrah fire was ablaze, too. Kenton doubted the soldiers were going to be able to contain their own fire.

Kenton pulled the chimney rubble away from the opening. He positioned himself at the hole and started to wriggle through. He noted that it was quite cool outside, though, and remembered the coat Callon had found for him. He fetched it, pushed it out through the hole, then worked his way into the opening himself. It was a tight squeeze.

When he was halfway out, he heard footsteps, and froze. Two soldiers trotted by the cabin, mere yards from him. He lay there, head and torso sticking out of the ragged hole in the chimney, and watched them pass. One side glance in his direction and he would be revealed. But they were distracted, apparently concerned by that same pistol shot Kenton had heard, and did not notice him.

Kenton pushed and wriggled and scratched his way farther out of the hole, but suddenly found himself stuck. He pulled and writhed, but to no avail.

He looked up toward the chimney top, the silhouette of which was a darker shadow against the night sky. Was the chimney moving and swaying a little as he tried to extricate himself, or was it just an illusion caused by the scudding clouds? It would be a ludicrous way to die, he thought, to be smashed like a bug beneath a falling chimney. Even if it didn't kill him, the clamor of the chimney falling would certainly get him caught.

Kenton gave one more great pull, twisting his body as he did so. He broke free, and was outside.

Rising, wincing at the astonishing soreness of his battered frame and fighting dizziness, he dusted himself off, picked up and slipped on the slightly oversized coat, and made for a burned-out building nearby. There he dropped into the shadows to rest briefly, hide, and assess his situation.

The woods were blazing brightly; out around the bonfires he saw the dark forms of moving soldiers. To the north, however, the woods had not yet been set aflame. It was very dark there. Instinct pulled him in that direction, but one worry stopped him: it was from that direction that he'd heard the sound of the gunshot.

Soldiers passed near, and Kenton ducked behind the remnants of a burned wall, trying to figure out what to do next.

"I'm quite fine, thank you, Sergeant," Colonel Ottinger was saying. "He got in a couple of swings, but the stick never struck me. He was quite intent on killing me, however. A shame I had to shoot him."

"Let us accompany you back to your quarters, sir," the

sergeant said. "Perhaps the doctor should examine you."

"No need for that," Ottinger said. "I already told you he connected with none of his blows. Not for lack of trying, however. I can't quite understand it. I offered the man a fine journalistic opportunity, the chance to write an authoritative account of what happened at this place, and he responded by attacking me! It's a mystery indeed."

"I'm glad you're not injured, sir." In truth the man would have hardly minded had Ottinger been killed. In the time since he had manipulated his way to Fort Brandon, he had made himself a most unpopular figure among the soldiers he commanded.

"Thank you," Ottinger said. "See to this man's body, will you?"

"Yes, sir."

"How goes the burning operation?"

"Quite well, sir, as best I can tell, if we can keep it under control. The control is the great concern . . . the wind is becoming a problem."

"If it spreads, it spreads. The point is to completely burn off this mountaintop. Rest the men in shifts and continue as long as necessary."

Ottinger walked back toward Gomorrah. He paused to watch the burning going on to the south, his lanky body outlined for a few moments against the flames. Then he went on.

"Let's get this corpse out of here," the sergeant said to three soldiers near him.

"Sergeant, may I ask you a question first?" said a corporal, who had the reputation of being too forthright for his own good.

"Go on."

"What the hell is going on here? Why are we burning off a mountaintop that's already been burned over once? Are we trying to cover something up?"

The sergeant paused. "We're following the Colonel's orders. That's what we're doing."

"Because I don't know that I like what we're doing here. This was the hand of God at work, and it ain't right for us to try to cover up what was done here. You've heard those people talking about that fellow who prophesied it all. I tell you, what happened here was intended as a warning to the nation. And now, here we are, trying to burn it all off and hide it. We'll be held to account for this. It ain't right, Sergeant."

"It isn't up to us to decide if it's right. It's up to us to obey orders."

"One more question, Sergeant?"

"What?"

"Is it true that the Colonel plans to send us to overrun Confederate Ridge?"

"Enough of the questions," the sergeant snapped. "Haul that dead man up and out of here, and let's get back to work. I'm afraid those fires are going to keep spreading and burn the entire damned mountain range before they're through."

Kenton left his hiding place behind and moved cautiously toward the edge of town. The farther he proceeded the safer he felt, because the fire and light were concentrated south and east of the town for now. He could take to the forest north of town, circle toward the west, and head down the road toward Fort Brandon.

What he'd do then he had not fully decided. The survivors of Gomorrah would probably be ensconced within the fort, out of reach. Somehow he would have to find out if one of them was Rankin.

That was a problem for another day, however. At the moment the challenge was merely to leave this place without being caught.

As he moved along, he wondered again about Gunnison,

seen by no one since Callon departed from him in the forest. Kenton wondered if Gunnison might yet be lingering and hiding in the woods, watching the developments in Gomorrah. Or perhaps he'd moved on.

Wherever he was, Kenton hoped he was safe and well. That gunshot he'd heard earlier in the woods worried him. He wondered where Callon was, too.

CHAPTER SEVENTEEN

OTTINGER WALKED RAPIDLY, HANDS CLASPED BEHIND HIS BACK to hide their trembling. He could scarcely believe he'd actually killed that young journalist. But one does what one must.

And there was one more journalist to be dealt with, too. Unless Kenton had changed his mind, he'd have to be gotten out of the way, like the other one. Even if Kenton declared now that he *had* changed his mind, Ottinger wasn't sure he could trust him.

The air was rich with smoke from the rekindled fires, and Ottinger sneezed several times. He looked around at the weird, yellow-orange light of the flames. The wind was whipping up fast, the flames rising higher now. The soldiers were working very hard to keep them from spreading farther than they should. Ottinger wasn't sure they were succeeding; it appeared to him that the fire might be spreading here and there past the previous burn area and into previously unburned parts of the forest.

He didn't really care. Let it burn, as long as the fallen trees around the town burned too.

He turned his back to the forest and studied the little house where Brady Kenton was held. Now was probably the best time to deal with that troublesome matter.

But Ottinger found he didn't have it in him at the moment. His nerves were already on edge . . . particularly when he considered the sounds he had heard in the dark woods. The idea that someone witnessed his murder of Paul Callon was cause for great concern.

He was about to turn away and continue on to his tent when something about the chimney of the cabin caught his attention. He looked closely, then advanced.

There was an opening in the side of the chimney, a big hole right through the chimney wall into the cabin! With his heart rising to his throat, Ottinger drew his pistol and advanced to the cabin, crouching and cautiously looking into the opening.

The cabin interior was dark; Kenton could still be hiding in there, unseen. But why would he? Ottinger knew full well that the cabin was empty. Kenton had made himself an exit right through the chimney.

As he rose from his crouch, Ottinger was startled to hear the chimney make a cracking, shifting noise. He looked up and saw the chimney move against the sky, tilting . . . then he dodged with more speed than he'd mustered in years as the chimney, weakened by the hole Kenton had put through it, gave way and fell.

Ottinger swore loudly, barely missing being crushed beneath the stones. A moment later, a handful of soldiers ran toward him.

"Sir! Are you hurt?"

Ottinger glared at them. "Hell, no, I'm not hurt, but the prisoner has escaped!"

"Escaped?"

"Yes, damn it! He made a hole through the chimney and crawled out . . . blasted chimney almost crushed me, falling! Go find him! I want him brought back, fast!"

"Do you know which way he went, sir?"

"How the hell should I know? Who's responsible for leaving this man unguarded, Sergeant?"

"We were all put to duty in the woods, sir, with the fires."

"Forget the damned fires—let them burn! I want these woods scoured until he's located. Round up every man if you have to! And if he flees, kill him!"

The soldiers glanced at one another, wondering why the Colonel was so wrought-up over the escape of what had seemed a harmless enough man to them. The Colonel was not to be questioned, though, especially now, when every vein in his neck bulged and his teeth were very nearly grinding in anger.

"Yes, sir. Right away. We'll find him for you, Colonel."

Twenty minutes later, Kenton paused, panting hard, winded.

It was very distressing, and downright embarrassing. He'd always prided himself on his physical strength and stamina at an age when many men begin to grow soft and weak, but right now he felt like an old man.

It was a terrible time to grow weak and slow. The forest was crawling with soldiers looking for him. He'd hoped that his escape from the cabin wouldn't have been detected so quickly, so he could have gotten much farther away than this before they began looking.

He wondered if Ottinger had personally ordered this great manhunt for him. Probably so. Only Ottinger would have reason to care so much about his escape, and only Ottinger would have had authority to pull so many men away from tending the fires—fires rapidly spreading out of control, it appeared, engulfing parts of the forest not burned the first time—to search for one strayed journalist.

Kenton leaned against a tree and sucked in air, lungs burning. He ached to cough in the smoke-tinged atmosphere, but feared his pursuers were too close. Someone might hear him. He fought against the urge . . . then coughed anyway.

"There!" someone yelled. "I can see him!"

Blast it all! These young soldiers with their keen eyes . . .

how could anyone possibly see him in this darkness? The fires were nowhere close. Then Kenton realized that in stopping where he had to rest, he'd unwittingly limned himself, from certain angles, against the vaguely luminescent sky.

He ran on, ignoring his body's demands for him to stop. He'd later decide to blame this lack of stamina more on his injuries than his age. It took a lot out of a man to be beaten unconscious by a highwayman, after all. At the moment, however, all Kenton could think was that he was surely going to burst his heart like an overwound clockspring, trying to escape these fleet young soldiers.

He determined that, catch him though they might, they'd not catch him before he'd run for them the best chase he could. He redoubled his efforts and ran along a ridgetop, then crossed it and dropped out of sight on the far side. He ran down, then cut left, right, up another hill, down the far side, across a gully and into a stream, then right again.

There was no way to keep up with exactly which direction he was moving. All he wanted right now was to throw off this blasted uniformed hunting pack. He used the light of the fast-spreading forest fires as a landmark, though, so that despite all the turning and crisscrossing and redoubling, he was always moving farther away from the light, farther away from Gomorrah.

Kenton wondered how many of the soldiers knew who they were chasing, or why. Most were probably just following orders.

The chase went on, Kenton never relenting despite his mounting exhaustion. He'd run until he dropped. Then he'd crawl, if crawling was all he could do.

He still had a little life left in him, though, and he pushed himself hard. Whenever he wanted to relax, to slow or stop again, he forced one thought through his mind: *You let them catch you, and you'll never find Rankin. You never find Rankin, and you'll never find what he knows about Victoria.*

Kenton looked behind him. He saw movement back there in the dark. Two men, maybe three, still in close pursuit. This was actually encouraging, though. There'd been many more than that to start with.

You're doing it, old boy. You're outrunning them! Keep going, keep those legs moving. No matter what.

A shot blasted behind him, and a bullet ripped through one tree and smacked into another, just a few yards to his right.

Dear Lord, they *were* serious about this!

His heart hammering that much harder, he ducked and ran as hard as he could, up a slope, around a jumble of boulders, and across a ridge, looking for a safe way down.

Someone shouted for him to halt, and he considered it. But some instinct said no, that Ottinger was more dangerous to him now than he could have thought possible, and that he must run now, or in the end he would die.

He pushed himself all the harder, so weary and straining now that his head ached, his lungs burned, and he was beginning to grow dizzy. A strong urge to vomit gripped him, but he fought it down, somehow.

Kenton reached the base of another rise—*Oh, no, I can't possibly climb another one!*—but he did climb, because he had no choice. His pursuers were now down to two men, he thought, but they were fast and drawing too close.

Before the next shot came, he somehow sensed it, cringed even before the blast came. Something sang loudly less than an inch from his ear, and he thought how strange all this had turned. All he'd wanted was to reach this mining town and meet a man who might—*Let it be true, Lord!*—lead him to Victoria. How was it he was now running through dark woods, pursued by soldiers of the same nation he'd almost died for more than once, being shot at—

His thoughts were cut off when his feet tangled on a protruding root. He fell forward, striking chest-first against a stone. The wind was jolted out of his lungs. He rolled, tumbling down a steep slope, striking stumps and stones, scraping down rough ground.

Sometime later, how much later he couldn't tell, Kenton was dimly aware of movement around him. He was lying on rough ground, very uncomfortable. His eyes were open, but he saw mostly darkness, though there were faintly lighter areas above him, and in them shadows moving. And sounds. Voices, he thought.

He felt hands on him. Rough and strong, moving him, trying to lift him.

Kenton closed his eyes and sank again into unconsciousness.

Once again, Alex Gunnison wished he had a spyglass.

Far above and behind him, the top of Gomorrah Mountain was in flames again. He could see the distant orange flicker on the mountaintop in the darkness. What could have rekindled the fire? It was puzzling. If he had a spyglass, or binoculars, at least he could get a closer look and maybe tell whether the town was burning as well.

One thing he knew: the surviving townspeople of Gomorrah were no longer in their town. They'd been moved down the mountain to Fort Brandon; from a distance, he'd watched them being herded in, accompanied by soldiers. Once the delivery was through, most of the latter had immediately turned back and headed toward Gomorrah again. Meanwhile, the fire had started anew, and seemed to be burning much farther down the mountain than the first one, spreading rapidly, and widely. Something odd was going on, and it intrigued his journalistic sensibilities.

He took a deep breath. "Keep your mind on what you're doing, Alex," he said aloud. "You're looking for this man Rankin, not for a story." He sat down on a nearby log and pulled off his shoes, rubbing the rather flat arches of his feet gingerly. "And while you're looking, it would surely be fine to have a horse."

Gunnison was a strong young man, and following around Brady Kenton through the years had called upon him many times to engage in all kinds of strenuous physical exertion, but the truth was he was no natural hiker. He was somewhat flatfooted, and walking for long distances wore him out and gave him all kinds of aches and pains. Right now his calves were cramping and his lower back ached almost as badly as his feet. His thoughts of obtaining a horse were quite serious. There was no telling how long it would be until he'd track down this Rankin and his cohorts. His feet might not be able to stand the test. And even though it would raise some protests from the bookkeepers, he could recoup the expense of a horse and saddle from the budget of the *Illustrated American.* There were definite advantages in being the son of the publisher.

As he sat rubbing his feet and watching the distant fire at Gomorrah, the horse-buying idea made the transition from vaguely considered possibility to a thing firmly decided. He'd do it. There were ranches in this region, and a little town not far ahead. It shouldn't be difficult to find someone with horses to sell.

And food. He was growing very hungry, and was tired of the trail fare he carried with him. He longed for a thick steak, a stack of biscuits . . . even a good, hot bowl of beans would seem luxurious at the moment.

He put his footwear back on and stood. He wasn't sure how far it was to that little town ahead, but if he was lucky, maybe he'd get there in time to find someone willing to give or rent him a room for the night and steer him toward a trustworthy horse seller. And maybe he'd be able to find some new lead on Rankin.

Gunnison had cause to believe that Rankin and his companions had passed this way. Earlier, Gunnison had encountered a lone rider on the road, a ranch boy out searching for a strayed mare, and had been told by the fellow that a group matching the description of Rankin and company had passed up this road.

Gunnison began hiking again. He thought of Kenton again, and felt all over again that deep and aching sorrow that had now been with him long enough to become familiar. He wondered if that rekindled fire up on Gomorrah Mountain had consumed Kenton's corpse. He rather hoped it had. It still distressed him that he'd not been able to see to a proper burial for his old friend and partner.

Kenton . . . dead. Despite what he'd seen with his own eyes, he still couldn't quite put the two things together. Brady Kenton was the most vigorous, fully alive man he'd ever known. It was going to take Gunnison a long time to come to grips with the fact that Kenton indeed was gone.

He'd not yet gotten around to wiring or mailing word to the *Illustrated American* about what had happened to Kenton. There hadn't been a convenient opportunity, obviously . . . and besides, it was simply too painful to deal with it yet . . . to make Kenton's death public and official, so to speak. But he'd have to do it soon, or else Callon would get the word out first.

He trudged on, trying to ignore his aching feet.

CHAPTER EIGHTEEN

THE RANCH STOOD IN A WIDE VALLEY THAT WAS BISECTED almost exactly by a straight-running creek with high banks. Cottonwoods grew along the creek, and the prairie land all around was gently rolling, mountains framing the scene. The house was typical of Montana Territory ranches, made of logs, one story high, long and rather sprawling because it was, in fact, three cabins built side-by-side and joined. Nearby were sheds and corrals, a large garden, and a big barn. It was the barn that had caught Gunnison's eye above all the rest, because it was at the moment well-lighted, and seemingly full of people.

He walked through the dark toward the barn, keeping in the center of the wagon road and deliberately making noise so that his arrival would surprise no one. He'd heard stories about Montana people's tendency toward vigilantism, and just in case something of that sort was going on here, he wanted nothing he did to look in any way sneaky or surreptitious.

As he drew near enough to the barn to hear some of what was going on inside, though, he realized that this was no vigilante meeting. Far from it: what he was hearing was a man praying, very loudly.

There were thirty or so people in the barn, all crowded together and seated on benches improvised from lumber set on kegs, boxes, logs, and other such items.

The praying man said his amen about the time Gunnison entered. Heads lifted, turned, looked back at him.

"Welcome, young man," said the leader. "Come and join us . . . come and pray."

"Thank you . . . but the truth was, I'm just looking for someone to sell me a horse . . . if I can find one affordable."

"There's horses to be had, but now is the time for praying, young fellow. Do come join us. There may not be much time left for any of us in this old world."

Gunnison looked around. "What's this about?"

"It's about turning our lives straight and averting the wrath of God, young man. If you wish to join with us, you may, but if not, we won't be kept from our own prayers." With that, the man turned away, dropped to his knees, and began to pray aloud again.

Gunnison, uncomfortable here, turned to the door and slipped out into the night. He considered going elsewhere to look for a horse, but decided not to. The man had said horses were available. He'd wait out the meeting and hope to buy one afterward, and maybe also to find some place he could spend the night. It was growing late and he was tired of traveling for today.

Gunnison walked around the side of the barn, listening to the muffled voices from inside. He paused and looked across the distance toward the dim glow that was the burning top of Gomorrah Mountain.

He heard footsteps behind him, and turned. A boy of about ten, whom he'd noticed at the rear fringes of the group in the prayer meeting, had followed him out and around the barn.

"Howdy," the boy said.

"Hello, there," Gunnison replied.

"My name's Rory Wilson." The boy put out his hand.

Gunnison shook it. "Alex Gunnison. Pleased to know you."

"Why didn't you stay to pray?" Rory asked.

"Well . . . I didn't feel quite comfortable with it, being a stranger. Just what's going on in there, anyway?"

"Kind of a revival service. Folks here have really got revived in their religion all at once. Because of that up yonder." The boy looked past Gunnison toward the burning mountain. "You can still see it a-burning. The fire fell, then went out, and now it's back again. Goes to show you can't quench the fire of God, my pap says."

"Well, something's certainly sparked the fire up again." Gunnison thought about telling the boy that he'd actually been up on Gomorrah Mountain not long before. It would surely impress him. But Kenton had taught Gunnison that more was to be learned from letting others speak than from speaking oneself, so he kept quiet.

"It was the fire starting back again that got everybody to gather and pray here tonight. They figured the wrath had come down on Gomorrah another time."

"The wrath?"

"Why, sure! The wrath of God! Gomorrah was a wicked town, and God has smit it for its sins. That's what my pap believes."

"Is he the one leading the meeting in there?"

"No. That's Jim Spradley, who owns this here ranch. We got a spread of our own, starting on the other side of the creek yonder way. Our house—it ain't as big as Mr. Spradley's over there, but it will be once Pap expands it—stands about two mile away from here."

"Does Mr. Spradley sell horses?"

"When he's got them to sell. He's got some now. But you won't get him out of that prayer meeting for a good while. The first prayer meeting he had like this lasted a good four hours straight."

"When did he have that meeting?"

"Right after the fire fell."

"What do you know about that firefall?"

The boy straightened his shoulders and looked proud. "I seen it happen. From a long ways off, like we are now, but I seen it."

"So you're an eyewitness."

"Yep. I was outside when it happened, turned in the direction I am now, so I could see the line of the mountains against the sky. There was a big light in the sky, like a flame shooting across, heading toward the mountain. Then it just burst, all flaming and bright, and after that, Gomorrah and all the mountaintop was burning. You could see it just like you can now, but brighter."

"Lightning, you think?"

"Oh, Lord no. Not lightning. There ain't never been no lightning like what I saw."

"So what do you think it was?"

"Fire and brimstone! What else? Fire and brimstone from heaven. When you name a town after a wicked city like Gomorrah, you see, a city that was destroyed by God, well, you're what they call tempting God. Like double-daring Him to do it again."

"Why do you think the mountain is burning now, considering that the fire went out before?"

"I don't know. Maybe God decided to smite it one more time."

Gunnison scanned the sky, so vast in Montana, and felt very small. The stars twinkled in the blackness, looking very far away. "You really do believe that God struck that town with His own hand?"

"That's what my pap says. He's generally right about things. Besides, what else would it have been?"

Gunnison continued to examine the sky. "I think something fell from up there and caught the town afire."

Rory snorted. "Just fell, all by itself? You're a disbeliever, then. You ain't giving God credit for what He done. Besides, what just falls from the sky?"

In one of those rare moments in life when an unplannable event happens at just the right time, Gunnison saw a streak of light fire across the sky to the north. The quick turning of Rory's head told Gunnison that the boy had seen it, too. "*Those* fall from the sky."

"Shooting stars? Well, sure they do, but you don't never see one strike. They just glow and go out."

"Sometimes they do strike. Or come very close to the ground before they burn out . . . or explode from their own heat."

"You're a disbeliever! You're trying to say it ain't God who caused the fire to fall!"

"Why would you say that? If God wanted to smite a town, He could use a shooting star as easily as anything else, couldn't He?"

The boy mulled that over. "Reckon He could. I never thought of it like that."

"But I won't lie to you: I'm not yet persuaded that what happened at Gomorrah was an outright divine punishment. I know it was a wicked town, but surely no more so than many other mining towns. And Gomorrah was small as mining towns go."

"Well, *I* know it was God's punishment. The prophet himself told us so."

The significance of that comment took a moment to settle on Gunnison. "The prophet? The man who predicted the firefall?"

"You've heard of him, I see! Yep, the same one. He came down from Gomorrah Mountain and preached to us all, right there in this same barn. His name's Peabody. Parson Peabody."

"Is he still here?" Gunnison asked.

"No. He's moved on."

"Tell me all you can about him: who was with him. What he said, where they went. It's important."

"Well, he and them with him just sort of showed up here. He had another couple of men with him, and there was a woman. One of the two men, a fellow named Gib Rankin, did most of the talking. He's a gambler who got converted up in Gomorrah after the fire came down. Mr. Rankin asked my pap to call all the folks together from hereabouts that he could, said the prophet had something to say to them. Pap already knew about the fire falling—he'd seen it happen, like I did. And even before the prophet got here, we knew about him. We'd heard about him from a man who came down from Gomorrah right after the firefall. He was burned and scared half to death, talking about the fire and the preacher who'd predicted it."

"What did Peabody say in his sermon?"

"He said that what happened up at Gomorrah was just the start of God judging wicked folks across this nation. He said that the fire would fall on us, too, just like on Gomorrah, if we didn't repent from our sins."

"And let me guess: Rankin then took up an offering."

"Yes. He told them that giving was a sign of their repentance, and that if they gave, maybe God would spare them from having the fire and brimstone fall on them."

Gunnison nodded. This was beginning to make sense. "Tell me something, Rory. When Peabody preached, what was his manner? Did he seem forceful, bold, that kind of thing?"

Rory thought that one through before he answered. "No . . . he seemed serious about it, but kind of timid and nervous . . . kind of hollow and scared. He talked real soft. It made him hard to hear. But it made what he said seem more real and scary, too."

"What about Gib Rankin's manner?"

"Oh, he was different. He was kind of in charge of things. He talked loud and pretty much ran the show."

"I see. Any chance, you think, that he'd told Peabody what he should say?"

The boy stared coldly at him. "I think you *are* a disbeliever."

"Not a disbeliever in God, or even in judgment, Rory. But maybe a disbeliever in Gib Rankin."

"You'd believe if you heard Parson Peabody speak."

"Maybe I would. I hope I can hear him speak. I'm trying to find him, as a matter of fact, and Mr. Rankin, too."

"How come?"

"I'm a writer. A journalist for *Gunnison's Illustrated American*. Have you heard of it?"

"Of course I have! That's Brady Kenton's magazine, ain't it?"

"Yes."

"Do you know Brady Kenton?" The boy spoke excitedly, and Gunnison was struck anew by the extent of Kenton's celebrity. Here was a mere boy, maybe not even literate, out on a ranch in the wilds of the Montana Territory, yet who knew the name and reputation of Brady Kenton.

"I do know Brady Kenton," Gunnison said, smiling to try to stave off the gush of sadness that rose inside him. "He's my partner, in fact." He realized he was speaking in the present tense, but didn't have the will to correct it. It was going to take a long time to get used to thinking of Brady Kenton as part of the past.

"Is he coming here?"

"No . . . no." Deciding to spare the sad details, Gunnison said, "But I'm looking for Rankin and Parson Peabody on his behalf. Can you or anyone else here tell me where they went after they left here?"

"My pap knows, I think."

The sound of the prayer meeting was still coming through the barn wall; there was no sign the gathering was going to break up anytime soon. "I'll ask him when he's through. In the meantime, maybe I can look at his horses for sale. Can you show me where they are?"

Rory nodded. "Follow me."

CHAPTER NINETEEN

WHEN KENTON REJOINED THE SENTIENT WORLD, HE WAS GLAD to find himself alive but dismayed to see that he was back inside the same cabin he'd escaped. He remembered rolling down that bluff, being picked up and carried away by someone. Obviously it had been some of the soldiers.

But as he sat up and looked around, he realized abruptly that he wasn't in the same cabin at all. This one was larger, better-built, an entirely new place to him. It had walls of hewn logs and a ceiling that sloped down from back to front.

The door opened and a man he'd never seen before entered. The fellow was about Kenton's own age, burly, gray-bearded. He stopped abruptly when he saw Kenton sitting up.

"Well, howdy!" he said, breaking into a warm grin. "I was just coming in to see if you might have broke out of that daze you was in."

"Hello," Kenton said, standing, looking warily at this newcomer, whose most distinctive garment was a gray coat with the sleeves cut off.

"You rolled down a mighty sheer bluff, Mr. Kenton. As best I can tell, though, you broke no bones. You could have been hurt bad. If Ottinger's soldiers had caught you, I think they'd have killed you."

He knows my name, Kenton thought. This, however, was

not particularly surprising. Kenton was often recognized.

The stranger went on: "When I saw them chasing you, we thought to ourselves: 'That man there is in need of some help.' So we gave it to you. Any man being chased by soldiers under the likes of that massacring Ottinger is bound to be a man I'd consider a friend. Well, you can imagine our surprise when we got you back here and discovered who you are!"

"Thanks for your help."

"Welcome. Hey, hell of a thing that's happened at Gomorrah. I never seen such a thing before."

"Unusual, certainly. Tell me something: Am I at Confederate Ridge?"

"So you are, Mr. Kenton. I hope you don't mind it, having been a Union man and all."

"Believe me, I don't mind it. I'm glad to be away from Ottinger."

"You're lucky to be away. He's already murdered one fellow in cold blood."

"Murdered? Who?"

"Some young fellow who he was trying to get to write a story for him. I was close enough to hear some of it, but not all. Your name was called, though."

Kenton felt weak. He sat down again.

Callon! "Tell me what happened," he said.

"Don't know, really. This fellow and Ottinger were arguing. He wouldn't do what Ottinger wanted, I reckon. Ottinger even tried to bribe him and he turned that down, too. So Ottinger up and shot him. I could hardly believe I saw it happen. I thought about gunning Ottinger down myself, right there, but we got a policy against that here. No engaging any official representative of the United States in battle or doing any harm to such except in clear self-defense. In other words, we ain't here to fight, but to mind our own business." He paused. "But I swear, I think it would have been right to shoot Ottinger. It was hard not to do it."

"Poor Callon," Kenton whispered. "Dear God, I feel partly responsible."

"Can't be your fault. You weren't even there."

"No, but I'd earlier turned down the same offer Ottinger made to Paul Callon—the man you saw shot—and if I'd handled it differently, maybe Paul would have never been put in that situation."

"He got wordy with Ottinger, losing his temper and so on. I think that's really what got him in trouble."

"Paul could be that way at times."

"I can tell you're grieved by this. I'm sorry to have had to tell you."

"Tell me: Does Ottinger know you saw the murder?"

"I think he suspects that *somebody* saw it. He heard me, I'm pretty sure."

"Would you testify in court to what you saw?"

"Sorry, Mr. Kenton. None of us here recognize the courts of the United States. We're free citizens, not Americans."

"And still at war with the U.S., as you see it."

"No, not at war. The war is done, and sorry to say, the war was lost. We accept that. Like I said before, all we want is to live in peace. We have a firm policy against any kind of confrontation with the forces of the United States."

"But you exchanged fire with the soldiers who chased me."

"Yes," the man said, now turning very solemn. "We did. In pure, outright violation of our own policy. And though it may have saved your skin, I'm afraid it was a mistake in every other way. That's what Pernell says, anyway. He says that we've given Ottinger a truly good reason to send his soldiers against us. I think he's right."

"Are you talking about Pernell Jones?"

"Yep. You know his name well, I'm sure."

"Of course I do."

"You may even known mine." The man advanced and put out his hand. "Milo Buckner."

"Buckner!" Kenton repeated, shaking the hand. "I do know you. You were the chief lieutenant of Jones through all the war years. His right hand."

"That's me."

"Is Jones still the leader of your group?"

"The closest thing to one that we've got. The honest truth is that we've found a way to live that don't really need a lot of leadership in terms of one man being the strutting rooster over everybody else. We kind of just take things as they come, and when we got to, vote amongst ourselves. Majority wins."

"That's a simple system."

"We're a simple people."

"How'd you come to be all the way out here?

"We never patched things up with the Lincolnites. Just said hell with them, that's all. Never wanted to be part of their country after the war. After the war was done, we turned our horses west and kept riding, going wherever we had to stay out of the bluebellies' hands. We've had a lot of different refuges through the years, always in the wilderness, out of the way. But we've always been detected. I've been amazed many a time at how hard it is to mind your own business and let everybody else mind their own. We ain't lived nowhere that everybody and his brother ain't learned real fast who we are. Hell, we've had reporter folks, like yourself, come riding up to our gates wanting to talk to Pernell for some story or another."

"So finally you drifted this far."

"Yep. And it's been good here. We've had this mountain to ourselves, mostly, apart from a few redskins and hunters and so on, for several years. But since the mines came in, and the ranchers, well, there's no place you can go, it don't seem, that you can escape the growing of the cussed United States."

"The cussed United States is going to be on us again, far too soon," a voice said. Kenton looked up and Milo turned. The door had quietly opened and a man had entered from the darkness outside, unnoticed, while Milo and Kenton conversed. The newcomer strode across and put out his hand to Kenton, who knew as he shook the hand that he has just made the aquaintance of the famed old Rebel renegade Pernell Jones.

"Hello, Mr. Kenton," Jones said. "You *are* Brady Kenton, I believe?"

"I am," Kenton replied.

"Pleased to meet you, sir. It's an honor to meet the man who told the truth to the world about J.B. Ottinger," Jones said. For a former Rebel rural insurgent who had spent most of his life since living among roughcut folk on the edges of society, he spoke in a surprisingly urbane manner. Kenton abruptly remembered something he'd been told about Jones once, but had forgotten: Jones had studied briefly at Harvard, but had been forced to cut his education short after his aging parents fell ill back in Virginia. He'd returned there and taken over the family's farm.

"My 'Lincolnite' past doesn't stifle my welcome?" Kenton asked.

"The war is over," Jones replied. "And your exposure of Ottinger covered a multitude of sins, as far as I'm concerned."

"But yet it never brought down Ottinger himself. He was never charged, much less tried."

"And now he threatens our safety," Jones said. "Milo was privileged to overhear an extended private conversation of Ottinger's. It's his scheme to blame the fire at Gomorrah on us, and use that as a pretext to overrun us." Jones looked coldly at Milo. "Of course, that's perhaps a moot point now. He has new grounds for coming after us now."

Kenton nodded. "Yes. Because his soldiers were fired upon while carrying out their assigned duty of chasing me down."

"That's correct. Glad as I am you were saved—and even though I admit I'd have done the same as Milo if I'd been the one who saw them chasing you—the truth is, we've put ourselves in a truly fine fix."

"I feel responsible," Kenton said. "But let me suggest something. Milo has witnessed Ottinger committing a murder—a murder of a friend of mine. If he would testify to what he's seen, Ottinger could be prosecuted for that murder."

Jones was already shaking his head. "No, Mr. Kenton. It's no good. We don't recognize nor participate in the United States judicial system. Even more importantly, Milo's testimony would never be believed. The right hand of Pernell Jones, giving unsupported testimony against the same man Pernell Jones once mangled with a shotgun blast? No. It would be a waste of time."

Kenton thought about it, and nodded.

"What will you do, then?" Kenton asked. "Try to resist them?"

Jones stared at his own feet a few moments, then looked up at Kenton again. "Mr. Kenton, you've been run through the mill, I know, but do you have the strength and interest to attend a little gathering? To see how we do things here at Confederate Ridge?"

"Of course."

"Good. We'll try to round up some paper and pencils for you. This may be something you'll want to record, because it may be the last time that our people gather here together, ever again."

CHAPTER TWENTY

PETER WILSON, WHO AFTER THE PRAYER MEETING SOLD A good horse at a good price to Gunnison, bore a strong physical resemblance to his son, Rory, but lacked the boy's ebullient personality. As he sat sipping coffee from a cracked cup and nibbling on the last biscuit left from supper, Wilson looked back at Alex Gunnison in a way that at first made Gunnison wonder if he looked like a criminal. After a time, though, he began to realize that this was just Wilson's ordinary look. He flashed that same suspicious look at his son, his wife, his two plump daughters, both of whom were flashing very different kinds of looks at Gunnison. He was beginning to wish he hadn't accepted the invitation to spend the night here.

Gunnison, uncomfortable under the hungry gaze of the two girls, shifted his posture in his chair and laid his left hand across his knee to make sure that his wedding ring was visible. He glanced at one of the daughters, ignored the smile she flashed him, and continued the conversation he was carrying on with Wilson.

"Rory tells me that the preacher himself had a troubled manner about him as he spoke," Gunnison said.

Wilson swallowed the last of the biscuit. "Yes, it struck me that way, too. He seemed a man under a great burden . . . maybe scared by his own message."

"Did he strike you as sincere?"

"Oh, yes. He believed what he was saying. But he had little spirit about him. I figure I'd be much the same, if the Lord had laid such a terrible message on my heart."

"You really do believe that Peabody is speaking a word from God?"

"Yes."

"What exactly did he say?"

"He spoke about judgment, about God's wrath against sin . . . it was frightening. The kind of thing to bring you to your knees in prayer. I won't shy away from telling you I did just that."

"Did he say that there would be more fire from heaven?"

"He said that Gomorrah had gone across a line of sin that could not be crossed again. Its judgment was inescapable. But for others, for us, it wasn't too late to repent. And if we would, the fire might not fall."

"So you repented."

"We did."

"That's a good thing, I'm sure."

"Yes."

Gunnison cleared his throat uncomfortably. He glanced once more at the staring daughters. "Rory told me there was an offering taken for Peabody."

"There was. I didn't begrudge it. Even a prophet has to live."

"Did the preacher say, directly or indirectly, that giving his offering was an essential part of the repenting process?"

As Gunnison had feared, Wilson seemed offended by the question. "Listen, young man, if you're implying that I, or the other people around here, are gullible fools who emptied their pockets for no reason, then I think you should rethink your thinking, right fast!"

"Sir, I'm sorry. I'm not trying to offend."

"There was an offering took, yes. But the preacher said nothing about it, asked not a penny."

"But the man with him, Rankin . . ."

"Well, yes. That's who it was who took the offering, with the help of another fellow."

"Did Rankin equate giving to the offering with repenting?"

"Look, the Bible itself says the worker is worthy of his hire. It says the servants of the Lord should be supported."

Gunnison needed to hear no more; Wilson's defensive, evasive answer was tantamount to an affirmative.

"Yes," Gunnison said. "It does teach that."

Wilson stood and went for his pipe on the mantelpiece. He took down a tobacco bag that hung from a rack of antlers attached decoratively to the wall above the fireplace. As he filled his pipe, he asked, "Do you have a family, Mr. Gunnison?"

"I've got a wife," Gunnison said, raising his voice a little to make sure the Wilson daughters heard him clearly.

"Then you picture yourself in the kind of situation I was. You look up in the sky one night and you see fire flash across the darkness. You see a mountaintop go into flames. Then, not long after, you see people who've come down from that mountain, burned and hurting and scared to death, telling that a preacher prophesied it all, and by gum if it didn't happen just like he said. Then that same preacher shows up and tells you that the same blasted thing could happen to you and your family . . . you think you'd take chances with your own safety and that of your own? Would you?"

"No, I suppose I wouldn't."

"You'd pray to God, you'd turn from your wicked ways, you'd pay whatever offering was asked; that's what you'd do. You wouldn't risk the safety of yourself and your own loved ones. And if some slick-dressed little news scribbler came around asking you a bunch of questions to imply you're a fool, you'd not be very pleased about it."

"Obviously I've hurt your feelings. I do apologize."

The daughters smiled at Gunnison, and quietly sighed in unison. Apparently he had a very appealing way of apologizing.

Wilson shrugged and chewed on his pipestem. "Don't worry about it. Didn't mean to say so much."

"Mr. Wilson, you're right that I didn't witness these things myself, and indeed I might have reacted just like you did if I had seen them. But you and I both know that people are capable of cheating and lying, especially if there's money to be made. Maybe Rankin has sincerely changed his ways . . . or maybe he's using this prophet fellow as a way of gouging money out of sincerely frightened people."

Wilson exhaled slowly. "I know. And down inside, I've wondered." He looked at Gunnison. "Rory says you believe it was some kind of shooting star that might have caused the fire."

"I don't really know what it was. It's just a guess."

"Tell me why you're so interested in all this. Are you trying to write a story about it?"

"I'm trying to find Rankin for the sake of a friend of mine. Rankin maybe has some information he needs. About my friend's wife."

"I see. Well, too bad you didn't come sooner. He's long gone now."

"Yes. Any idea where?"

"Wherever there's people. The preacher said he was going to travel from town to town, giving warning about the fire from heaven. Getting people to repent."

"With Rankin collecting money at every place."

"Reckon so."

"Any idea which town he was heading to next?"

"They headed in the direction of Paxton."

Gunnison nodded. He'd heard of Paxton. Just another little mining town in the Montana mountains.

"That's where I'll look, then."

"Listen, if you're Brady Kenton's partner, then where is he?"

Gunnison didn't want to answer, but he did. "Brady Kenton is dead. He was killed in the fire at Gomorrah."

"Lord . . . I'm sorry."

"I am, too, Mr. Wilson. I haven't yet found it in myself to truly believe he is dead."

The Confederate Ridge compound, revealed to Kenton as he followed Jones and Milo out of the cabin, was bigger than he would have expected, had he had opportunity to develop any specific expectations. Kenton walked into a broad, packed-dirt central area and watched the people of the compound gathering around a well in the dead center of the enclosure, which was lighted by three bonfires. There was a small platform around the well; Pernell Jones stepped upon it, his expression solemn.

Kenton took a quick look around. The stockade stood about twelve feet high on all sides, with numerous cabins like the one he'd just left built all around. There were other buildings, all made of logs, scattered around the enclosure as well, but farther inside, not against the walls. There were a couple of small barns, a few sheds and privies, a sizeable stockpen in which cattle meandered, and a corral well stocked with horses. He counted no less than three gardens. He spotted one cabin with a cross mounted atop it: obviously a church building. Beside it was a small, enclosed graveyard with a few smaller crosses stuck in it. All in all, the whole thing reminded Kenton of typical stockades from the earlier days of what was now the East. It was neat, well-kept, and more impressive than Kenton had expected. Confederate Ridge was not some mere mountain hideout. This was a true community, maintained well and having about it the feeling of a small, peaceful village that just happened to be enclosed behind walls.

Kenton felt the familiar tug of his journalistic impulse. This was a surprising place, an unusual place, a place that deserved to be written about. This was a town that was on no map, a dwelling place of people who considered themselves not Americans but independent entities. He wished he had his sketch pad. All he had, though, were a few scraps of paper Milo had handed him, and a couple of stubby pencils. He could do a bit of note-taking, but that was about all.

Kenton spoke to Milo. "I didn't realize there were so many here. Especially so many women and children."

"We've established a fine place here," Milo answered. "Many of us here have married and brought wives here, raised children. Now some of the children have grown and married one another to start whole new families."

"I think you're about to outgrow this place."

"I don't think it's going to matter after tonight," Milo said.

Kenton might have asked how it was that such a community could be maintained without the support of commerce with the outside world. Self-sufficiency, in his experience, could only take people so far, and his impression was that Confederate Ridge had moved beyond that point. He wondered if there was some outside source of supply or subsidy . . . maybe some network of underground commerce, or some benefactor, who was helping keep this community alive. He'd try to find out later.

Kenton drew quite a few curious, hard stares as he neared the crowd. He suspected that it was rare indeed that a strange face appeared among this little population.

CHAPTER TWENTY-ONE

JONES CLEARED HIS THROAT AND SPOKE FROM THE PLATFORM. "That man there with Milo is named Brady Kenton," he said. "Many of you have probably heard of him. He writes stories and draws pictures for the *Illustrated American* magazine."

Kenton usually saw smiles and nods of welcome when he was recognized in a crowd, but these people didn't seem to care. They continued to glare at him, most looking even more mistrustful now that they knew he was a journalist. The few young children in the crowd scooted behind their mothers' skirts and peered at him unblinkingly, maybe wondering what breed of devil this stranger was.

"Mr. Kenton, you probably know, was brought to us by Milo and his scouts. They rescued him fleeing from Ottinger's soldiers, who were shooting at him."

The harshness vanished from most of the stares he was receiving. Any enemy of Ottinger's was apparently a friend of theirs.

Jones went on, "Mr. Kenton, though not one of us, and a Lincolnite in former days, is nevertheless a man who has done many good things. In my opinion, the best was that he wrote stories many years ago that exposed to the world the kind of beast that J.B. Ottinger is, and this despite the fact that he and Ottinger were both on the same side during the late war. So I hope you'll make him welcome during this brief time we have remaining together."

There was no general rumble of welcome, however, because that last sentence instantly drew all attention away from Kenton.

A man near the front of the crowd asked, "What do you mean, 'brief time,' Pernell?"

Pernell Jones had the demeanor of a man who has just lost a close loved one. He looked sadly across the group and appeared to be blinking back tears. "My friends, we've lived as a community for many a year. Like a family, we've been, making our own way, living in peace with one another, being our own little nation. We've lived as man was intended to live: free. We ought to be proud of it. I am. I think you are, too.

"This mountainside has provided a good home for us. We've lived quite a few places over the years, but this place here, I think, has been the finest of them all. It's a place I would have wished could go on forever. But it can't."

Jones paused to let his statement sink in. Kenton watched the crowd shift and whisper and murmur. Kenton did his best to commit the scene to memory, hoping to re-create it on a sketch pad later, and jotted notes to retain the gist of Jones's words.

"Few of those out there in the foreign nation who have known of us have understood us," Jones said. It took Kenton a moment to realize the "foreign nation" referred to was the United States. "They've thought of us as hostile and warlike. They've assumed we've pulled ourselves apart from them because we want to continue to fight them. We all know that's not how it is. We want nothing more than for them to ignore us as we ignore them."

He paused, struggling with rising emotion. "But there are those who refuse to ignore us. There are those who refuse to drop old grudges. As I'm sure you know, I'm talking specifically about Colonel J.B. Ottinger."

Mere mention of the name was enough to generate angry grumbles among the people.

Jones then began to reveal information that, until then, had been known only to a few. The crowd received it in stunned silence, for it was inherently shocking news. "I've decided to reveal to you all that on several occasions since the end of the great and lost war, Colonel J.B. Ottinger has made attempts on my life," Jones said. "I've not revealed it until now because I saw no need for it. In most cases, the attempts were rather pitiful, done by inept men Ottinger hired as assassins. Two of these men made the mistake of making their attempts in areas and situations in which I was able to defend myself. One of them admitted—before they died—that Ottinger had hired them. The remarkable thing was that this was done while Ottinger was still in Texas, and we were already here. From that far away, he tried to hire out my assassination! It shows the depth and persistence of the man's hatred."

Kenton could feel the tension and anger of the crowd growing.

Jones continued: "As time passed, Ottinger hired increasingly better, more dangerous, would-be assassins. Each failed, nonetheless. Some of them betrayed him, making no real effort to kill me, and I suppose satisfying themselves with however much of their pay he'd given them in advance. But I began to realize that, eventually, these failures and betrayals would only make Ottinger grow more hungry for my death. I knew that eventually, he'd involve himself directly in the business of seeing to the death of the man whose shotgun mangled his face.

"When Ottinger's wife died and he arranged for transfer to Fort Brandon, only a few miles from here, this bore grim tidings for me . . . for us. I knew his motive for coming. I knew he was moving himself into a better position, a place closer to me, so he could oversee my demise."

Kenton was intrigued. If not for what he'd personally seen of Ottinger's mad, manipulative obsession in the Gomorrah incident, he'd have probably wondered if Jones were simply being paranoid. But he knew enough of Ottinger to know this was no exaggeration. Back before his disfigurement, Ottinger was known as a handsome and very vain man, quick to pose for portraits, photographs, eager to be at the head of any crowd. It was no wonder that such a man would be so obsessively hateful toward the one who forever ruined his appearance.

Jones went on. "I had hoped against hope that somehow Ottinger would simply give up, or at the very least, that he would keep his attempts on my life aimed purely at me alone. But it hasn't happened that way. And now, with this strange event that has happened at Gomorrah, Ottinger has seized an opportunity to compromise us all.

"Our scouts, as you know, have been secretly watching the soldiers since they arrived. In some instances they've been able to overhear some important things as well. The gist of what they've learned is this: Colonel Ottinger intends to officially blame the destruction of Gomorrah on those of us in this compound. He'll label us as violent, obsessed, old unreconstructed Rebels who planted a bomb or set a blaze in the town as some absurd act of war against the United States. And he'll use that as a pretext to overrun us as common outlaws and seditionists."

"Pernell, can I ask something?" a man near the front said.

"Of course you can, Michael."

"I saw what destroyed Gomorrah. Several of us did. It fell from the sky, like a ball of fire, and exploded like no bomb I've ever heard of or seen. It laid the trees out like twigs and ignited near a whole mountaintop at once. How in the world could Ottinger hope to persuade anyone that we here could come up with an explosive big enough to do that kind of damage? Nobody will believe him!"

Jones succinctly explained Ottinger's apparent strategy of relighting the fire and destroying the evidence of the fall pattern of the trees.

"But we've got Brady Kenton here!" someone hollered. "Get him to write the truth!"

Kenton spoke up. "You can rest assured that I will indeed write the truth," he said. "I've exposed Ottinger once, and will happily do it again." *Particularly since he murdered poor Callon. I'll see the man tried and hanged!*

"I think we can trust Kenton to be true to that pledge," Jones said. "But there's one thing I don't want Brady Kenton to have to write. I don't want him to have to describe another Ottinger-led massacre. And that's just what will happen if Ottinger actually besieges us here. This isn't a normal man we're dealing with. This is a man obsessed by hatred, who'll use his authority and his troops for his own personal ends."

"We'll fight the bastards!" someone exclaimed. "This is a strong fort! We're strong men!"

"Kenneth, listen to me," Jones said firmly. "This is the United States Army we're talking about. We resist them, we're just giving them a reason to bring in more soldiers and swarm over us like ants. We'll hand Ottinger even more grounds to treat us like a hostile enemy. We can't engage them in any kind of fight. Remember what our philosophy here has always been: We aren't seeking to continue a lost war, only to continue our lives. We just want to leave alone, and be left alone. If we take up arms against an official United States military force, we will throw all that away."

"Pernell, you're just talking about rolling over and letting them kick us! We *have* to resist!"

"No." Jones swallowed hard, his next words obviously difficult to get out. "We can do only one thing: leave. Immediately and finally."

Silence held a few moments. A woman said, "You're saying we must leave our homes?"

"I can't order anyone to do anything," Jones said. "You're not soldiers and I'm not a commander. But it's my belief that the only sane and safe option is for us to abandon Confederate Ridge. Probably for good."

This generated several stunned reactions and protests. Kenton noted a few people beginning to weep.

"But where would we go?" a woman asked.

"It would be necessary for us to scatter. To dissolve ourselves as a society and a community . . . perhaps forever. Or perhaps until we could find a way to re-form ourselves, maybe north of the border of the United States. Maybe south of it."

"But if we separate, how would we ever come together again?"

"All of you know my brother. You know how and where to reach him. He could serve as our point of reference, to come together again. It would take a long time to come about, I think. But it could be done."

The people weren't eager to hear these words or to accept this option. Protests rose to the sky with the smoke of the bonfires, and the more distant smoke rising from Gomorrah Mountain, now burning out of control and spreading wildly across the countryside, though still far away from Confederate Ridge.

Jones lifted his hands again and spoke earnestly. "It's a hard thing to say, I know, but you have to understand our situation. Ottinger has found a pretext that will allow him to come after not only me, but all of you. And he's not using some private hired guns this time, but United States soldiers."

"I still say resist them!" the man called Kenneth yelled. Others shouted agreement.

Jones shook his head. "Don't even consider it," he said. "It would be suicide."

"Better to die a brave man than live a coward!" Kenneth replied.

Jones stared at him. "If you are implying that I'm a coward, Kenneth, I think you know better."

The man blubbered and blustered, then hung his head. "Yes. I'm sorry. It just burns in me to think of turning tail."

"You're like me, Kenneth. No wife, no family to consider. But think of it from the standpoint of some of the others here who *do* have families."

Kenneth thrust his hands into his pockets and stared at his feet.

Kenton was already dreaming up possible titles for the story he would write about this, picturing designs for the ornate frontispiece sketch that would sit like a crown on the head of the article. He played with ideas for how to word that crucial opening sentence.

"I can't bear for us to leave our homes!" a woman declared in a high, emotional bleat.

"It ain't right, Pernell!" her husband said.

Jones said, "There's no other way."

"A vote!" another man said. "We haven't took a vote!"

"Fine," Jones said. "All of you out there, grown men only, indicate what you want. Those of you who say stay and fight, raise your hands."

The man who had called for the vote, plus a few others, shot hands up. Jones counted them quietly.

"All right. Those who believe we must leave, like sign."

The hands went up much more slowly, but the numbers were far greater than those of the first voters.

Jones nodded. "It's decided, then. We go."

"When, Pernell?"

"This very night. I'm convinced Ottinger won't let this compound remain unmolested for even one more day. We must get out of here before dawn."

CHAPTER TWENTY-TWO

As battered and exhausted as he was, Brady Kenton felt almost none of it as he observed, from a participant's perspective, the evacuation of Confederate Ridge.

It was a remarkable and moving sight. Despite their emotion, despite knowing that the odds of every single one of them coming together again as before were slim, the people moved with a fluid efficiency to gather what they needed and to abandon the rest. They saddled horses and pack mules, cried and hugged and cried some more, then within an hour of having made the decision, abandoned the Confederate Ridge enclave.

Kenton stayed close to Jones, as did Milo—still Jones's right hand after all these years, Kenton observed. Jones was generous, giving Kenton a horse, an old but efficient saddle, and even a good Colt pistol and ammunition. He tried to persuade him to take a rifle as well, but Kenton would not do so.

As the group moved through the dark mountains without the benefit even of torchlight, two things were evident: They knew every mountain trail intimately, and they were no strangers to fast group flight. Kenton marveled at their efficiency, their trail skills, their determination. He'd never be able to endure their familial, cloistered way of life, nor share their isolationist philosophy, but he found he could understand them nonetheless, and even admire them.

Jones in particular he thought admirable. The man might view himself as just one more resident of the Confederate Ridge community, but Kenton saw that he was far more. Jones had the qualities of natural leadership. It was no wonder he had been so effective as a guerilla warrior during the great civil conflict, and so feared by the Yankee squads he stung like a hornet time and again in the wilderness regions of Virginia and Tennessee.

When the great moving pillar of people began to disperse at key points along the way, Kenton realized that this flight was in no way random. *They've planned this all . . . long in advance!* he thought. This was made evident by the natural and orderly way the group broke apart, different individuals and families taking different mountain trails. He wondered how it must have been to live in a society that was so insecure, so subject to interference, that it had been necessary to develop an advance pattern for its self-destruction.

The group went on, growing smaller all the while. Jones spoke little, withdrawn inside himself, yet also wary and attentive, keeping watch for pursuers. Kenton himself worried about this, especially at the beginning, but less as time passed and it became clear that no one was on their trail. Kenton realized that the out-of-control forest fires that were spreading from Gomorrah Mountain were actually working to the advantage of the Confederate Ridge refugees, diverting the attention and manpower of the soldiers, giving more time for flight.

Kenton found much satisfaction in knowing that Colonel Ottinger had made a fundamental miscalculation. He had assumed that Jones and the people of Confederate Ridge would remain where they were. He had assumed he had all the time he needed to deal with them.

He'd find himself overrunning an empty stockade. The mental image made Kenton smile.

By the time dawn came, Kenton, Milo, and Jones were

alone. The populace of Confederate Ridge had entirely broken up, like smoke dissolving to nothing.

As Kenton lay down at last to sleep, hidden away with his two companions in a mountain hollow, only then did he realize that he had not the slightest idea where they were going, or even if Jones and Milo wanted him along.

At this point, he was far too tired to care.

About the time Kenton was falling asleep, a band of exhausted, ash-covered soldiers stood in the midst of the Confederate Ridge compound and watched Colonel J.B. Ottinger seem to fade away before them.

He stood alone, unsmiling, unspeaking, the morning sun bright on his disfigured face but murky in his dead eye. He looked very old.

His troops hated him by now. They'd begun to hate him slowly, by stages, almost as soon as he'd arrived to take command at Fort Benton. The soldiers had known of Confederate Ridge a long time, just as they knew of the personal history between Ottinger and Jones. If any had doubted that Ottinger's coming to Montana had nothing to do with his hatred for Jones, they'd lost that doubt now. The entire Gomorrah incident made it undeniable.

The nearby ridges flamed now, burning over many miles, hopelessly out of control. For a time the soldiers had tried to contain the blaze once it spread beyond the planned reburn area, but the wind and the dry mountains, which had seen no rain for a month other than that one storm that had put out the original Gomorrah fire, combined to make it impossible. Stopping the fire the soldiers had started was now in the hands of God and nature alone.

As exhausted as they were after all their slavish labor, though, Ottinger had ordered them to ready their arms and march to Confederate Ridge, there to demand the surrender of the enclave and to take into military custody its leader, Jones.

But Jones was gone. The stockade was empty. And after a feeble effort at tracking and pursuit, even Ottinger had to realize that it was hopeless. His men were far too weary, and Jones and his people had too great a start.

So Ottinger stood there near the Confederate Ridge stockade well, alone, old, his spirit seeming to die while his men silently watched.

An under officer approached him. "Do you have orders for us, sir?"

Ottinger said wearily, "Set the stockade ablaze."

"Ablaze, sir? Begging your pardon, sir, but we've already lost control of the earlier fires, sir. It could happen on this ridge as well."

"I've given my order. Carry it out."

They did set the log fort ablaze, and all the buildings inside it, and for an hour watched it all burn. Then, at Ottinger's orders, they returned to Gomorrah, there to rest for a few hours and break their camp before beginning the march back to Fort Brandon, a place they normally deplored, but which by comparison to what they'd endured at Gomorrah, now seemed a welcome refuge and familiar home.

When they'd rested for a time, Kenton, Jones, and Milo Buckner made a fire, cooked food and coffee, and talked about the immediate future.

Though these men were quite different from him, and during the war had been his enemies, Kenton was naturally drawn to them. They were tragic figures, in their way, attempting to live an independent, autonomous life that could never fully succeed, yet this was part of what was intriguing about them.

"You said you'd write about us, Kenton, and tell the true story. Did you mean it?" Jones asked.

"I did. I only regret I saw so little of your way of life . . . I saw only the end of it all."

"It's not the end yet," Jones said. "We'll find our way together again, most of us, anyway. And someday find a place far enough away that we can live and truly be left alone."

"Pernell, you have to face the facts: That would be easier said than done," Milo Buckner said. "It would be hard indeed to survive if we were too far cut off from your brother."

Jones watched the steam rise from his coffee, and nodded. "Yes. I know."

"I never knew you had a brother," Kenton said. He'd known a fair amount about Pernell Jones back in the war days, but had never heard of a brother until Jones had mentioned one during his final talk to the people in the Confederate Ridge compound.

"I do," Jones said. "A fine brother . . . and Milo's right. Without ready access to him, I don't know if we could have survived here like we did." He stood, swore softly, and began pacing about. "I don't like to say it, don't even like to admit it to myself, but I suppose we haven't been as self-sufficient at Confederate Ridge as it might appear. Without my brother's support, we would have been a very impoverished people at times."

Kenton paid close attention. He'd wondered almost as soon as he'd seen the cloistered community of Confederate Ridge how such a group could have survived so well without outside commerce or subsidy. Evidently they hadn't.

"So your brother has helped you?"

"Yes. Yes, many times. He has always believed in us, understood us, and helped us . . . all without really being part of us. He's deeply involved in the commerce of the Foreign Nation. Quite wealthy, he is. His generosity has, from time to time, been what allowed us to go on."

Kenton felt mildly disappointed. The idea of a self-sufficient, self-sustaining community of stubborn isolationists appealed to his romantic side more so than that of a group that required occasional injections of support from the outside in order to survive. Rather than being independent from the commerce of the "Foreign Nation" of the United States, Jones and his people had actually been indirectly dependent on it.

"Where does your brother's wealth come from?" Kenton asked.

Jones said, "Tell you what—why don't you come see for yourself?"

Milo Buckner grinned. "I was hoping that's where we were going, Pernell!"

"So you don't care if I travel with you a while longer?" Kenton asked.

"I was counting on you doing so."

"So was I," Kenton replied. "There's still much I need to learn about you and your people if I'm to write about it as I should."

"Then meet my brother you shall." Jones went back to the battered coffee pot, which Milo had brought out of Confederate Ridge slung by a string to the horn of his horse's saddle, and poured a fresh cupful for himself. "Tell me something, Mr. Kenton: What brought you to these parts in the first place? The fire at Gomorrah?"

"Oh, no. I came earlier than that. I was to meet a man in Gomorrah. He'd contacted me, telling me he had information that would be important to me. I was about halfway up Gomorrah Mountain when I was attacked by a highwayman and robbed. The sorry thief left me unconscious in the forest, took my possessions, even my original coat and pistol, everything, and apparently headed on up toward Gomorrah. Actually, I suppose the poor devil saved my life. He was apparently just outside town when the fire came down.

Burned him to a cinder. I was farther down the mountain, unconscious on the ground, so I survived with nothing more than a fairly mild scorching."

"Speaking of that fire . . . what do you think it was?" Milo asked.

"I couldn't say," Kenton replied. "It certainly wasn't man-caused, and was nothing volcanic, or lightning-related. I can only surmise that something fell from the sky and exploded just above the town."

"A meteor," Jones said. "That's been my suspicion from the outset. One bursting through the atmosphere so fast it generates intense heat and disintegrates with an explosive force."

"A meteor . . . like a falling star?" Milo said.

"That's right."

"Mercy!"

"It's an amazing thing to consider," Kenton said. "It's a telling thing about Ottinger, too, that the man could find nothing in such a fascinating event except a handy pretext for trying to settle a personal score."

Jones stared across the mountains. "I hate him. I thought about slipping away, heading back, and finding him. If he wants to kill me, let him see if he's man enough to do it face-to-face."

"I'm glad you didn't do that, Pernell," Milo said.

Kenton shifted the conversation back onto its original course. "Where does your brother live, Pernell?"

"A couple of days' ride from here. You may be surprised to meet him. But what about this man you were to meet in Gomorrah? You never met him, I'm sure."

"No, I didn't," Kenton said. "Now I don't know if he's dead or alive. If alive, he's at Fort Brandon, a place I certainly can't safely go."

"So what will you do?"

"Hope he's alive, and that he contacts me again through

the offices of the *Illustrated American*. It's all I can do at the moment."

"Tell you what. Let's take a look at Fort Brandon first, from a distance, anyway. Maybe we'll spot him.

"It's a good idea. Can you spare the time?"

"Fort Brandon's not far out of our way."

"I do appreciate it."

"Glad to have you with us, Kenton. Glad to have you writing about us, and about Ottinger."

"I intend to bring him down completely this time."

"He had his men shooting at you, Kenton. He wants you dead. He'll try to get you again, as he's tried with me many times."

"Let him try," Kenton replied. "Let him try."

CHAPTER TWENTY-THREE

THE OLD SADDLE ALEX GUNNISON HAD PURCHASED FROM Peter Wilson fit his newly purchased horse perfectly, but his own rear very poorly. As he dismounted near a clear brook that ran down from the mountains and went to it to drink, he did so gingerly, his legs sore and chafed, his rump more sore yet.

Gunnison knelt where the brook swirled into a tiny, bay-shaped recess in the stony bank, forming a slow-moving whirlpool of water deliciously cool and fresh. Gunnison looked at his moving reflection as he drank and thought, with secret pride, that his days of roughing it had certainly toughened him. His skin was browned, his face ruddy, his whiskers darkening his jawline. The grime of travel covered his clothing, masking the fine cut of his trousers and the tailored lines of his shirt. With his coat on and his hat jammed down low over his slightly curling hair, Gunnison thought he looked as rugged as any denizen of this territory he was likely to encounter.

He stood, stretching, and fed his horse some oats out of the supply he'd bought from Wilson. He was in an isolated area, no visible dwellings around, no chimney smoke rising from beyond the next hill.

He wondered how long it would be until he reached the community of Paxton. Also, he wondered if Parson Peabody, Rankin, and company had even come this way at all. Though he told himself he was tracking the group, the truth was he was counting much on luck. The Wilsons had said Parson Peabody's group had headed generally toward Paxton, and on that basis alone he was traveling this way.

He'd just started to sit down on a rock and rest his bones a few moments when the sound of a man's singing voice reached him from the other side of a hill just beyond the spring. He stood, wary, not fully pleased to be meeting a stranger in this unfamiliar region. He reached beneath his coat and thumbed off the leather thong holding his pistol in its holster, just in case.

The man who came over the hill stopped singing as soon as he saw Gunnison, but after only a couple of seconds, picked up his tune again. He was astride a mule, his long legs sticking down straight as sticks on either side, booted feet in stirrups that seemed set just a little too low. He was armed with a pistol stuck backward in a holster on his left side, and with a battered Henry repeating rifle sleeved on the side of the saddle.

The song was one Gunnison had heard before, either in a saloon or in church. Funny how so many drinking songs and hymns had similar-sounding tunes.

The man pulled the mule to a halt and looked squarely at Gunnison as he finished his song's last line:

". . . and home again I go, to see my sweeeeeeeeeet lady!"

He warbled a little on the extended "sweet," and grinned at Gunnison when he'd finished.

"Well, now! Did you hear that?" he asked. "I've long wondered how them truly good singers make their voice have that little quiver like that, and now here I've gone and taught myself to do it!"

"It sounded very good," Gunnison said. This wasn't just prudent flattery. The fellow's voice was indeed a fairly good baritone, and that warble had been worth hearing.

"I thank you, sir," the man said. "Mind if I have a bit of water from your spring?"

"Isn't my spring. I'm just passing through."

"I know. I pass it all the time myself. Just trying to be polite to you, that's all."

Gunnison grinned. This cheerful fellow was hard not to like.

The man swung down off the mule and advanced toward the spring. The mule went with him, and they drank together. Gunnison noted that the man drank downstream from the mule, so that what it slobbered out he instantly imbibed. It didn't seem to bother the man at all, though it did rather bother Gunnison.

"My, my, ain't nothing better than fresh water when you're thirsty," the man said, rising. "Young man, my name's Peabody . . ."

Peabody!

". . . Millard Peabody. I'd shake your hand if the stream was a bit more narrow, you obviously being the fine young Christian you are."

"My name's Gunnison. Alex Gunnison. Pleased to meet you, Mr. Peabody."

"Got a question for you, young fellow: You ain't going to rob me here, are you?"

"No, sir."

"Well, good. I thought you might. A fellow about your age once tried to rob me here at this very spot."

"It wasn't me."

"No, no, I'm sure 'twasn't. 'Less you're a ghost. He lies buried over yonder, right where I planted him. I don't allow myself to be robbed, you see. Really hated to pull the trigger on one so young."

"You needn't worry about me, Mr. Peabody. All I ask from you is some information, if you've got it."

"What I know, you'll know. Ask right on."

"I happen to be looking for a man with the same last name as you. A sort of preacher that might have passed through here, maybe heading for Paxton. They call him Parson Peabody. I don't think anybody's ever told me his first name."

"Peabody, huh?"

"Mister, you wouldn't be the same Peabody, would you?"

"Afraid not. Honest truth is, I ain't named Peabody at all."

"Beg pardon?"

"I don't usually give my name out to strangers on the road, young man. For reasons of my own. You ought not be so ready to give yours, if you'll take some advice from a stranger."

Gunnison knew this attitude well. He'd traveled with Kenton enough to learn that the farther west of the Mississippi one traveled, the more private a man's name and business became. Rare was the occasion when one could ask a man what he was doing, where he was going, even who he was, without generating great offense. Even those who readily told their names, as "Peabody" had, often—like he—were not giving their real names at all.

"Wasn't trying to pry, mister. It's just that I need to find this Parson Peabody, and some people with him."

"I know where he is . . . if you're looking for the man who said the fire would fall on Gomorrah."

"That's him."

"You'll not find him at Paxton. He's done been there and gone. I seen him there, heard him preach. His name's been fresh on my mind, which is why it's the name I gave you instead of my real one, which is Tom Smith . . . or maybe Luke McGlue, or maybe something else entirely."

"Did he still have a couple of men and a woman with him?"

"He did. One of them was right keen on taking up offerings, I'll tell you."

"Where did they go after Paxton?"

"My belief is they went about ten miles on beyond, to Pearl Town."

"Don't recall I've ever heard of Pearl Town."

"Ain't much there. A little town, mostly cabins and shacks. One fine hotel, though. Not that it's needed. It's just there because old Johansen wants it to be."

Johansen . . . that name tried to connect with some vein of memory or recognition in Gunnison's mind, but didn't quite make it. "Who is Johansen?" he asked.

"One of the richest men in the Montana Territory. He owns three good mines there near Pearl Town. Didn't find them, just bought them from them who did, at a high price that he's earned back again many times over. He grew up back East somewhere, poor family, and became a sea captain. He made himself rich in shipping, then decided to put the sea behind him, head out West, and get into mining. Built himself a fine house, that big hotel—just because he wanted a fine hotel to lodge the folks who come to visit him—and stuck a big ship's mast down square in the middle of the town street. They used to call the town Mast Town before Livesay Johansen named it Pearl Town after his wife. What Johansen wants, Johansen gets, you see. He owns not only his mines in his own vicinity, but parts of several others all across this territory, not to mention so much grazing land back in the eastern end of the territory that you could walk all day and never leave Johansen land. Even without his mines, Johansen would do quite well from his ranching."

"Why do you think Parson Peabody's at Pearl Town?"

"Because when he left Paxton, he and his friends did it in company of some of Johansen's men, riding in a Johansen carriage. You know Johansen's things by the big fancy 'J' printed on their side. It's on his vehicles, his hotel, and half the other buildings in town. Hell, he'd stamp it on the people of his town if they'd let him. Bunch of folks walking around with big 'J' letters on their faces, that's what it would be."

"I wonder why he'd want to see somebody like Parson Peabody?"

"He probably didn't. It was probably his wife who sent for them. Strange, strange woman, that Pearl is. Kind of witchy and peculiar."

"You seem to know a lot about the Johansens."

"Worked for him a spell while the place was still called Mast Town, back before I went into business for myself. I tended bar in the Johansen Hotel. Poured many a drink for Mr. Johansen during that time. Sort of got to know him, and a more salt-of-the-earth fellow you'd never find. But only one time did I even lay eyes on his wife. She spends most of her time in that big house he built for her, talking to the souls of dead people and doing what she calls 'spirit traveling.' Claims she can make herself leave her body and go wherever she wants. All the way to Boston, if she wants, without her body ever leaving her chair. Hell, she might be flitting right over us right now, like a jarfly, and us not even know it." He glanced skyward, tipped his hat, and said, "Afternoon, Mrs. Johansen."

Gunnison grinned. "She sounds like a peculiar woman indeed."

The other put a finger to his lips. "Hush that! She might be hovering around above you, listening."

Gunnison laughed. "Why would somebody like her want to see a common preacher like Parson Peabody?"

"Common preacher? You call rightly predicting the destruction of a town by fire from above, of all things, as the act of a common preacher? It's very *uncommon*, and just the sort of thing to thrill the soul of Pearl Johansen."

"Well, that makes sense. Tell me how I can get to Pearl Town."

"Head on like you are, up this road, until you reach Paxton. Take the left fork in the road and bear down toward the river. You'll reach Joe Rush's trading post and ferry before long. Once you get across the river, stay on the road for maybe six more miles, and you'll find Pearl Town."

"I appreciate your help . . . Mr. McGlue."

"Always glad to be of service."

He went on, traveling the opposite direction from the one Gunnison was going, singing his song again. Gunnison watched him until he was out of sight, and at that moment appreciated very much his line of work, prone though he was to often resent its rigors, the separation from his wife that it inevitably involved, and the frequent loneliness. Still, it brought him into contact with interesting human beings, like this fellow.

He thought, *Wait until I tell Kenton about this fellow. This is just the sort of character he enjoys.*

Gunnison winced. He'd forgotten yet again. His days of sharing anything with Kenton were forever gone.

Sorrow overwhelmed Gunnison, but also another feeling, one that had been arising steadily, though nonsensically, since he'd left Gomorrah Mountain. It was the notion that Kenton, somehow, was still out there, alive as ever. It couldn't be, of course—he'd seen his dead body, *smelled* it, for heaven's sake—but even so, the feeling persisted, strong enough that Gunnison had not yet felt any strong impulse to rush to notify the *Illustrated American* of Kenton's death.

He knew it was only wishful thinking. If only it could be true, though! If only Kenton really could be alive!

This surely must be the way Kenton felt when he thought about his lost Victoria, Gunnison considered. There's something in us that just won't let go sometimes, something that won't let hope die even in the face of the most overwhelming evidence.

Gunnison rested a few minutes more, then remounted and continued on down the road toward Paxton.

CHAPTER TWENTY-FOUR

GUNNISON'S HORSE THREW A SHOE AS HE REACHED PAXTON, and he spent the rest of the day finding a blacksmith to deal with the problem. By then it was too late to travel farther, so he took up lodging in a flea-ridden, low and long cabin with a sagging roof and a bad smell—a typical kind of hotel in far too many Western towns that Gunnison had visited.

The night, spent in a big room with three soggy, sunken beds and six snoring men, was miserable, but had one interesting aspect: before they fell asleep, the men, most of them strangers to one another, talked among themselves. The topic was Gomorrah, and the man who had prophesied its destruction.

The story was becoming distorted, Gunnison noticed. Peabody's prophecy, it was said, had been made in the center of the town, spoken to the entire populace. It had forecast not only that the town would be destroyed, but at precisely what minute, and who would die and who would live. And the fire, Peabody had reportedly said, would not be quenchable for a month.

It was remarkable to watch folklore in the making.

The snores echoed through the hotel like unending rolls of thunder. Gunnison, though exhausted, lay awake most of the night. By the hour just before dawn, he was praying for morning like a man dying in a desert prays for water.

* * *

Gunnison reached the Joe Rush trading post late the next morning. Built of logs still in the bark, facing at an angle toward the river, it was an ugly building, poorly designed and inconsistently chinked, so that from certain angles one could see light penetrating the building back to front.

He sniffed the air and smelled cooking meat, borne on the smoke that rose from the chimney. Ah, yes. He was very hungry. Suddenly the place looked much better.

Gunnison was halfway across the stony yard of the trading post, just about to come around the corner of a big woodshed, when he was shocked to hear the blast of a gunshot from inside the trading post. His horse nickered and reared, just a little.

"Whoa, whoa there!" he said softly. "Settle down now."

He backtracked a few yards, dismounted, and tethered the horse securely to a sapling. Another shot sounded from the trading post, then a third.

Gunnison, though no coward, was as human as anyone, and the thought of just mounting up and riding past this place by some alternate and unseen route crossed his mind. Whatever trouble was going on there—if it was trouble at all, and not just some harmless target practice out back—needn't involve him.

A couple of things kept Gunnison from riding away, though. One was the fact that he knew he'd be ashamed of himself if he did. The other was that, between the last two shots, he'd distinctly heard the pleading cry of a distraught woman.

Gunnison went to the corner of the shed and peered around it at the trading post. Through some of the unchinked portions he could see movement against the daylight coming in from behind, but could not make out any details.

Another shot, another scream.

Without knowing enough facts to make a plan, he could

only follow intuition. He holstered his pistol, went and freed his horse, and rode it around the shed into the trading post yard, acting casual, a man just happening upon the scene.

He dismounted and tethered his horse to the hitchpost, then walked toward the trading post door.

He entered just as the next shot blasted. Gunnison let out a yell of apparent surprise. "What the . . ."

"Howdy, friend!" said one of two burly, roughly dressed men who stood in the middle of the room with pistols drawn. On the floor between them was a crockery jug of homemade whiskey. "You come in just in time to watch the dance!"

"What's going on here?" Gunnison asked. He glanced toward the corner, where two middle-aged women and a boy of about ten stood looking very frightened and worried.

The only other person in the room was an old man who stood in the opposite corner from the women and boy. He was trembling like an aspen leaf and looked like he might faint.

"Just a little bit of fun," the other gunman answered. "We found us a good dancer here. See?"

He lifted his pistol, aimed at the floor just beneath the old man's feet, and fired.

The old man yelped a little and went into a weary jig. The men with the pistols laughed.

"I thought this only happened in dime novels," Gunnison said.

The men laughed and fired again.

The old man looked pleadingly at Gunnison as he continued his frail dance. A glance at the women and boy revealed the same pitiful expression.

"Why are you treating that old fellow that way?" Gunnison asked.

Neither gunman answered. One paused to reload his pistol while the other took a swig from the whiskey jug.

The old man, looking ready to drop, stopped dancing. "Uh-uh, old fellow! No stopping! Keep a-jigging!"

Gunnison feared the old man would fall over dead at any point. He wondered what motivated this bit of cruelty. Maybe there was no motivation beyond alcohol, opportunity, and meanness.

Gunnison took a step forward. One of the roughnecks wheeled to face him. "Where you going, swell?"

Swell? Gunnison was honestly offended. Everywhere he went, no matter how dirty, rumpled, and whiskered he became, there was always someone telling him he looked like a swell. The curse of his urban raising, he supposed.

"Just wanted to get a better view of the dancing," Gunnison replied.

The men glanced at one another, then laughed. "Yeah. Well, watch this step!" one said. He fired a shot that very nearly clipped the heel off one of the old man's shoes.

The gunmen howled in mirth.

"Please!" one of the women begged. "His heart is weak . . . you must stop!"

"Shut up, cow!" one of the pair replied, aiming and firing a shot that struck even closer yet to the dancing man's feet.

Gunnison grinned and chuckled. "He's a good dancer," he said.

"Hell, yes!"

"How long you had him at it?"

"Why, half an hour or more. Hey! Don't slow there, nimble-toes! Step lively!" The pistol blasted again.

Gunnison sneezed. "Mighty lot of gunsmoke you're filling this place with."

One man took a swig, passed the jug to the other.

"I think you ought to stop now," Gunnison said. "That old man will die if you don't."

The pair ignored him. One leveled his hot and smoking pistol again.

Gunnison reached over and grasped his wrist.

The man turned and stared at him in astonishment. "What the hell!"

The old man didn't quite quit dancing, but he slowed down.

"You trying to kill yourself, young man?"

"Just trying to keep you from killing an old one."

The man looked down at his wrist, still gripped in Gunnison's hand. "Let go my arm."

"If you'll quit shooting at the old man."

"I might just shoot you instead."

The man's partner, amazed at Gunnison's effrontery, raised his pistol and aimed it at Gunnison's temple. "If'n I don't do it first."

Gunnison's heart hammered, but he kept his expression calm, and stared without blinking at the man whose wrist he held. Kenton had taught him that trick: an unblinking stare, he said, adds five measures of courage to a man. Gunnison was praying hard, meanwhile, for he had no real idea what he was going to do. These men could kill him at any point, and probably would.

He could think of only one possibility. "If you want someone to dance for you, I'll do it. You just let the old man rest."

The two ruffians looked at one another, both breaking into a grin. "You just made yourself a bargain!" the man said. He yanked his wrist free.

Gunnison went to the corner where the old man still shuffled, not quite sure whether it was safe yet to stop.

"Go to yonder corner," Gunnison said quietly, clapping his hand on his shoulder. "Sit down and rest your heart."

The old man nodded, reached up and touched Gunnison's hand on his shoulder. "Thank you," he whispered.

The old man shuffled off to his grateful loved ones, and Gunnison faced the ruffians.

One lifted his pistol, aimed it at Gunnison's chest . . .

The blast made Gunnison jump in surprise. He looked down at his body, expecting to see a gush of blood, but there was none. The pistoleer had jerked the pistol downward at the last moment and fired it into the floor.

"Step up to the music, boy!"

Gunnison got himself to breathing again and began stepping. He clicked his heels on the puncheon floor, kicked his legs, did everything he could to put on a satisfying show of buffoonery in hope he could soon satisfy these drunkards and they would go on their way.

He looked past them to the people in the corner; one of the women, in tears, silently mouthed, "Thank you."

Gunnison, feeling very foolish but also knowing he was the hero of the hour in the eyes of the grateful audience in the far corner, gave his dancing all he could. He turned, bowed, curtsied . . . all to the occasional blast of a pistol.

When one of the bullets nearly caught him in the calf, Gunnison stopped dancing abruptly.

"Enough of that!" he shouted, out of breath. "I'm dancing willingly—no need to shoot at me!"

The answer was another blast. Gunnison began dancing again.

He began to think he'd made a mistake. He'd anticipated that these men would soon tire of such juvenile amusement, but they seemed content to go on this way as long as the whiskey lasted.

On it went, another ten minutes, then fifteen . . . Gunnison was growing exhausted, and angry. He even resented the silent people in the corner for standing there and staring and doing nothing. Didn't they have a rifle or a shotgun hidden somewhere?

Another shot, and this time the bullet ripped through the cuff of his trousers.

Gunnison had had enough. Sweating, weary, he reached

under his coat and yanked out his pistol from its holster. He leveled it at the nearer of the two gunmen, who in turn lifted his own pistol. The second ruffian, as luck would have it, had just emptied his pistol and was about to reload.

"No reloading!" Gunnison shouted. "Drop it, or I'll kill your partner!"

"I'll kill you first!" the one with the raised pistol said.

In fact, neither man fired. Both stood there, pistols raised at each other, both frozen in place.

"Looks like we're in a standoff," the ruffian said at last.

"Afraid not," said a new voice.

Gunnison shifted his eyes just long enough to see who had spoken. It was the same singing traveler he'd encountered earlier at the spring. He was standing in the doorway with a shotgun raised, leveled at the two ruffians. The barrels were sawed off horrifically short, and the stock as well. The weapon was so small it could have been concealed in nothing larger than a good-sized saddlebag, which is exactly where Gunnison figured it had been.

"The pattern of this shotgun is mighty broad," the man said. "One shot, and both you gentlemen will go down. I suggest you drop your weapons and haul your backsides out of here, and far away, before I give you a demonstration of this shotgun that neither of you will live long enough to be impressed by."

The men complied, glowering, faces and eyes red from anger and liquor. "We'll not forget this!" one said. "We see you again, you're a dead man. Same goes for all of you!"

"Out!" the man at the door said, sidestepping carefully to give them egress while also keeping them covered.

They left, took their horses from the corral, and rode away, shouting obscenities as they did so.

The newcomer fired off a high blast from the shotgun in answer. They hastened their flight and were soon gone.

Gunnison holstered his pistol and walked toward the

man, hand outstretched. "I thank you, sir. I'm quite happy to see you again, believe me."

"Good to see you as well, Mister . . . Gunnison, if I recall?"

"Yes. And you are named McGlue and several other things as well, I believe."

"In fact, my name is Rush," the man said. "Joe Rush. Welcome to my trading post."

The details of what had happened made Rush's face go red and sent a vein to visibly throbbing in his temple. But it established Gunnison at once as virtually an honorary member of the Joe Rush family. He was given food, drink, assorted free supplies, and more praise than he'd received at any one time in his life.

The old man whom Gunnison had saved from dancing to death was Rush's father. One of the two women was Rush's wife, the other his widowed sister-in-law, who was also mother to the boy.

"I'm sorry I was so cagey with you about who I was when we met there at the spring," Rush said. "I've just learned it don't always pay to be overly forthcoming with information. Folks sometimes tend to believe a man who operates a post like this one probably has money on him at any given time."

"All I care about is that you came back at just the right time to save my bacon," Gunnison said.

"Pshaw! You'd have done fine even without me. You got gravel in that craw of yours, young man. You ain't the swell you look to be."

There it was again: once more he was being labeled a swell. And once more he ignored it.

Rush continued, "I go from time to time to pay a visit on my cousin, who lives a mile beyond that spring we met up at," he said. "I was on my way there when I met you.

Danged if he wasn't home when I arrived. A neighbor fellow there told me he'd gone off in the direction of Fort Brandon, where there's been a lot of religious revivaling going on because of the Preacher Peabody's prophesying."

"I'm glad he wasn't there. Otherwise you'd not have come back when you did. But I'm . . ." Gunnison cut off and glanced at the women, boy, and old man. He drew closer to Joe Rush and said in a whisper, ". . . I'm concerned about those two. I'm moving on, so I'm not likely to encounter them again. But they know where to find you."

"That they do, but talk is cheap, particularly when it's soaked in whiskey. I'll keep an eye out for them. You do the same. Paths cross sometimes in ways you don't expect."

CHAPTER TWENTY-FIVE

WELL-FED, WELL-WATERED, AND WELL-SUPPLIED, GUNNISON crossed the river on Joe Rush's ferry and went on his way toward Pearl Town. The weather was good, the journey pleasant and uneventful, and he reached the town hours before he expected he would.

The imposing Johansen Hotel was one of only two things worth noticing in Pearl Town, and that only because it looked so out of place amid the more typical plain houses and outright hovels that dominated the rest of the town.

The other thing was the Johansen house, which stood roughly across the street from the hotel. In a city setting the three-story house would have been mildly noteworthy for its size and excellent construction, but against the backdrop of Pearl Town it looked absolutely ostentatious. Gunnison would have liked to have had a clearer look at the place, but his view was blocked by a high, heavy, wooden fence that completely surrounded the house's grounds.

Gunnison dismounted at the front of the hotel and tied off his horse. Walking inside, he approached the desk clerk.

"Got some rooms?"

"Yes, sir. Four available."

"Give me the cheapest you have—preferably on the third floor, facing the street."

"We have a room available there, but it's one of our better ones. Certainly not the cheapest."

"I'll take it," Gunnison said. In that his expenses were faithfully recouped by the *Illustrated American*, he never worried too much about costs, except when his traveling money got exceptionally low. At the moment he was holding up fairly well for cash, though, even after purchasing the horse and saddle from Rory Wilson's father. And with the supplies heaped upon him by the grateful Joe Rush, he had little need to buy much. A better room would be fine. He hadn't slept on a truly good bed in days.

"A street view is indeed the thing to have," the clerk small-talked while he signed Gunnison in. "Always interesting things to watch on the street."

Gunnison decided to play ignorant in hopes of ferreting out some new information. "Tell me, whose house is it across the street from here?"

"Oh, that's Mr. Johansen's house."

"Johansen, like the hotel name here?"

"Yes. He owns us."

"I see. Must be a wealthy man."

"Mr. Johansen has done well for himself."

"It seems a shame he hides that beautiful house behind such a tall fence."

"Oh . . . well . . ." The clerk glanced from side to side and leaned over the desk a little, dropping his voice. "That's not really Mr. Johansen's doing, but his wife's. She's somewhat . . . well, I'm not sure how to describe her . . ."

"Fearful? Reclusive? Eccentric?"

"Eccentric. Yes. That's the word."

"I hear she has that preacher with her, the one who predicted the destruction of that mining town."

"She might. I, for one, don't believe that whole fire-from-heaven story."

"I'm a journalist . . . any chance, you think, of getting to meet Pearl Johansen and her guests?"

The man laughed. "Don't waste your time. *Nobody* sees

Pearl Johansen unless she wants to be seen. And both she and her husband have no use for journalists. Rich people, you know, don't like people nosing around in their business." He looked around quickly. "But don't say I said that."

Kenton had always said that the direct way usually was the best way, and Gunnison tried it the next morning despite the discouragement the hotel clerk had given him.

Gathering his courage, wondering why he was so nervous, he crossed the street to the front gate of the big wall around the Johansen house, and hammered the big iron knocker there.

Minutes passed; he hammered twice more. Finally a small door built into the gate opened and a gruff-looking man, who gave the impression of being a groundskeeper or some sort of other general worker about the place, stared out at Gunnison without speaking.

"Hello," Gunnison said. "My name is Alex Gunnison, with *Gunnison's Illustrated American*. I've come hoping to speak with the preacher named Peabody, and particularly with a man with him whose name is—"

The door slammed, cutting him off.

Persist, Kenton had always said. *Persist.*

Gunnison knocked again. This time the man jerked the door open violently and glared out. "Do you not understand the meaning of a slamming door, friend?"

"It's very important that I—"

The door slammed again.

Gunnison did understand. He sighed, turned, and walked back to the hotel.

That afternoon, after an excellent lunch in the hotel's fine cafe, he sat down in the airy lobby with a pad of paper, a pen, and some ink. After staring several minutes at the blank sheets, he at last forced himself to begin to write.

The letter was addressed to his father, back at the *Illustrated American.* Though normally words came easily for Gunnison, this time he had to fight the pen to get the words onto paper. Slowly the page filled, then another, and another.

When he was finished, Gunnison read what he'd written: the sad story of the death of Brady Kenton.

When he'd read it, he read it again. Then he tore it up, wadded the shreds, and put them in the nearest garbage bin. He still couldn't accept it. Still was not ready to make it official. No matter what, he couldn't really accommodate the idea that Brady Kenton was dead.

He returned to his room to take a nap.

Many miles away, Brady Kenton knelt on a hillside overlooking Fort Brandon, looking through Milo's spyglass. He focused it, and after a few moments handed it over to Jones. Jones readjusted it to his own eye and watched the scene below.

"No question about it," he said. "Those are definitely some of the Gomorrah residents leaving the fort. I recognize some of the faces. That last one was a storekeeper I've done some business with. Oscar Morris. I'm glad he survived the fire."

"You used to show yourself openly in Gomorrah?" Kenton asked.

"People don't really know me anymore, Kenton. Not by appearance. I could go there and be just one more of many unknown faces."

"Interesting that they're all leaving pretty much at once," Milo said.

"Ottinger's got little reason to hold them anymore," Jones said. "When we gave him the slip, it was over. Why waste time trying to concoct an elaborate scheme to pin the blame for Gomorrah on us, when we were nowhere to be found? He locked up all those people to keep his lie from being contradicted . . . and now it doesn't matter. He's got nothing to gain by keeping the game going any longer. We're out of his reach."

"For now," Milo said.

"No," Jones replied. "More than that this time. I can feel it. This time we're through with Ottinger."

"Optimism's a good thing, I suppose," Milo said. "I can't say I have as much of it as you do."

Kenton was thinking of other things. "I wonder if Rankin is among any of those we've seen?"

"Only one way to find out, Kenton," Jones said.

"Right," he replied, rising.

Twenty minutes later, having circled down from the hillside, keeping as hidden as possible from the fort, they reached the road and intercepted the storekeeper Jones had recognized. Despite Jones's earlier talk of having been anonymous during his Gomorrah visits, it was evident that at least some there—including this man—knew him for who he was.

The man blanched at the sight of Jones. "Good Lord, Pernell—you'd best not be showing yourself in this vicinity! If Ottinger gets his hands on you . . ."

"He'll not," Jones replied confidently. "Oscar, I want to get some information from you. There was a man in Gomorrah, name of Rankin, who was to meet my friend here." He gestured toward Kenton, but did not introduce him by name. Best to keep this simple. "Do you know if he survived the fire?"

"Oh, yes indeed. He wasn't even there when it happened. But he came back soon enough, all attached to Parson Peabody, like a shadow. And he left with him, too." The storekeeper told the story, all he knew of it. "And now, from what I hear passing around the fort, Peabody and Rankin are traveling from town to town, preaching and warning and taking up quite a lot of money from folks, so that other towns and people won't be burned up, too."

"How are these towns supposed to avoid that fate?" Jones asked.

"I don't know. All I know is what I heard the soldiers saying among themselves in the fort."

Kenton, who had instantly become quite energized when he learned that Rankin was alive, said, "I hardly care about what Peabody is doing. The key matter to me is that I can still meet the man who may know something about my wife." To the storekeeper he said, "Sir, do you know if there is a woman traveling with Rankin and Peabody?"

"There was one in Gomorrah," he said. He briefly described Princess, her manner, looks, general age, her association with Rankin.

Kenton had trouble drawing his breath. He turned away, excited and nearly overcome. "Dear Father above . . . it sounds like it could be her . . . it could be Victoria herself!"

"Do you know which direction Peabody and the others went after they left Gomorrah?" Jones asked.

"They left by the Fort Brandon Road, so if I had to guess, I'd say they headed through the valley in the direction of Paxton and those towns."

"The same direction I need to go, anyway, to reach my brother," Jones said to Kenton. "Looks like our two paths are for the moment merged into one."

Gunnison had deliberately requested a room that would allow him a good view of the Johansen house. Being on the third floor, he could even see a little over the wall, past that gate that remained forever closed.

There seemed to be a fair amount of activity always going on beyond those walls, though none of it seemed particularly significant or unusual—just a lot of going back and forth by apparent household employees and so on. Many people were admitted in and out of the big gate that remained closed to him. He had the impression that most were men associated with Johansen's mine operations, because they generally bore papers or satchels in hand in their hurried, businesslike comings and goings from the house.

Gunnison wondered if Peabody, Rankin, and company were at the house at all. After hours of watching the place, he saw no sign of them. But it was a big house, sprawling and dark. They could be inside there anywhere.

Gunnison attempted to talk to a couple of the people who came out of the house, but got nowhere. These were men in a hurry, with no time for inquisitive strangers. From their earnest and concentrated manner, Gunnison drew the conclusion that Johansen must be a tough and no-nonsense businessman, not one to put up with employees who shirked their duties. Initially this seemed at odds with Joe Rush's description of Johansen as a "salt-of-the-earth" fellow, but Gunnison ended up drawing a comparison to Kenton himself: hard-working, dedicated, not prone to endure fools gladly, yet with the ability to relax and drink and ham it up at social gatherings with the best of them. Maybe Johansen was like that.

Johansen and everyone associated with him began to become objects of mystery and intrigue to Gunnison, if only because he could never so much as catch a glimpse of them.

Conversations in the cafe and saloon of the hotel revealed that Johansen apparently had given up his old habit of drinking at the bar, as he'd done during the days Joe Rush worked for him. This apparently was because of his wife, who apparently was an ever-changing woman, obsessed with metaphysics, spiritualism, quack sciences, and religion of the more esoteric variety. Gunnison was told by the friendly barkeep at the saloon—a man who remembered Joe Rush fondly—that about a year back, Pearl Johansen had received a "communication" from some spiritual source telling her that nothing intoxicating should ever pass the lips of mankind. She'd taken the message to heart and had urged her husband entirely off his liquor. Devoted to his wife, Johansen had gone along, and no longer ever visited the saloon.

Gunnison was disappointed. He'd hoped he might be able to strike up an acquaintance with Johansen and get inside the gate.

One thing Gunnison was able to verify in the saloon was that the well-known Peabody was indeed at the Johansen residence. Pearl Johansen has sent for him as soon as she heard the story of his fulfilled prophecy about Gomorrah. The saloonkeeper by chance had actually witnessed the arrival of Peabody and company, having been taking a break on the hotel porch, smoking a cigar, when the carriage rolled in. He'd caught a glimpse of three men, and perhaps a woman, though he wasn't really sure about the woman.

Gunnison asked the barkeep how he could get to the occupants of the Johansen house, if only for a few moments. The answer was a shrug; that big gate and high wall were never passed by any except a select and predetermined few who had legitimate business there. Pearl Johansen was quite reclusive, and her husband allowed her full rein with her eccentricities and self-isolationism.

Gunnison was beginning to grow discouraged. It appeared that his only hope of getting to Rankin might be to simply wait him out. Pearl Johansen couldn't keep Peabody and his entourage inside those walls forever.

CHAPTER TWENTY-SIX

THERE WAS NO QUESTION ON KENTON'S PART THAT ALL OF THIS would lead to what might be the best and most amazing story he'd ever written.

It wouldn't be merely a story of a seemingly inexplicable destruction of a mountain mining town, as poor Callon would have written. Kenton would use the Gomorrah destruction as merely the starting point of a strange tale of nature turned hostile, of human weakness and human bravery, of the wickedness of a revenge-obsessed military man, and the stoic determination to survive on the part of an old wartime Rebel who now wanted only to be left alone.

And at the end, God willing, would come the most wonderful ending of all: a reunion with his own long-missing wife. He hardly dared hope for it, so unlikely did it seem, but hope he did.

Kenton was pleased that Pernell Jones, who had spent so many years trying to cut himself off from the eyes and ears of the world, was now so eager to open himself for public inspection. From the time they'd fled Confederate Ridge, he'd talked candidly to Kenton, seemingly hiding nothing, eager for the hundreds of thousands of readers of the *Illustrated American* to understand who he was and what had been his purposes in trying to live a life cut off from the "Foreign Nation," whose laws and jurisdiction he could never personally embrace.

But as he rode along beside Jones, Kenton had just found one door into his life that Jones declined to open.

"My brother cannot be identified," he said. "I'll not hide his identity from you personally, but in no way can he be named or even described in any way that would make it likely that he would be identified. I don't even want it said that I have a brother at all. You may merely describe him as an anonymous benefactor whose generosity has made it possible for the free people of Confederate Ridge to survive as a community at times they otherwise would have been forced to disband and disperse."

Kenton replied, "But how can I tell your story in any complete way if I'm not to mention your brother?"

"You're a skilled man, Kenton. You'll find a way. This is not negotiable. Either you agree, or there will be no further conversation between us, and you and I will go our separate ways."

Kenton had never liked being dictated to. It didn't fit his personality. Besides, he was accustomed to most people all but falling over themselves to cooperate with him in hopes of having their names forever enshrined through mention in an authentic Brady Kenton story. This time, though, he was in a box, and had to admit it.

"Very well," he said grudgingly. "Though I don't like being dishonest with my readers."

"There's nothing dishonest about it. You can speak the truth about him . . . just very, very little of it. You have to understand, Kenton, that it's not necessarily a safe thing to be known as my brother, particularly now, with Ottinger out to get me. I could conceive of that devil actually trying to threaten my brother, or his interests, to get to me. He can't know about him."

Kenton had to admit the sense of that, and did.

"It could also be very harmful to my brother's business interests if it were known that he and I are brothers."

"Your points make sense. You have my firm word. But how does your brother manage to disguise his relation to you otherwise?"

"By use of a false name, for one thing. And the presentation of a false family history."

"Since I'm to meet him, can you go ahead and tell me his name?"

"I don't see why not. His name is one he took from an old seaman we knew as boys, a fellow who had come up from the Carolinas to settle in Virginia. Livesay took on that name, as a matter of fact, when he got into trouble with the law for having very nearly beaten a scoundrel to death, and fled to the sea to avoid the consequences. He's been Livesay Johansen so long that I don't even think of him as Livesay Jones anymore."

"Livesay Johansen, the mining magnate, is your brother?"

"He is."

"I'll be! So I suppose it's Pearl Town we're going to."

"It is."

They passed into a broad valley and passed ranch houses, corrals, wide and rolling grasslands, and barns. The day was bright and clear, the air crisp. Kenton, despite all the hard knocks he had endured, felt good and vigorous.

Milo, however, didn't. He'd begun to suffer a terrific stomach ache shortly after the trio had ridden away from the vicinity of Fort Brandon, and for the last hour had been declaring that if he didn't soon obtain a bottle of wine, he'd surely die. "The grape heals the belly," he said.

"Or makes you feel so good that you no longer notice you feel bad," Jones countered.

"Please, Pernell. Let's see if we can't find somebody hereabouts who'd take mercy on me. Just a few swallows of wine, that's all I need."

They soon relented, and before long Kenton raised his arm and pointed at a ranch house ahead, not far off the road. The riders turned their horses onto the dirt avenue leading toward the house.

A boy emerged from a barn and shaded his eyes with his hand. He peered, then came closer. Kenton noticed that the boy seemed most interested in him.

"Hello, young man," Kenton said, smiling. "Is your father or mother close by?"

"You look like Brady Kenton," the boy said.

"Do I? I've been told that before. What's your name?"

"My name's Rory. Rory Wilson."

"Pleased to meet you, Rory. We came over to ask a favor: If you have any wine about your place, my companion Mr. Buckner back there could use just a small amount to settle a stomach ailment."

"We used to have a bit of wine, and sometimes my father had whiskey," Rory replied. "But not no more. He's rededicated himself to the service of the Lord, and put away strong drink."

"I see." Kenton looked back over his shoulder. "Sorry, Milo."

A man came riding around the barn. He paused to study the newcomers, then came in closer. "Howdy," Peter Wilson said.

The three said their hellos.

"Pap, he looks like Brady Kenton," Rory said. "Just like that picture that they always print."

"You'll have to excuse the boy," Wilson said. "He's recently met a fellow who worked with Brady Kenton, and I guess it's on his mind."

Kenton rose in the stirrups and almost came out of his saddle. "Alex has been here?"

"Alex Gunnison, yes . . . my word, sir, there's no chance you actually *are* . . ."

"I'm Brady Kenton. Yes. I am."

Rory went white as snow and backstepped several paces. Peter Wilson blanched as well.

"But you can't be Brady Kenton!" he said. "Brady Kenton is dead! Mr. Gunnison told us he was killed in the fire at Gomorrah!"

Now Kenton did come out of the saddle, and despite the fact that he was a tall and powerfully built man, touched the ground with the lightness of a ballet dancer. He advanced toward Peter Wilson. "Sir, Alex no doubt believes what he told you is true. He found a corpse at Gomorrah, wearing my coat and carrying my pistol. It was a highwayman, who had robbed me. I myself, though unconscious, was alive. And still am, as you can see."

"How can I know you're really Kenton?"

Kenton frowned, thinking, then bent to the earth and dusted off a broad expanse of bare dirt. Kneeling, he looked at Rory and began to draw with his finger, his hand moving so fast it was hard to follow. Curiosity drew the Wilsons near. From the house emerged Rory's mother, then the two Wilson daughters. After watching from a distance a few moments, they too came forward to see what was happening.

Kenton stood. In the dirt was a nearly perfect rendering of Rory's face. Even in such a crude medium, the distinctive, universally recognizable drawing style of Brady Kenton was evident.

"Dear Lord!" Peter Wilson muttered. "Corey, do you see that?" He pulled his wife close to him, and with his arm around her shoulder, stared at the remarkable rendering. He looked up at Kenton. "You *are* him. You really are."

"Have been since birth, sir."

"I'll be!" Peter Wilson laughed. "Who'd have thought we'd be visited by Kenton's partner, and then Kenton himself!"

"I have to find Alex," Kenton said. "Where is he now?"

"Gone. On up the road. Chasing after a preacher who foretold the falling of fire on Gomorrah. Parson Peabody, this fellow is, and with him a man named Shafter, another one named Rankin, and a woman."

Jones spoke. "Your partner must be planning to write about this preacher."

"It's not that," Rory said. "He said he was looking for Mr. Rankin, who had information about the wife of a friend of his."

Kenton lowered his head, unable to speak. On what had begun as a day of lightheartedness, Kenton was suddenly overcome with emotion. *Alex is looking for Rankin for me, because he believes I can't. He's trying to find what he can about Victoria, in my place!*

"Mr. Kenton, are you well?"

"I'm very well, thank you," Kenton wiped his eye. "Very well indeed."

"I think perhaps everyone should come inside," Mrs. Wilson suggested.

"Kind of you," Kenton said.

Milo Buckner grinned. "I ain't sure all that's happened here, but I gather it's good that we stopped. Fortunate thing I had that bellyache, eh?"

Jones was the last to enter the house. As he reached back to pull the door closed, he noticed two mounted men on a low rise a a few hundred yards away, watching. Squinting, he looked back. One had a spyglass against his eye and was looking back at him.

Disturbed, Jones closed the door, but said nothing to the others of what he had just seen.

CHAPTER TWENTY-SEVEN

AFTER NIGHTFALL, THE SAME DAY. COLONEL J.B. OTTINGER stared at his reflection in the mirror, and hated what he saw. Once handsome and admired, now he was disfigured, physically ruined, and growing old to boot. It had been so many years since Pernell Jones's shotgun blast had damaged his face that it seemed he should be accustomed to it by now, yet he wasn't. He never would be.

Sometimes he stared at himself like this for an hour or more. Especially since the loss of his wife, the one good and fine thing in his life for most of his years. After the war and the incident in Virginia that had made him so infamous, she had been the only stable factor in his life. She had stuck by him, been loyal, never believing the stories told about him. She'd once burned a copy of *Gunnison's Illustrated American*, page by page, to demonstrate to him her belief in him and her disdain for those who dared to criticize him. He smiled at the memory; that copy had been of the very edition that included Kenton's ruinous, famous article, the one that very nearly destroyed his military career.

Ottinger stared at the scars marring his face, and the marble dullness of that unseeing eye.

He hated Pernell Jones. Hated Brady Kenton. Hated all who whispered about him, pointed their wagging fingers . . . hated even God Himself, for having taken away his wife and leaving him alone.

He would not go to his grave until he'd evened every balance. He vowed it to his reflection.

Turning away from the mirror, Ottinger paced back and forth in the small bedroom. He despised this place. Fort Brandon was a squalid hellhole, miserable and cramped and all in all one of the worst posts in which a military man could find himself. But Ottinger had come here willingly, sure that from this vantage point so close to Confederate Ridge he could at last achieve his vengeance upon the despised Pernell Jones.

Vengeance . . . he'd been so close! But even that had been taken away.

He couldn't believe they'd escaped him so efficiently. An entire compound full of people, vanished, dispersing into the mountains like mist dissolving in sunlight, and just as untraceable.

Standing in the midst of the empty Confederate Ridge, he'd felt something inside grow tired and old, and for the first time he'd faced the possibility that he'd never have the privilege of seeing Pernell Jones pay at all. Ottinger would go to his grave, and Jones would go on . . . and that would be the greatest of many injustices that an uncaring universe had thrown in his lap.

Ottinger would gladly die and put it all behind, but not without the satisfaction of seeing Pernell Jones pay for what he'd done. And Brady Kenton, too, if it could be achieved. A damned assassin, Kenton was. Nothing but a damned assassin, but one who used words instead of bullets.

Words were worse. They brought pain that lasted much longer.

Ottinger poured himself a glass of whiskey from a decanter on a desk in the corner. He sipped slowly, and let his eyes drift over to the wardrobe, which stood ajar, the faint glow of lamplight penetrating into it and revealing the clothing that hung there.

Civilian clothing. In his position, Ottinger seldom had reason to wear his civilian garb.

The thought had come lately that maybe he should change that. Put that civilian clothing on, and toss away the uniforms for good. Take into his own hands the matters he wanted to see dealt with . . .

A rap on the door startled him. He turned. "Yes!"

"Colonel, sir, you have a man who has come to see you."

"Who?"

"He says his name is Pride. He says you know him and will be glad to see him and hear what he has to tell you."

Pride? Ottinger tried to think who this would be. The last man named Pride he'd known was . . .

He swore softly. Could it be?

Ottinger tossed down the rest of his whiskey and wiped off his mouth with the back of his hand. He quickly hid the glass and whiskey bottle, checked to make sure his pants were hitched, and went to the door. He hoped they wouldn't smell the whiskey on him too strongly. He'd imbibed more than once tonight.

He opened the door and stared at the civilian who stood there beside the soldier who'd knocked.

"Sir, this man says he has important information for you."

"Yes . . . right. He can come in. You can go."

"Yes, sir."

When the door was closed, the whiskered, weathered newcomer grinned at the Colonel, displaying more gaps than teeth. "Hello, Colonel Ottinger. Didn't expect to see old Robert Pride at your door, did you?"

"I must say I didn't. Given my past experience with you and your partner, I'm surprised you have the courage to show yourself to me."

"What happened before just happened, sir. We gave it the best effort we could. Pernell Jones was just too slick to be caught, much less killed."

"How difficult can it be to kill a man?"

"Not hard at all, if you're talking blowing a man's head off from behind a tree on a road somewhere. Mighty difficult, if you have such requirements as you put upon us. You weren't content for us just to kill Jones. No, you had to have him suffer this way and that first, and know before he died that it was you who arranged his killing. We just couldn't make that happen with all them restrictions."

"Why are you here now at this time of night?"

"Because I think we might be able to do better for you than we did last time."

Ottinger took a moment to realize what this implied. "You have Jones?"

"We know where he is, let's put it that way. Murph's keeping watch on the place right now, to make sure he stays put. Me, I just put in a long, hard ride to get here. Didn't expect to find you awake, to tell the truth."

"I don't sleep much at my age. Tell me where he is!"

"We'll do better than that for you. We'll bring in the sumbitch's head on a stick, if you want it. But only if the same arrangement as before stands."

"How do I know you really have him?"

"You got to take my word, I reckon."

"You'll be wanting advance money, I suppose?"

"Like I said: same arrangement as before. But this time, we don't fail. This time we really bring him down."

Ottinger shook his head. "No. The prior arrangement won't do."

"What? You don't want him dead no more?"

"Oh, I want him dead. But this time, I'll not trust the job to be done by two men acting unsupervised. How far away is Jones right now?"

"I rode over three hours to get here. Without a fresh horse, it'll take me quite a stretch longer to get back."

"You'll have a fresh horse."

"In that case, I can be back there by sunrise, no problem."

"Jones is nighting over somewhere?"

"Look, I ain't answering no more questions until I know I'm getting paid for this."

"You'll be paid."

"But you said—"

"I said the same arrangement as before won't do. I'll not have you do this unsupervised. I'm coming with you."

"What?"

"You heard me."

"Colonel, you'll stand out like a sore thumb."

"I'll not be in uniform."

"Listen, Colonel, me and Murph can do this job best on our own."

"You'll do it my way or not get paid. You take me with you, no money up front, and you catch Jones and let me take a direct part in sending him to his hellfire reward, and you'll get twice the money I promised you before."

Pride's eyes gleamed. His grin broadened to reveal more black space, but no more teeth.

"You got a deal, Colonel."

"Just see you don't fail to catch him this time."

"We done got him. Murph is keeping watch on the house where he's spending the night. If Jones should chance to leave before we get back to Murph, he's going to follow, and leave a clear trail of sign for us. But it looks to me like Jones is doing no more than taking the main road toward the river, and Paxton."

"The one that passes by the Rush trading post?"

"That's the road. The trading post won't be there much longer, though. Me and Murph are going to burn it down. We had a bit of fun there right recent, and got mistreated for it."

"I don't care what you do, or to whom, as long as you give me Jones."

"You'll have him, Colonel. You'll have him."

When Ottinger rode out of Fort Brandon that night, clad in common civilian clothing, he found himself pondering the possibility of not returning to this place at all, never again donning a uniform. But there were such things as pensions and public face to be considered. He'd be back.

But tonight he'd be no military officer and represent no one but himself. Tonight he'd be only James Bertram Ottinger, a man out to avenge himself for an offense that stared back at him every time he looked in a mirror.

He'd received strange looks from the sentinels as he left the fort in the company of the to-them-unknown civilian Robert Pride. There might be questions later, things to be explained.

The hell with that, Ottinger thought. *There are always questions. I don't care what happens as long as I see Pernell Jones die with his own face ruined, like he ruined mine.*

He swore beneath his breath. He'd intended to bring his shotgun with him, for use on Jones. He wanted the man to feel exactly what he'd felt when the shot ruined his face all those long years ago in Virginia. He wanted Pernell Jones to die knowing who had killed him, knowing who was the victor at last. Well, if a shotgun wasn't to be had, he'd just make do with his knife. It would be a pleasure to work on Jones with a keen blade.

"Can you find your way to the right place in the dark?" Ottinger asked Pride.

"Can't miss it," Pride answered. "It's not far off the main road."

"I want nothing to go amiss this time."

"Nothing will. I promise. Twice the money you say? You'll not try to back out on that once the job's done?"

"You lead me to Jones, you clear the path to let me get to him, and you'll have your money. Every cent."

"That's what I like to hear, Colonel. That's the very music of the heavens to my ears."

They rode on, pushing the horses hard.

CHAPTER TWENTY-EIGHT

IN THE JOHANSEN HOTEL, ALEX GUNNISON GAVE UP TRYING TO sleep and rose. He couldn't account for his restlessness, certainly couldn't blame it on the bed, which was exceedingly comfortable, or on any lack of weariness, for he was quite tired.

Frustration, probably. A sense of wheels spinning but the wagon going nowhere.

He was beginning to wonder if he'd lost all his common sense.

Gunnison walked across the dark room and sat down in a chair at his window. It was very late; most of the businesses in the little town were shut down and dark, except for a couple of saloons up the street, and a dance hall. He could see the faint glow of doorway lamps burning one street over, in a section of town he'd been told wasn't frequented by the more upstanding sort of folks. Just a typical mining town.

Except for that atypical house right across the street. Gunnison stared at the place, at the high fence that made it a virtual fortress, and marveled at how difficult it was proving to be merely to make contact with the people inside. He knew Peabody was in there, and Rankin. Yet they might as well be a hundred miles away.

If they wouldn't let him in, he'd just have to wait it out. All he could do. He could, of course, try to come up with some ruse to get inside—"delivering" something on a wagon, or pretending to be a U.S. Marshal on official business, maybe—but he doubted it would work. And once he revealed his true identity and profession, Johansen might have him prosecuted, if he was authentically the journalist-hater he apparently was.

Wait them out. Kenton would do that. But Kenton had been one of those men who was a remarkable contradiction: seemingly restless and mentally active at all times, but also remarkably patient when he had to be. Gunnison wasn't like that.

A light came on in a window in the Johansen house, drawing Gunnison's eye. He dusted off the window pane and looked closely. Through the thin curtains on the other side of the window he could see someone moving, back and forth. Pacing, it seemed.

Apparently he wasn't the only person who was restless this night.

He felt somewhat voyeuristic, watching a stranger's window from the seclusion of his dark room, but it really didn't amount to much. He couldn't even tell if the figure in the lighted room was a man or woman.

The curtain drew back, and he saw the outline of what appeared to be a man's head and shoulders, and the arm holding back the curtain. He could make out no features, but the man appeared to be rather shaggy-headed, whiskered . . .

I'd place a wager that I'm looking at Parson Peabody right now, he thought. *He'd be ragged like that.*

The figure didn't let the curtain drop, but stayed where he was for at least two minutes, looking back and forth, then finally craning his neck and looking out the window to his left—Gunnison's right. Then the man opened the window and thrust his head and upper body out, holding to the sill and looking off in that same direction.

Gunnison realized he was looking toward the saloons.

He almost came to his feet when he saw the man draw

back inside his window, tuck the curtain up to one side, then thrust a foot through the opening. He poked his leg about outside, then stilled it, apparently having found a small ledge or some other such foothold.

Great day! The fellow was trying to climb out!

Gunnison watched, breathless, as the man shifted his weight, raised his other leg, and stuck it out the window. He was now seated on the sill, upper body still inside the room, legs out.

Don't do it! Gunnison mentally urged. *You'll fall!*

He wondered if he was duty-bound to raise his own window and holler across at the man. The other hotel guests would like *that* at this hour, no question! But a man's life could be at risk.

Gunnison rose and began to raise his window. The man, however, remained perched on the window sill as before, not having moved to venture farther out. Gunnison paused, hoping the man was reconsidering his plan, growing sensibly scared about the danger. Gunnison could recall seeing no substantial ledge of any kind outside that house.

He was relieved when the man pulled his legs back inside and closed the window. The curtain fell back down.

A moment later, Gunnison saw the man's moving silhouette on the curtain, pacing back and forth, back and forth, faster than before.

Whoever this fellow was, he was even more restless than Gunnison, and judging from his staring in the direction of the saloon, probably craving liquor.

Brady Kenton, lodged safely in the house of Peter Wilson and family, had anything but a restless night. He slept on a rather thin pallet on a hard floor, but like usual, rested soundly. His ability to rest with full satisfaction in almost any circumstance was something that made Kenton's roving life much easier for him to bear, but which had always tended to drive Gunnison rather crazy. Kenton had always taken a secret delight in that.

He awakened to a marvelous breakfast cooked by Mrs. Wilson, and to a sense of hope and happiness that almost overwhelmed him. Gunnison was alive and safe, he now knew, and performing the very touching act of taking on Kenton's quest as his own, thinking as he did that Kenton was forever gone. Better still, Kenton also now knew that Rankin was alive, and where he was . . . and that he had a woman with him.

Dear Lord, let it be her! Let it be Victoria! It was the most fervent prayer Kenton could put forth, and it played through his mind every moment, even as he laughed and talked with the others over breakfast.

Staying the night with the Wilsons had, of course, been unplanned in that they'd stopped only in hope of finding some wine to settle Milo Buckner's stomach. But there had been much to talk about with these people, and by the time the talking was through, it had grown late, and the Wilsons' invitation to stay the night had seemed a sensible thing to accept.

Only Pernell Jones seemed uncomfortable with it, Kenton had noticed. He'd gone repeatedly to the front window, looking out toward the rise on the far side of the road. Kenton had asked him what he was looking at, but Jones had answered only with a shake of his head.

Had he not been so preoccupied with the things he was learning from the Wilsons, Kenton might have become a little more concerned than he did about Jones's strange restlessness.

Kenton was fascinated to hear in some detail the story of Parson Peabody and his prophecy. He was also rather proud of Gunnison to hear that he'd theorized that the destruction of Gomorrah might be accounted for by a meteoric explosion. Kenton had already settled on that as the most likely explanation. Gunnison was beginning to show signs of level-headedness and rational thinking, two things that Kenton prized highly.

They lingered after breakfast only long enough to help Peter and Rory perform a few chores about the place—the standard kind of repayment for hospitality in these parts. Then they mounted up and prepared to move on, Kenton eager to track down Gunnison and Rankin, Jones to reach his brother in Pearl Town. As for Milo Buckner, whose stomach ache had evidently passed if the size of his breakfast was an indication, he seemed happy to be wherever Jones was and to go wherever he went. Kenton admired the man's devotion to his friend. He was obviously still Pernell Jones's right hand after all these years.

They said their good-byes at midmorning, saddled and mounted their horses, and rode out.

Jones glanced behind them several times as they rode, as if looking for something or someone, but Kenton remained too distracted to much notice. Milo Buckner noticed, though, and asked about it, but Jones had no more of an answer for him than he had for Kenton the night before.

Ottinger lowered the spyglass. His heart hammered fast and he was full of tense energy and alertness, despite his drinking the night before, and the long nocturnal ride that had brought them to this spot only half an hour before dawn. Here they'd found Murph faithfully waiting, having spent the entire night hidden on the rise, watching the ranch house below.

"I'll be damned!" Ottinger exclaimed. "That's indeed Jones—and I'm shot if one of the men with him isn't Brady Kenton!"

"Kenton? Who's that?" Murph asked.

As much as Ottinger deplored Kenton, he couldn't help

but look down a little on anyone who had never heard of so famous a journalist. "He's a man who assassinates other men with words on paper," he said. "And he's a man I want to see dead almost as much as Jones. You take care of that for me, gentlemen, and there's an extra hundred dollars in it for both of you."

This was heartily welcomed news. "We'll take care of him," Pride said. "Who's the other one?"

"I don't know," Ottinger said. "Probably one of Jones's Confederates. Whoever he is, he's in damned bad company, and so much the worse for him because of it."

"We'll kill him, too, then. Don't want no witnesses remaining, nohow."

"We'll have to follow them," Ottinger said. "And that worries me. If we keep them in our line of sight, we stay in theirs."

"Hell, it's evident where they're going," Pride said. "They're heading toward the river. They'll take the Rush ferry across it, most likely. Probably stop in at the trading post to eat."

"There's a place before you reach that post where a man could set him up a fine ambush," Murph said.

"Just what I was thinking," Pride responded.

"Only one problem I can see with that, gentlemen," Ottinger said. "They're ahead of us. We can't reach this ambush spot without passing them."

"There's a shorter way than the road," Pride said. "Rougher, and overland, but it can get us there ahead of them, and they'll not see us going."

"We take a risk, letting them out of our sight," Ottinger said. "What if they turn off some other way? What if they cross the river somewhere besides the ferry, and don't go by the trading post?"

"They could do that, but it ain't likely, Colonel. There's no good road except the one they're on, and since they don't know they're being followed, they've got no reason to be evasive."

"I wonder if they do suspect someone's after them," Ottinger said. "Jones has looked over his shoulder several times."

"All the more reason to give him nothing to spot. I think it's a reasonable chance to take to assume they'll keep to the main road. If they do, we can ambush them. If they don't, we'll just have to find their trail again and get them somewhere else. It shouldn't be overly hard to do."

Ottinger watched the trio of riders moving down the road, growing more distant by the moment.

"You're sure we can reach that ambush point before they do?"

"If we ride steady, and start now."

"You know the way?"

"Like the back of my hand."

"Lead on, then, Mr. Pride. I'm putting my trust in your judgment. Don't let me down."

Parson Peabody sat up as the door to his room opened. Rankin thrust his head inside, his face wearing a frown.

"You're *still* in bed? Great God, man, the woman's waiting for you! You were supposed to be giving her more of your 'teaching' almost an hour ago! You've been sleeping all this time?"

Peabody brushed back his hair with his finger. "Please, Mr. Rankin, I'm sick. I'm really sick . . . I need medicine bad."

"Hell, drop this 'medicine' nonsense! You're aching for liquor because you're a drunkard who can't live without the stuff, and you may as well admit it. But you know we can't risk you drinking here. The old woman'll smell it on you, and that would be the end of this little party! She's strong against whiskey, and she'd never stand for her little pet prophet drinking any of it."

"I don't want to be here, Rankin. I'm tired of this, I'm sick . . . and I don't have nothing more to teach her. I've said everything I can say, over and over again. And I can't understand the things she asks me. She believes in some strange things." He rubbed his face with his hands. "God help me, I need a drink!"

"You'll get all the drinks you want when we're finally through here." Rankin stepped all the way into the room and closed the door. He approached Peabody's bedside and pulled up a chair beside it. As hard as it was to retain any kind of patience with this simple, whiskey-ruined man, he forced himself to speak softly and kindly. Peabody was at the moment the best moneymaker he'd ever found for himself, and he intended to use him until the last cent that could be made through him was in his pocket. "Listen to me, Parson," he said. "I know this is hard for you. I know that Mrs. Johansen is a strange woman, and talks in ways you and I can't understand. I know she believes in things you don't. But it's important that you go along with all this for now. I believe it's God's will for you to. Do you realize who her husband is? Do you realize how much wealth he has, and how freely he lets her spend it? If we can spend even just a few more days here, with you 'teaching' her, we'll leave this place with more money than either one of us have ever seen in our lives." He paused. "Money for you to use to spread God's word far and wide. Maybe even build you a church of your own. She's already paid us more than a thousand dollars, Parson! Far more than we were getting through those collections at your preaching services. And she'll give a lot more before we're through."

In fact she'd already given a lot more than Rankin had revealed. In his possession was a little more than three thousand dollars given to the Parson's "ministry" by the very odd and eccentric Mrs. Johansen. Peabody knew of only a third of that amount, and Rankin planned to keep it that way.

Peabody listened, thinking hard, but shook his head. "It's just too hard, not having whiskey. Too hard."

"You can do it, just a while longer. You'll have whiskey soon, I promise. But not in this house. We just can't risk it."

Peabody looked at Rankin. "I need to know something . . . about you. Do you really believe in me? That God spoke through me about that fire?"

"You know I do."

"You still blaspheme God's name. You don't seem to care about nothing but the money."

"The money is what will let us build you a church to spread the word."

"And you're cruel to Princess. You were so mean to her you made her go away."

Rankin's cheek twitched just a little, under his left eye. Peabody had touched on a sensitive topic. Princess had in fact left him, only the day before. He hardly cared, in one way—Princess had become much less important to him since Parson Peabody had turned into such a money factory. But it hurt his masculine pride that she had deserted him.

If he found her again, in private circumstances, he'd make her regret embarrassing him.

"Princess left because she didn't really believe in you," he said. "Forget her."

"Where is she now?"

"I don't know. Forget about her. And get dressed. Come downstairs and get some food, and then get started with today's teaching."

"I don't know what to tell her. I don't have anything to say."

"Say what you've said to everybody."

"I've said those things already."

"Then say them again, damn it! Or make something up. It doesn't matter—she'll believe whatever you say. The most important thing is to tell her how important it is that she keep on supporting you with her money. Tell her . . . tell her that if she doesn't, the fire will fall here, too."

"I'll not say that. I'm not a prophet. Not really. I feel like I'm lying when I say I am."

Rankin stuck his finger right between Peabody's eyes. "You *are* a prophet. Don't you forget it, or stop saying it. Especially to *her*. You understand me?"

Peabody looked away. "I understand you."

"Get dressed. And make it fast. She's waiting."

Rankin walked out, slamming the door behind him.

CHAPTER TWENTY-NINE

About an hour before Kenton and his partners left the Wilson house many miles away, Alex Gunnison had walked out the door of the Johansen Hotel, pulled in a lungful of fresh air, and stretched. Beautiful day. Perhaps he'd take advantage of the good weather to take a walk around town, and for a time, forget his frustrations.

A pup came bounding around the corner of the hotel and up the steps to the porch. Gunnison grinned at the lively little creature and reached down to pet it. The pup, however, scampered on past, leaping into an empty rocking chair near the end of the porch, almost losing its balance when the chair tilted. Instantly it leaped out again and began nosing around under the chair and in the corners of the porch.

Gunnison pulled a pocketwatch from his vest pocket and glanced at the time. As he closed the watch to put it away again, it slipped through his fingers and clattered to the porch at his feet, its fob being unattached.

He stooped to retrieve it, but the pup was faster than he. It shot by, snatched the watch in its mouth, and ran down the steps to the street.

"Hey!" Gunnison called. "Bring that back here!"

He ran down the steps after the dog. A man standing nearby, whittling on a stick, laughed at him.

The pup bounded on down the street and veered right into an alleyway. Gunnison turned in after it in time to catch sight of it making a left turn around the rear of the next building over. Gunnison did the same, and found himself in a narrow backlot filled with heaped refuse, including a big pile of dirty and discarded rags. The pup was trapped in the enclosed space.

Or so Gunnison thought. The pup made for a hole near the bottom of the fence. The hole was barely enough to accommodate its body. The pup squeezed through and got away, but Gunnison was no longer concerned with it: his pocketwatch lay on the ground near the hole, dropped by the dog.

Gunnison picked it up and made a face because of how wet he found it. Thick canine saliva covered the watch and also his fingers. He walked to the pile of discarded rags, picked one up, and began wiping the watchcase clean.

He dropped the watch in surprise, however, when suddenly the entire pile moved, and a human form arose from its midst. Gunnison let out a little howl of fright.

"Who the devil . . ."

"I'm sorry," the ragpile dweller said. A woman! Gunnison was surprised again. "I wasn't trying to startle you. I felt the rags shift and thought someone was trying to find me."

Gunnison drew in a slow breath and relaxed. He stooped, retrieved his watch, and put it in his pocket. "All I was doing was trying to find a cloth to clean off my watch," he said. "A dog carried it back here in its mouth."

The woman nodded. She had a very sad face, Gunnison noticed. A face that was nicely formed, but beginning to age. In her young days, she would have been a beautiful woman.

Realizing that she must have spent the night here in this ragpile, he felt his heart go out to her. "Ma'am, are you all right?"

"Yes, I'm fine."

"I mean . . . did you have to sleep back here last night?"

She nodded and would not look at him; the question seemed to have embarrassed her.

"Have you been out here long?"

"Last night was the first night. I was somewhere else before that."

Gunnison, trying to tread lightly on the line between helpfulness and intrusiveness, asked, "Do you not have a home?"

"No. Not of my own. Until last night, though, I'd been staying here, in this town, I mean, in someone else's house." Her eyes flicked in the direction of the street.

In this part of town, there were no real houses except one. "You mean, you were in the Johansen house?"

"Yes, sir."

"So why are you out here now?"

"The people I traveled here with had begun to mistreat me. I left because I was afraid he would hurt me."

Gunnison was thinking hard. "Ma'am, by chance might any of the ones you traveled here with be named Rankin?"

She looked at him in sharp surprise. "Yes . . . how did you know?"

Gunnison felt a sense of awe. It had surely been written in his destiny for that pup to steal his pocketwatch at just this time, and lead him around to this particular back alley while this particular woman was here.

He stepped closer and looked into her eyes. He could hardly find his voice.

"Victoria Kenton? Is it really you?"

Oliver Rush, father of trading post operator Joe Rush, was growing old, and he didn't like it at all.

He'd never much realized his advancing years, not until that recent humiliating episode in his son's trading post. Forced to dance, like some dime-novel greenhorn, before the blasting pistols of two drunken ruffians! He'd never felt so degraded and helpless . . . so much an old man no longer able to stand up for himself.

It had haunted him ever since it happened. But what haunted the most deeply wasn't simply that he'd not been capable of taking care of himself, but had balked as well at trying to help out the young fellow who had stepped in to take the abuse in his place.

Maybe I'm too old to be any good to anyone anymore, he'd taken to thinking. *Too old to even be willing do what's right. I should have resisted them. In my younger days, I would have.*

He was wandering alone along the cottonwood-lined creek that ran behind and beside the trading post over to the river near the ferry crossing. Here there was enough vegetation that a man could move about unseen, and think without being bothered. Oliver Rush had come here to mull over his advancing years, and his failure, and to grieve in his shame.

He wished he could do it over again. Face those two devils and make them pay for making him feel this way. He'd not dance again for them, that much he knew! He'd let them kill him before he did that.

Oliver Rush leaned up against a cottonwood and pulled his pipe from his pocket. Before he could fetch out his tobacco, though, he noticed that someone was moving in a surreptitious manner over in the thickets atop the rise overlooking the road before it curved around to head toward the trading post.

Something inside warned him, and he knelt slowly, putting the pipe away. He peeped around the trunk of the cottonwood, squinting . . .

It was *them!* His heart almost failed him. The very two scoundrels who had humiliated him, and with them, a third man, much older, and with half his face badly scarred. All of them were armed, and from their postures and placement, Oliver knew right away that they were planning to ambush someone. He himself had often thought about the fact that the area they were overlooking was a prime ambush spot, and had worried that thieves might take to the place.

Who might they be planning to ambush? Whoever happened to come down the road next? Not likely. Sometimes nobody came down that road for days. Whoever they were after was someone they *expected.* Someone they knew was coming.

Joe. Maybe it was Joe. He's the one who had run them off, after all, sent them scurrying like cowards. And he was away from the trading post today. Probably they knew that and were waiting for him to return.

Oliver Rush felt a swell of dread combined with a sense of opportunity. There were three of them—who the older, disfigured one was he had no idea—and he was only one man, but by care and planning, and preserving the element of surprise, he just might be able to deal with them.

He turned and crept back to the trading post and around to his cabin behind it. He went in and fetched his old but reliable shotgun off the pegs on the wall. He put shells in each barrel and extras in his pocket. He also strapped on the fine Colt pistol that he spent much more time cleaning than shooting, and made sure every chamber was loaded. Then he paused, heart thumping, and said a prayer in a whisper.

"Lord, I may die today. I pray I won't, but if I do, wash my soul clean and take me to Your glory. I thank You for this opportunity to make up for failing to do what I should have before. If I die, I die. Just let me take them with me. Amen."

He left the cabin and sneaked back toward the creek, planning to approach them from behind.

He was more scared than he'd admit, and shaking badly. It was breezy and not very hot today, but sweat kept dripping in his eyes.

He kept going anyway.

* * *

Miles away, Parson Peabody was sitting in a straight-backed chair, looking across a table at the strangest woman he'd ever met.

The worst part was she insisted on him holding her hands while he "taught" her. He didn't want to hold her hands. He didn't like touching her, and didn't like the way she looked at him like he was some sort of great wise man, nodding that silver-haired head with long, foreign-looking decorative pins stuck all through her topknot. Long, dangling earrings that looked like little carved idols to Peabody hung from both her overstretched lobes. And her breath was bad, and had a long reach.

He hated this. He wanted to pull free, tear away, run out the door and into the nearest saloon. But Rankin was there, standing by and watching him with that grin that really was just a cover for a threat. Thomas Shafter was near, too, seated somewhat behind Rankin and looking almost as unhappy as Peabody felt. Peabody had yet to figure out what part Shafter really played in all this. Mostly he just loitered around, looking increasingly dissatisfied, and made Peabody feel threatened. Come to think of it, maybe that *was* his function.

"Tell me, Prophet, that there is a way I can share your gift," Pearl Johansen said. Her voice was a raspy squeak that reminded Peabody of a bad hinge. "If I could know the will of the Most High Creator, if I could speak His words as you do . . . oh, it would be all I ever longed for!"

"Well, generally, I just recommend reading the Bible," Peabody said. "I don't know that I have a way to actually *share* any power or nothing with somebody else . . ."

He felt Rankin's glare and glanced up at him. The smile was on the lips still, but gone from the eyes.

Peabody cleared his throat. "Of course, I suppose it could be done . . . in the right circumstances . . . if, uh, well, if you were worthy . . ."

Rankin cleared his throat. "What Prophet Peabody is too kind to say, ma'am, is that the gift can certainly be shared, but only to one who has demonstrated the full level of dedication and devotion. He and I discussed this only last night. If there were one who could make it possible for the prophet to fulfill his dream, the dream given to him by God himself . . ."

"What is this dream?" she said, eyes wide.

"A dream of a great church, a sanctuary, where the searching could come and find the truth."

"A church!"

"Yes. It's the prophet's vision. Deeply personal, deeply private . . . hard for him to speak of."

She looked at Peabody and smiled, squeezing his hands. "Oh, if only you had let me know sooner! I am a woman blessed with means, you know. I can make this dream possible, Prophet. I can be the very answer to your prayer!"

Rankin's smile was quite sincere now. He foresaw a few prayers of his own about to be answered.

"Tell me how much, Prophet Peabody. Tell me, and it is yours! And then, give the gift to me! I long for it! I wish to follow you, to be a prophetess just as you are a prophet!"

"Well . . . I don't really know how much," Peabody said. "I reckon a hundred dollars could go a right smart way toward—"

"Again," Rankin cut in quickly, "he's being too humble. It isn't his way to seek wordly wealth—he cares so little for it." Rankin reached into a pocket and pulled out a slip of paper and a pencil. He scribbled a figure, folded the paper, and handed it to Pearl Johansen. She removed her right hand from Peabody's—he took advantage of this to yank that freed hand back under the table and out of reach—then let go of the other hand to open the note. The left hand shot under the table, too, where Peabody wiped his fingers on his trousers. The dang woman had the sweatiest hands he'd ever held.

She read the figure, smiled up at Rankin, then beamed at Peabody. "Sir, it's a great gift you ask . . . but it's a great gift I ask from you in return." She licked her lips, and with a hungry look said, "Will I be able to foresee the coming of judgment, the falling of fire, as you can?"

Peabody opened his mouth and tried to find an answer. Rankin, meanwhile, was all but trembling in anticipation of the wealth he envisioned being just about to come to him. Shafter just looked angry, like always, a dark shadow in the background.

Suddenly Parson Peabody could bear it no more. A sense of clarity overwhelmed him, and he saw the situation as it was—even himself as he really was. He stood abruptly, almost jarring the table over. He shoved his chair back so fast it tipped and fell.

"No!" he boomed. "No!"

Rankin's eyes all but shot flame. Shafter looked puzzled, but interested for once. The woman almost fell out of her seat and looked up at Peabody as if she expected the fire from heaven to suddenly fall on *her*.

"Parson . . . Prophet—what are you doing?"

"You shut up, Rankin! Shut up! And don't call me 'Prophet'! Don't even call me 'Parson,' for I'm neither one! I'm just Forrest Peabody, a drunk who wishes he wasn't a drunk, but can't seem to be nothing else! I ain't no man of God! I don't speak no divine truths, ma'am. I'm just a man, just a common old sinner, not fit even to call the name of God, much less pretend to speak for Him."

Rankin looked ready to explode, Pearl Johansen to faint.

"This is all false. It has been from the start. I mouthed off some nonsense before Gomorrah fell, but that's all it was—just nonsense. I've said the same kinds of things before, other times and other places. The only difference was, this time it happened. I can't explain it, but it did. And it scared the holy fire out of me, ma'am. 'Cause I sure didn't cause it, and I surely didn't foresee it."

Rankin's mouth was moving, but he was too furious to make words come out.

"Rankin there pretended to think me a prophet and almost convinced me I was. He hauled me off like a monkey on a string and made me preach to people, threatening to burn up their towns and homes with God's fire, too, if they didn't give money. And they did give, but he kept it. He don't want your money to build a church, ma'am. He just wants it to spend on gambling and whiskey and whores, if you'll pardon my forthright speaking. That's all."

The woman was white as death, Rankin as red as Gomorrah's flames. Thomas Shafter, meanwhile, burst out laughing.

"I wish you'd never heard of me, Mrs. Johansen. Then you'd never have sent for me, and I'd not feel so guilty for having sat here and lied to you and all like I have. I ain't no prophet. Really I ain't. The only thing I can teach you, ma'am, is that . . . well, you ought not be so gullible. You ought not be so ready to believe any nonsense somebody throws at you, for people will lie, ma'am. People ain't to be trusted."

"Damn you!" Rankin exploded. "Damn you, you sorry old drunk—do you realize what you've just thrown away!"

"I'm leaving," Peabody said. "I want a drink."

Rankin swore obscenely, and put his hand under his coat. When it came out, it carried a small pistol. He aimed it at Peabody.

"I wouldn't."

The voice was that of Livesay Johansen, who had burst through the door into the library just as Rankin had drawn out the pistol. The Colt in Johansen's hand was much larger than the little gun in Rankin's.

"Drop the pistol, sir," Johansen said to Rankin, and Rankin did, at once. "Leave it on the floor, and prepare yourself to face the consequences of the law. I've been standing behind that door there since this little session began this morning, for I had suspicions about you. God knows I've been lenient with Pearl's eccentricities through the years, letting her call in her seers and sages and gypsies . . . but I'll not be defrauded so blatantly as this. Pearl, give me that note."

Trembling, the woman handed the slip of paper to her husband. He glanced at the figure on it, and swore. "Pearl, you think I'd have let you give this much away to so obvious a fraud? Do you think you married a fool?"

Pearl burst into tears and fled the room.

"What about me?" Shafter said.

"You may go. I've not seen you take any direct part in this fraud."

Shafter was out the room's opposite door in a moment.

"I'll go to jail, if that's what I should do, sir," Peabody said to Johansen.

"No, sir," Johansen replied. "I saw what you're made of, sir, when you spoke the truth just now. Consider yourself a free man."

Peabody grinned. "Thank you, sir. Thank you."

"As for you, Mr. Rankin, if that's really your name, you've got some money to cough back up. I know that Pearl has given you gifts already, probably sizeable. I'll have that back from you . . . or perhaps you'd like to make a quiet and permanent exploration of the bottom of one of my old mines, hmm?"

Peabody heard no more. He was out the door and into the yard, then out the front gate, feeling like a man just set free from a dungeon.

He realized all at once that he'd left his few possessions behind, including his Bible in its sack. Well, never mind.

He'd get him a new one. He wasn't going back into that place, not with that strange woman, not with all the unpleasant associations the place possessed. And so strange had Pearl Johansen been, talking about ghosts and souls traveling outside their bodies and so on, that he'd come to think there were some bad spirits floating around in that house.

Peabody had no use for such. He knew the kind of spirits he liked.

With the fleetness of a youth, he ran straight for the nearest saloon.

CHAPTER THIRTY

OTTINGER, THOUGH OLDER AND ONE-EYED, WAS THE FIRST TO spot them.

"There!" he whispered sharply, pointing.

The trio of of would-be ambushers crouched, all in a similar posture.

If he hadn't been so nervous and so intensely in concentration, the old man watching them from behind might have found it funny. Three cowards all in a line, all ready to kill men from cover. Oliver Rush despised them.

He heard a voice out on the road. A man singing. It had to be Joe—Joe always sang while he rode, usually that song about his "sweeeeeeeet lady."

But this was a different song, Oliver realized. And a different voice. Not Joe at all.

So it wasn't Joe they were after! Someone else instead . . .

Oliver hesitated. It was one thing to shoot at men who were trying to kill his own son, another to shoot at them when he really didn't know who they were after. The men on the road might be as bad as they were. Rats, after all, often attacked one another.

He saw one of the pair raising his rifle, aiming.

There were three men on the road, if the voices were an indication. Talking, one of them still singing, none of them with any idea they were about to be ambushed.

Unanswered questions be hanged! Oliver Rush hesitated no more. He raised his shotgun and fired.

Murph Scott, hired assassin and lifelong piece of outlaw trash, died without ever knowing he'd been shot, the pellets striking him squarely in the back of the head.

How you like that *kind of dancing*, friend? Oliver Rush thought.

On the road, the singing stopped, horses nickered and reared.

The two surviving ambushers rolled to one side and looked behind them to see who'd just killed their partner. But Oliver Rush was nowhere to be seen. He'd just ducked behind a cottonwood. He cracked his shotgun and removed the spent shell, replacing it with a fresh one.

The older, disfigured ambusher headed for cover. The other seemed unsure what to do. Going from being the ambusher to the one ambushed was obviously a most unexpected turn of events.

Oliver Rush peered out from behind the cottonwood just in time to see Robert Pride lift his rifle and shoot back in his general direction. The old man ducked back and the shot went wide, but he knew he'd been seen.

He wondered where the older fellow was. He'd managed to disappear.

Out on the other side of the road, Brady Kenton had his pistol out and was crouched in a shallow ravine beside Milo Buckner. Pernell Jones was off the right, hiding in some brush and at the moment out of sight.

"What's the shooting about up there, you think?" Milo asked.

"My thought was we were being ambushed," Kenton said. "But nobody's shot at us yet."

That changed an instant later. A shotgun blast ripped out of the thicket above and blasted dirt and grit off the road and into Kenton's eyes. He yelled and dropped back, momentarily blinded.

Milo fired beside him, the roar deafening.

Milo's shot passed above Ottinger's head. The Colonel, surprised by the attack from behind, had managed to roll to a new and protected position, and by chance had found that from this new location he had a clear view of where Brady Kenton and that third, unidentified man, had taken cover. He'd not been able to resist trying to put some shot through Kenton's face, and wasn't sure he hadn't succeeded.

Ottinger shifted position slightly, raised his shotgun, and fired again.

Milo Buckner was struck in the forehead. Blood splattered over Kenton, who screamed out, "Milo!"

Milo Buckner never heard his name called. He was dead where he lay.

In the thicket, Ottinger grinned and began to reload his shotgun.

Pernell Jones came out of his hiding place, knowing by Kenton's yell what had happened. Fully exposed, he ran down the road toward the place Kenton was, and dropped beside Milo's body.

"Oh, no . . . Milo, dear Lord, no . . ."

Ottinger had seen his old enemy appear, and it struck him with such a fever to shoot at him that he fumbled his reloading and lost the clear shot. Ottinger swore, but decided that maybe it didn't matter. As he'd fantasized before, it would be far more satisfying to kill Jones with Jones knowing who was doing the killing.

Ottinger looked around for Robert Pride, hoping for help in dealing with Kenton and Jones, but Pride had left his position. Ottinger twisted his head and saw Pride creeping back toward a big cottonwood, rifle ready . . .

A surprisingly old man appeared from behind that cottonwood and shot Robert Pride with one barrel-load of shot through the stomach. Pride doubled over, and the old man finished him with a second blast to the top of the head.

Ottinger winced. Ugly sight. And bad news for him. He was alone now.

He'd have to run for it, and he wasn't sure he would make it. They'd catch him, and that would be the end.

So I'd best take my opportunities while I can, he thought.

He leveled the shotgun, aimed at Pernell Jones below, and fired.

Jones grunted, spasmed, and rolled out of view in the ravine. Kenton dropped right after him, ducking for cover.

Ottinger rose and ran, angling off generally in the direction of the trading post, keeping cover between himself and Kenton while also avoiding allowing that shotgun-toting old stranger from getting a clear shot at him. He veered at the edge of the clearing where the post stood, ran toward some cabins in the rear, then lost himself among them and headed for the next stand of trees.

Ottinger could hardly believe how things had fallen out. The two men he'd hired to kill Jones and Kenton had themselves been killed—by an old man, of all people! Who the old fellow was and why he'd taken it on himself to spoil the ambush was something Ottinger couldn't know. Right now he didn't care.

The important thing was, he'd managed to shoot Pernell Jones. And though he couldn't be sure, he believed he might have killed him.

The shooting had drawn the attention of the women and the boy at the trading post. Nervous as cats already because of the ordeal they'd recently gone through, they initially hid on impulse. The boy, Bart, saw an old man with a strange, half-ruined face briefly dart out of the woods and around the rear of the trading post, but the women had their heads down and didn't see him.

They remained hidden until there was a rapping on the

door. They didn't answer it, full of terror, but the boy did.

"Please," Brady Kenton said as he stood with Pernell Jones's arm draped over his shoulder, keeping his limp form upright. Jones had blood on his side. "My friend's been shot. He needs help."

Duty overcame fear, and the women emerged from hiding. Jones was led in; one of the women quickly spread a pallet and Jones was laid down.

Oliver Rush, holding his smoking shotgun, appeared in the doorway. Even in the tumult of the moment the boy noticed something about him: he looked younger, for some reason. Stronger and more upright. Like a burden was gone from him.

"That's Pernell Jones," Rush said. "I've seen him before."

"It is," Kenton replied. "He's been shot. And a man named Milo Buckner has been killed out there beside the road."

"Milo Buckner!" Oliver exclaimed. "I've seen him before, too."

"We were ambushed," Kenton said, beginning to remove Jones's coat and shirt.

"You'd have been ambushed a lot worse if I hadn't fired first," the old man said. He looked at the women and the boy. "The ones who made me dance . . . it was them. I've killed them both."

"Milo's dead," Jones said, his voice straining. "Milo's dead."

"Yes," Kenton said, exposing Jones's wound. It was raw and bleeding, but Kenton was actually pleased to see that it didn't appear quite as severe as he had expected. "I'm sorry about Milo, Pernell. Who do you think ambushed us?"

"Ottinger," Jones said, grimacing as the women began to gently wash the wound. "It had to be Ottinger behind it." He began to weep, and Kenton knew it wasn't because of the pain of his wound, but because of the loss of his closest friend.

Joe Rush arrived at the post just before sundown, and walked into the middle of a situation he never could have expected.

In his trading post was the most famous, if seldom-seen, former Rebel in the Montana Territory, with a bandage around his chest, and with him the nation's most famous traveling journalist. And his own father, looking back at him with pride in his eye because, this time, he'd fought like a man.

When introductions were done, stories were told. Rush was stunned to learn of the ambush—particularly stunned to learn of his father's role in keeping the carnage in innocent blood from being even worse.

Milo's body, meanwhile, had been moved from the roadside to a shed in the yard.

Joe Rush, himself a former Confederate soldier, knew much about Pernell Jones, and was familiar also with the name of Milo Buckner. "I'll consider it an honor to lay him to rest here on my property, if that will be suiting to you, Mr. Jones," he said.

"It will be suiting indeed. Thank you."

"How bad is your wound, sir?"

"More painful than serious. Nothing vital was struck. I'll have an ugly scar, but no more."

"These ambushers . . . do you think there's danger that the third one of them might still be lingering around?"

"I doubt it," Jones said. "Probably just another of Ottinger's hired assassins. With his partners dead, he'll have fled far away by now, whoever he is."

"My nephew over there got a look at him, sir," Joe Rush said. "Did you know that?"

"No."

"Bart said the man was on the older side, and had a face badly scarred up on one side."

Jones looked at Kenton. "Ottinger himself, then. I'd have never thought it."

When the others were not nearby to hear, Jones said quietly to Kenton: "We must get away from here as quickly as we can. If it's Ottinger himself out there, he won't run away like a hired assassin would. He'll linger around, and be a danger to these good people as long as I'm here."

"I agree," Kenton said. "Are you fit to travel, though?"

"I can travel. If we can reach Pearl Town and my brother's home, we'll be safe."

"That may be a big 'if,' if Ottinger is tracking us."

Jones thought deeply, frowning. "Yes. And the fact is, I can't lead him to my brother's house. If he were to learn that Livesay Johansen is really the brother of Pernell Jones, and if he were to figure out that Livesay has been a crucial supporter of mine and my people's over the years, he'll find a way to cause him trouble. Try to portray him as a traitor or insurgent . . . it would be very hurtful to a man in Livesay's position."

"So we can't stay, and we can't go to your brother. What do we do, then?"

Jones clamped his mouth into a tight line for a moment, then said, "The question isn't 'we,' Kenton. This is up to me. I'm going to have to face him. Alone."

"It's absurd," Kenton said. "Don't even consider it. Nothing can be put past Ottinger. The man has hired killers to go after his enemies. He's used the United States Army as a tool for personal vengeance. He's tried to distort the truth about a natural disaster just to discredit an old enemy and provide a pretext for what probably would have become the second massacre of his career, with the people of Confederate Ridge the victims. He's even murdered a young journalist who dared to threaten to expose him. He's a wicked man, not to be trusted at all. You can't afford to face him alone. He's far too treacherous."

"You're right, of course," Jones said. "We'll discuss it more come morning."

Kenton looked out a window into the night. "Do you think he's out there somewhere, Pernell?"

"I think he's out there. Watching."

They stood watch through the night, fearing that Ottinger might resort to such a crude crime as arson in an attempt to get at Jones. Joe Rush spelled Kenton sometime after midnight. Before Kenton went to his pallet to sleep, though, Rush told him about the earlier visit of the two now-dead ambushers to the trading post, and the way they'd made his old father dance in such a humiliating manner. But a young man had come along, he said, who'd stopped the situation at great risk to himself. He was a journalist, like Kenton, and on the trail of that preacher named Peabody everyone's been talking about. His name was Gunnison.

It was late, and to say much would lead to long explanations that Kenton didn't wish to indulge in at this late hour, so he did not reveal to Joe Rush that the young man who'd done so fine a thing was his own partner. But the pride Kenton felt in Gunnison right then was as deep as that a father feels for a son who has done a noble thing, and it was difficult to fight back tears.

"Where is this Gunnison now, you think?" Kenton asked.

"He was going after the preacher Peabody, and Peabody, I told him, would likely be found in Pearl Town, at the house of Livesay Johansen, for I know he was sent for by his wife. She's a strange woman, very interested in such kinds of things as preachers and prophecies and so on."

Amazing, Kenton thought, how sometimes divergent trails meld so unexpectedly into one. The very town, the very house, to which he and Jones were bound was the very place that Gunnison would have gone—the very place Rankin and maybe even Victoria might be!

Kenton quietly said a prayer of thanks for the way the patterns of life, usually unseen, sometimes revealed themselves in the most remarkable of ways.

He lay down and closed his eyes, listening to Joe Rush humming quietly to himself as he stood sentinel, perched on a stool and looking out the dark window.

CHAPTER THIRTY-ONE

KENTON WAS SHAKEN AWAKE AT DAWN. HE SAT UP STIFFLY, confused.

Joe Rush's expression was serious and maybe a little afraid.

"I made a terrible mistake, Mr. Kenton. Lord forgive me, but I fell asleep at watch. And now Mr. Jones is gone."

"Gone?"

"Yes. I don't understand it. His pallet is empty."

Kenton got up quickly. "I understand it," he said. "Quickly . . . there's no time to waste!"

"Where's he gone?"

"Out to face that third ambusher, alone."

"Why?"

"Because that ambusher is Colonel J.B. Ottinger, a man who has hated Pernell Jones ever since the war, when Pernell disfigured his face with a shotgun blast. I knew it was him when you told me your son had seen a man with scars over half his face."

"Why in the devil is Jones facing him alone, though?"

"He feels it's the only way. Ottinger has tormented and chased him for years, hired would-be assassins, all that sort of thing. I think he's ready to bring it to an end."

They dressed and armed themselves quickly. Joe Rush sent Bart out to the stable to saddle and prepare two horses for his and Kenton's use.

Oliver had spent the night in the trading post with the rest of them, rather than in his cabin, and readied himself to go as well, but Joe stopped him. "Pap, we'll need you here, to guard this place in case he shows up while we're gone."

"I can handle myself as good as either one of you!"

"I know. You proved that yesterday. But I want you to stay here, and keep watch. It's important, Pap."

The old man nodded, reluctantly, but obediently positioned himself by the window on a stool.

"A brave man, your father," Kenton said as he and Jones loaded weapons and made their final checks.

"I'm proud of him," Rush said. "He was bitterly ashamed at having been made to dance like he was, but after yesterday, I don't think he has a thing left he needs to prove to anyone. That was some piece of fighting he did."

They left the house and headed to the stables. When they got there, they found that Bart had saddled no horses for them. Bart, in fact, was not to be found.

"Where the devil is that boy?" Joe Rush said. "Bart! Show yourself—and you'd best have a good explanation as to why you ain't . . ."

Rush trailed off into silence as, from behind a big feed bin, Colonel J.B. Ottinger stepped, with Bart before him, standing with a tear-stained face and a shotgun thrust against his spine.

Ottinger grinned a very ugly grin at Kenton. "Well, hello, Mr. 'Houser.' Fancy seeing you here!"

"Let the boy go, Ottinger," Kenton said.

"I'll let this shotgun go, that's what I'll do," Ottinger replied. "Can you imagine how big a hole it would blow through this lad? Both of you, toss your weapons into that feed bin."

"You won't kill the boy. The moment you do, you're a dead man, and you know it."

"Yes . . . but he'd also be a dead boy. Can you live with that?"

Kenton and Rush glanced at one another, in silent communication. Ottinger had them. With great resentment and reluctance, they disarmed themselves and tossed the weapons into the grain-filled bin.

"All right," Ottinger said. "That's how I want it. And now, Kenton, you take some of that rope yonder and tie up your partner there, good and tight. Then come tie this boy."

Kenton despised cooperating with a man he was sure would murder them all, cooperation notwithstanding, but he had no option. He obeyed.

"Now," Ottinger said, "you're going to go fetch me Pernell Jones back in the trading post. And you're going to carry him out, and all of us will go off to a private area and have ourselves a score-settling party."

"A bit of a problem there," Kenton said. "Jones is gone."

"He's not gone. The man was wounded. He's inside and you know it."

"He's gone, I tell you! Why do you think we were getting ready to ride out? We were going to look for him."

"Going for a doctor, that's what you were doing. Or maybe for a territorial marshal."

"Both of us? Not likely. We were going to look for Jones, and that's no lie."

Ottinger was clearly debating whether to believe this. "It's true," the trussed-up Joe Rush said. "We kept watch last night in case you were still around. I fell asleep before dawn, and he slipped out. He wasn't hurt as bad as you might think."

"Running from me!" Ottinger declared.

"More likely coming out to find you," Kenton said. "He was talking about doing that. He didn't want to bring danger down on other people. It's the same reason he disbanded his people at Confederate Ridge before you could overrun them with your soldiers . . . and no doubt find an excuse to massacre them."

"You sing the same songs forevermore, eh, Kenton? Any I've 'massacred,' as you choose to put it, have been killed because they merited the fate. War is ugly, Kenton. You clearly didn't have the stomach for what war sometimes requires."

"There are crimes, even in wartime. And the war is long over now, Colonel. If you'd killed any at Confederate Ridge, you would have been killing citizens of a territory of your own nation, not at war against you."

"As I understand it, Jones and his people didn't consider themselves citizens, and for them, the war was still on."

"They wanted only to be left alone. And whatever they considered themselves, citizens they were, and are."

"It doesn't matter now. I care only about Jones . . . and you. You should have never assassinated me in your journal, Kenton. The words you wrote, the lies, have hurt me through the years almost as much as this!" He pointed spastically at his ruined face. "I intend to see you pay for what you did to me, just like Jones!"

A shadow moved somewhere behind Ottinger; a rear door opened and sunlight spilled in.

Pernell Jones, outlined against the light, stepped inside. "Hello, Colonel," he said. "I should have realized you'd not have gone far away. It would have saved me some searching this morning."

"Jones! Come around here where I can see you, out of that light!"

Pernell Jones walked slowly into the shadows, where his features became visible. He moved somewhat gingerly because of his wound, and pain was in his eyes, but the brighter light in them was that of hatred for Ottinger. When Jones was beside Kenton, he stopped.

Ottinger stared at him, face-to-face. "You have a weapon hidden on you anywhere?"

Jones lifted his arms, then lowered them, slipped off his coat with much stiffness and wincing, and did a slow turn so that Ottinger could see he bore no weapon. "I dropped my rifle outside," he said.

"You're a damned fool, then. You could have shot me from behind and been done with it."

"I thought about it. But I feared I'd injure one of these others. Besides, that's not how I settle my scores. If you want to settle our longstanding differences, Ottinger, do it in a manful way. You and I will go off, together. Fight this thing out however you want it. Knives, pistols, bare fists. But leave these people alone."

"You'll not set the terms for my actions, Jones. But you and I will go off together, indeed. And when you die, you'll die in the kind of suffering you've caused me all these years. Do you know what it is to be mangled? To have children stare at you, and women turn their heads?"

"I wasn't trying to mangle your face when I shot you," Jones said. "I was trying to blow your head completely off—due retaliation for the massacre you led. My aim was just a bit off."

"Too bad," Kenton muttered.

"Yes, it is too bad," Jones said. "My life would have been much different through all the years afterward if I hadn't had to spend so much of it dodging your hired assassins, Ottinger. What's the matter with you, anyway? Do you not have the courage to fight your own fights? Do you hire out every dirty job, afraid to take it on yourself? When I shot out your eye, did I blow off your manhood, too?"

"Damn you!" Ottinger hissed. "Damn you, Jones, I'll not hear that from you! We'll end this right now, right here!"

He shoved the boy with the muzzle of the shotgun, pushing him down. Raising the shotgun, he aimed first at Kenton, and fired.

Kenton, though, ducked just before the blast went off, and felt only the sting of a couple of pellets barely grazing the top of his head, scraping off a little hair and flesh, but doing no real damage.

Jones, despite his prior wound, dove through a stall door beside him and out of sight. Ottinger could have easily shot him right through the wall of the stall, but he couldn't see exactly where he was, and dared not risk expending the second barrel and leaving his shotgun empty.

Ottinger stepped forward to look into the stall. Kenton rose and lunged toward him, but the shotgun swung toward him and he was forced to stop.

"You . . . scar-face!"

Kenton looked up to see old Oliver Rush coming in the same rear door that had admitted Jones. The old man had his shotgun raised, aimed at Ottinger.

Ottinger swore and raised his own shotgun . . .

But not in time. Oliver Rush fired.

Most of the pellets missed Ottinger, but enough of them caught him on the left side of his face to blow out his only good eye and shred his flesh. He screamed and fell back, dropping his shotgun. Blind, he lay on his back, blood gushing, then pulled himself upright, feeling his ruined face.

The noises he made were terrible, and Kenton found himself, to his surprise, actually feeling a burst of pity for the terrible man. Then he reminded himself that many of those Ottinger had massacred had no doubt been just as pathetic in their last moments, and he had shown them no mercy at all. And what mercy had Callon seen? Or Milo Buckner?

Ottinger pushed himself to his knees. Bleeding and unseeing, he waved his arms around in the air, like a child playing blindman's buff. Then he bent over, hands on the strawy floor, groping until he found the shotgun he'd dropped. Kenton feared for a moment that Ottinger was going to fire it blindly in whatever direction he thought it would do the most damage, but almost instantly it became evident that this was not his intention.

Ottinger put the muzzle of the shotgun beneath his chin, propped the butt on the stable floor, and simultaneously with giving out a terrible cry, pushed the trigger.

Kenton stared at Ottinger, too stunned to move right away. Then he broke out of it, stepped forward, reached down, and took the shotgun from the man.

Ottinger's voice was gurgly, blood coming out of his mouth. "What happened? Why did it not fire?" he asked.

"The shotgun malfunctioned," Kenton said. "The shell didn't go off."

Ottinger moaned, for a long time, making the kind of noise that surely must rise out of hell. "Kill me!" he blubbered. "I can't live like this! Just like before . . . just like before . . ."

"Just like before, but with one difference," Kenton said, gently. "This time I don't think you're going to survive, Colonel."

The truth of this was obvious. Ottinger was losing blood rapidly.

"I'm blind . . . *all* my face is ruined now . . . all of it . . ."

"That's of no importance now," Kenton said. "I suggest, sir, that you take these final moments to make your peace with God."

Ottinger, though, did nothing but keep up his moaning. But it grew weaker; he slumped to the side.

Pernell Jones walked up slowly to him, looking down in horror at the man who had been his bane for years. It was hardly like looking at a man at all now.

Jones knelt, right in the spreading pool of blood. "Ottinger . . . you're dying."

"Jones? Jones . . . damn you, Jones . . . damn you . . ."

"Don't talk so, Colonel. Not at this time. Make your peace; you're a dying man."

Ottinger groped about him, searching for a weapon. "I'll kill you, Jones . . . I'll kill you, and Kenton too . . ."

Jones shook his head, stunned at the persistence of this man's hatred. He pulled away, stood, and stepped back.

Ottinger continued to moan and threaten, his voice growing weaker by the moment. Finally his strength was gone, and he lay on the barn floor, dying faster now, his voice gone.

Kenton watched Ottinger's chest heave spastically, drawing in its final breaths now, until finally it stopped moving.

"The depths of the man's hatred were incredible," he said. "I don't know that I've ever seen the like of it."

Jones, looking solemn, nodded, turned away, and would look at Ottinger no more.

It took a long time to settle down the women.

They had not been a part of all the violence that had erupted around them, and did not for some time understand what had happened. When finally they did, they urged that someone go find a territorial lawman—a suggestion not popular with any of the men.

Joe Rush said, "We have nothing to gain by involving the law in this. No one was here to witness any of this. And I don't want my father dragged into a bunch of trouble with the law. Not at his age. Everyone who was killed here, with the exception of Milo Buckner, was killed with perfect justification. I don't need my father hauled off into some courtroom, in his dotage, to suffer through some kind of legal nonsense just to reach the same conclusion we already know." He turned to Kenton. "And I don't want to see this little adventure recounted in the pages of *Gunnison's Illustrated American*, either, with all due respect."

Kenton nodded. “Some stories can’t be told. This is one of them.” It was a hard statement for him to make, for this was a grand story indeed, from the firefall on Gomorrah through the final, ironic death of the most wicked military man Kenton had ever known. Yet to tell the tale would be to compromise the safety and reputations of good people.

“What about Ottinger?” Jones asked. “Obviously there will be some sort of attempt to track down what happened to him. A high-ranking officer disappears from his command, then never returns . . . it will stir a lot of questions.”

“If we bury him deeply enough and keep our mouths closed, those questions will simply remain unanswered,” Kenton said. “As for those ambushers who died, I doubt any search for them will ever be made. They were probably just lone wolves, no family, no real connections. I’ve seen plenty of the type.”

“And good riddance to them two,” Joe Rush said.

Kenton turned to Jones. “But what about Milo? I hate for his end to be in some anonymous grave.”

“We’re all anonymous in the grave, Kenton. I’ll make sure that those who need to know what happened to him, will.”

“The Confederate Ridge folks?”

“Yes. That was the only family Milo had left.”

“But they’re dispersed now to Lord only knows where.”

“Not forever. They all know about my brother. They all know where to establish communication with me. We’ll come together again, if there is anything I can do about it.”

“Ottinger is gone, and so is his threat . . . unless his report blaming you for the destruction of Gomorrah comes back to haunt you.”

“If he ever filed that report at all. That report, I figure, was probably a pretext he would use to justify overrunning us. When we escaped before he could do that, he may not have cared anymore about blaming that fire on us. But who can know? We'll deal with that situation as it comes."

"So mum's the word on all that happened here," Kenton said. "Is that our agreement?"

"It is," Joe Rush said. "Now, let's round up some shovels. We've got some gravedigging to do."

CHAPTER THIRTY-TWO

THEY RODE INTO PEARL TOWN AT DUSK THE NEXT DAY.

Kenton, normally on top of almost any situation, was nothing but nerves. *She* might be here . . . or at the very least, the beginnings of a trail that would lead to her in the end.

What if he really did find her? What if he looked on her face after so many years? What would she look like? How would she respond to him?

There was another question, too, one a little too painful to dwell on: if she did prove to be alive, why had she remained apart from her own husband for so long? As high a profile as Brady Kenton possessed, it was obvious she could have reached him if she chose.

Unless something was wrong with her. If that long-ago railway accident hadn't killed her body, perhaps it had killed her mind.

The uncertainty of it all, the big questions and fears lingering, were a torment. In the back of his mind, Kenton prayed, and prayed some more . . . and dared to hope.

The fence around the Johansen house would have surprised Kenton had not Pernell Jones talked at length about his brother and his esoteric wife along the way. In other circumstances Kenton would have looked for ways to write about so unusual and eccentric a woman, but at this point he cared nothing for journalism.

He wanted only to settle the questions tumbling around in his head.

They reached the front gate. Kenton remained in the saddle, but Pernell Jones dismounted, went to the gate, and rapped.

The door opened and the same groundskeeper who had sent Gunnison on his way appeared and broke into a grin at the sight of Jones.

"I'll be, sir!" he said cheerfully. "We weren't expecting to see you!"

"It's an unexpected visit," Jones replied. "I've brought a friend, as you can see. But it's all right. He already knows pretty much everything. And we believe there's somebody here that he needs to meet."

Kenton waited as patiently as he could while brother met brother. Pernell Jones had much to explain to Livesay Johansen, who greeted the news of the dissolution of the Confederate Ridge compound with fury, and vowed that indeed the scattered ones would be reunited.

Jones held nothing back in his recounting, telling his brother every detail, including the facts of the death of Colonel Ottinger, and that his body was now hidden and his death itself a secret all who had witnessed it had sworn never to reveal.

"Let him be forgotten—it's fine with me," Johansen said. "I'll never speak a word of what you have told me to anyone, not even to Pearl."

"Where is Pearl?" Pernell asked.

Kenton, who had been walking slowly around the library where this meeting was taking place, examining the covers of books and studying the strange, occultish paintings Pearl Johansen had hung all about the walls, turned upon hearing that question. The subject was now moving around to his own area of interest here.

"Pearl has put herself in isolation," Livesay said. "I'm afraid she's angry at me for having run off a certain swindler who was foisting off some self-styled backcountry preacher as a prophet of God—all in hopes of getting his hands on as much of my money as he could, a process Pearl was all too willingly going along with."

"Excuse me, sir," Kenton said.

"Certainly, Mr. Kenton."

"This swindler . . . was he named Rankin?"

"He was."

"And you've run him off?"

"I have, sir. I held him for a time, made him believe I was going to prosecute him into the very bowels of the deepest prison in the nation, but in the end I let him go. I think he's learned his lesson, at least so far as bothering the Johansen household again. He'll not come back here, I don't think."

Kenton slumped into the nearest chair.

"Mr. Kenton!" Johansen exclaimed, rising. "Are you sick?"

Pernell Jones said, "He's not sick, Livesay. Just very disappointed. He'd been on his way to meet Rankin in Gomorrah when the fire came, and he's been trying to track him down ever since. Rankin claims to have information about Kenton's wife . . . who he claims apparently isn't dead, as Kenton has believed for years."

"Oh, my," Johansen said. "If I had had any notion of this, I'd not have let the scoundrel go. Wait a minute . . . might this wife of Kenton's have been *with* Rankin?"

Kenton came to his feet again. "It's possible," he said.

"There was a woman with him, you see, when he first came here. But she left after a short time. Rankin didn't seem to mind her leaving."

"Where did she go?"

"I don't know. I'm sorry."

"What about the preacher . . . Peabody, or whoever he was?"

"Gone, too. He's the one who finally broke down and confessed that Rankin was trying to defraud us, although I'd already figured that out from some quiet observation and eavesdropping. He left after that, and I let him."

Kenton thought he might be ill. To have built up so many hopes, to have come this far through so much trial and danger, only to have it all vanish like smoke before him, was nearly overwhelming.

"I'm very sorry, Mr. Kenton," Johansen said. "I feel I've unwittingly done you a great disservice."

Kenton forced himself to remain composed, even to smile. "You certainly had no way to know, sir. All you did, from your vantage point, was run off a confidence man preying on your wife."

"Rankin could yet still be in town. Any of them could be, for that matter. There was another man, too, besides Rankin and the preacher. A quiet fellow named . . . Shafter, I think. Seemed to be sort of just along for the ride. I sent him off even before I did Rankin. Shafter seemed to get a great lot of amusement out of seeing Rankin caught in the act."

Hearing that Rankin and company might yet be in the vicinity put a new spark in Kenton's spirit. "Indeed," he said. "Perhaps the thing for me to do is to begin exploring the town a bit, asking questions."

"Yes, indeed. As a journalist, I'm sure you're quite familiar with that process," Johansen said. "If they're to be found here, you'll be the man who can do it." He cleared his throat. "And though I must say I don't have much use for journalists in general, in this case I wish you great success."

"Livesay's been hounded for years by journalists wanting to take his time and have him discuss his own private fortunes with them in great detail," Pernell said.

"Indeed I have," Livesay said. "Why, just this week, my groundskeeper told me there was some young journalist at the gate, asking to come inside."

Kenton froze. "Young journalist . . . was his name Gunnison?"

"I have no idea."

"My partner's name is Gunnison . . . he thinks I'm dead, but apparently knows I was trying to find Rankin, and decided to take up my quest in my place."

"It might have been him, then. Rankin was here at the time. I suggest you find my groundskeeper and—"

Kenton was already out the door before Johansen had time to finish.

The groundskeeper was a suspicous-minded fellow, not eager to answer questions. Kenton was so intense in presenting them, though, that the man eventually relented, maybe in fear that Kenton would hurt him if he didn't.

"I don't recall if this fellow told me his name or not," the man said. "All I knew was he was another nosey word-scribbler, and I'm under stern orders never to let such a one in. So I sent him on his way."

"Did he leave town?"

"Far from it. I've seen him coming and going from the hotel yonder ever since. Saw him just today, as a matter of fact."

Kenton was out the gate almost at once, yelling his thank-you across his shoulder.

Gunnison, feeling poorly, had turned in early, but he wasn't resting well.

Illnesses, especially minor ones like the one that had him now, tended to give him nightmares. Dreams of ghosts, usually, people from the dead returning, sliding through the shadows, rapping on his door . . .

Rapping on his door . . .

He opened his eyes. Someone *was* at the door. He sat up, blinking, wondering what time it was.

"Just a minute!" he called. He lit a lamp and cranked it

up bright, then took time to light another. He didn't like it when nightmares melded too closely into reality. When the knocking had awakened him, he'd been in the midst of dreaming that he was back home with his wife, arms wrapped around her as she slept, when a rapping at the door had awakened him, and he'd gone to open it, as he was now, and before him stood the reanimated corpse of . . .

"Kenton!" Gunnison shouted the name as he opened the door.

Kenton cocked up one brow and smiled at him.

Gunnison did a slow turn and collapsed to the floor in a dead faint.

When he woke up, he was back on his bed and Kenton was in a chair beside him, bathing his brow with a cool, damp cloth.

"Don't worry," Kenton said in a voice that sounded very flesh-and-blood. "I'm no ghost."

"But I . . . there was your Mason's pin . . . there were maggots on you, and . . ."

"No need to get gruesome, Alex. That wasn't me. That was the highwayman who robbed me and took my coat, my pistol, and so on. I was lying unconscious out in the woods. It's probably what saved my life when the fire came down."

Gunnison stared at Kenton, then began to weep.

"Thank God," he said. "Thank God you're alive. I never could get it in my mind that you were really dead, even though I was sure I'd seen your corpse with my own eyes."

Overcome, Gunnison reached up and hugged his partner.

Kenton would have none of this. He quickly pulled away, stood, and walked a few paces from the bed. "Good heavens, Alex! We're not two sentimental old women, you know!"

Gunnison jumped out of the bed. "Oh, no."

"What is it?"

"I sent off a letter, just today, telling the *Illustrated American* of your death."

"And asking for my job, no doubt."

"I'd tried to send one before, but couldn't bring myself to do it."

Kenton laughed. "So now the world will think I'm dead! I think I like the idea. Good excuse for some time off from working."

"Kenton, how did you find me here?"

"It's a long story. I'll tell it later. For now I want to know if you ever found Rankin . . . and . . ."

"I never found Rankin, Kenton. I never could get to him in the Johansen house."

"What about . . ."

"Sit down, Kenton."

Kenton did. He was going a little white, looking a good deal like an authentic ghost now.

"Kenton, I think Victoria really may be alive."

"Did you find her?"

"No. But I found her sister."

Kenton went a shade whiter. "Katherine?"

"Yes."

"But Katherine died, too . . . in the same railway accident that killed Victoria."

"She didn't die. But she was hurt, her memory lost to her for years. Within the past two years, it's begun to return to her. She remembers the accident now, remembers crawling away from it, then walking. And Kenton: she remembers Victoria doing the same."

Kenton closed his eyes. "Dear Lord," he whispered.

"But she remembers nothing more, really. Nothing significant. She talked to Victoria, saw that she was hurt, but alive . . . somehow they were separated. The details after that are gone."

"But Victoria lived."

"Yes. She lived."

"Where is Katherine now?"

"I couldn't make her stay, Kenton. She slipped away from me. I first found her sleeping in rags outside a building near here; Rankin had apparently gotten tired of her, preoccupied with his prophesying preacher scheme, and she'd left him. I brought her in, fed her, talked to her . . . I first thought I'd found Victoria herself."

"But she wouldn't stay?"

"Kenton, I told her what I thought was true . . . that you'd died. So she didn't know you would come here. Also, she's a damaged woman. Very shy, fearful . . . she talked a lot about a man named Shafter, who traveled with Rankin and herself. She'd developed the idea he would find her and hurt her. So she left, even though I tried to make her stay."

"I wish she had."

"Kenton, I gave her my identification card. I told her how to reach the *Illustrated American*, if ever she remembers more about what became of Victoria. I suppose I had it in mind to find Victoria myself, even if you couldn't. I didn't know, of course, that you'd show up alive and well at my door."

"What was Rankin's purpose in sending for me?"

"A swindle. Katherine, you see, lived a very hard life. With her memory gone for years, with no connections, no work, no money, she wandered through the cities, one after another, doing what she could to survive. Some of what she told me is not at all a pretty story. Other parts she didn't tell were probably worse.

"In any case, she wound up somehow with this Gib Rankin fellow. Thought she was in love with him at first, though that faded as time went by. But she stayed with him for security, and when her memory began to return, she told him the things she recalled. Who she was, and who her sister was . . . and that her sister had married Brady Kenton."

"I see."

"Apparently, Kenton, Rankin heard somewhere the tale about how you have been searching for clues about what happened to Victoria, and hoping she is alive . . . I have to tell you, Kenton, that this search of yours for Victoria isn't as secret as you might have thought. Most of your professional peers, anyway, know about it, and some of them, I suppose, talk."

"I suppose."

"Rankin developed the idea that he could pass Katherine off as Victoria. He figured that the passing of years and the fact you couldn't know what Victoria would look like after all this time would give him a chance to make it all seem persuasive. What facts Katherine didn't know, or what things about her that didn't seem to fit, could probably be passed off as resulting from her damaged memory."

"The scoundrel . . ."

"Yes. But it was a clever scheme, in its way. Katherine went along with it, but she didn't favor it. She was afraid to defy him. Rankin's plan was to seek some big reward from you for reuniting you with your lost wife."

"I can guess the rest," Kenton said. "Rankin was waiting for me at Gomorrah, and then came this strange firefall, and the coincidental ravings of a drunken self-proclaimed preacher that chanced to fit the facts of what happened, and suddenly he saw before him a chance for bigger and better money than he could have gotten from me alone. He rode the crest of the terror over what happened at Gomorrah, told people, through the preacher, that he could assure them of escaping the same fate if only they supported the preacher's 'ministry' . . ."

"Absolutely right. And it worked well, until finally he landed here, with the rich and gullible wife of Mr. Livesay Johansen across the street, where even yet, I'm sure, he continues to roll in abundant donations."

"Not any longer. The preacher 'fessed up. Blew the whole scheme to pieces—apparently an honest soul at heart—and Johansen sent them packing."

"What? How do you know?"

"I just came from the Johansen house."

"You were *there?* For how long?"

"I only arrived today. Alex, I've got a long and amazing story to tell you, one that, unfortunately, I'll never be able to put into print without endangering the lives and welfare of people who don't deserve for that to happen to them."

"I'm eager to hear it."

"Let's go downstairs, then. I talk better over a cup of good coffee."

While Kenton and Gunnison talked late into the night in the cafe of the Johansen Hotel, Parson Forrest Peabody was enjoying himself immensely.

Rankin hadn't given him much money out of the "donations" they'd collected during his brief tour as a preaching prophet, but he'd gotten enough to have some fine times in the saloons here. He'd drunk his fill, which was a lot, and still had money left.

Given all the trouble over at the Johansen house, Peabody figured it would have been the better part of discretion to have left Pearl Town by now. But he'd made it no farther than the edge-of-town saloons.

Stepping out into the night with a cheap cigar clenched in his teeth, Peabody paused to light it. This required several attempts because his hands wouldn't stay still, but kept waving about in front of him, the match missing the cigar. Finally it connected, and he blew out a thick cloud of smoke.

As it cleared, he saw Gib Rankin striding toward him, his face dark with anger.

Peabody dropped the cigar. His eyes went wide, and he turned and ran.

Rankin caught up with him beneath the balcony of a cheap boarding house in which the upper rooms had permanent female occupants whose duties were to make sure the males who rented beds for the night were anything but bored.

Rankin grabbed Peabody by the collar and shoved him up against a porch rail.

"Do you know what you cost us, spouting off your mouth to Johansen? Do you realize how much money that old coot-woman was ready to hand us?"

"I'm sorry! I wasn't trying to make you mad!"

"Oh, but you did! I'm so mad I could kill you right here! Maybe I will . . . nobody in this damned town would care, or even know!"

Peabody tried to think of something to say. "God would know," he said.

Rankin laughed.

"Yes, sir, God would know!" a voice directly above said. "And send down fire from heaven on you, He might!"

Rankin looked up in time to see Thomas Shafter, his arm gripped by a grinning saloon girl, hold up a lighted kerosene lamp.

"Let the fire fall!" Shafter yelled. "Glory hallelujah!"

The lamp dropped right onto Rankin's shoulders, breaking and spilling burning coal oil down Rankin's back. Though his heavy coat protected him from immediate severe burns, it did render him a human torch.

Howling, he let go of Peabody, ran across the street, and immersed himself in a watering trough, splashing about, putting out the flames.

"Look there, preacher!" Shafter declared. "Got us a baptizing going on! *Ree*-vival time!"

Rankin came out of the water swearing, pulling out his soaked pistol.

Shafter already had out a pistol of his own. "Wouldn't do it, Rankin. I can send down some fire from my little heaven up here that would do a lot worse damage than that lamp did."

Rankin swore some more and shoved the pistol back into its holster. "Devil take all of you!" he declared. "Ain't neither of you worth fooling with!" He stomped off toward the edge of town, vanishing into the darkness.

"Believe we've seen the last of him, Parson Peabody," Shafter said.

"Yes." Peabody hardly had a voice.

"Well, evening to you. Been nice working with you, as long as it lasted. Ain't no bad thing that it's over. He wasn't ever going to share much of that money with us nohow."

"Yes . . . no . . . right." Peabody swallowed and tried to stop trembling. "I'm not feeling too well, Mr. Shafter. I think I'll go get myself another bit of medicine."

"You do that, preacher."

Peabody tipped his hat to Shafter and the lady, tucked his coat together, cleared his throat, and stumbled back toward the welcoming light of the saloons as off to the west, a shooting star cut a swath across the velvet-black sky.

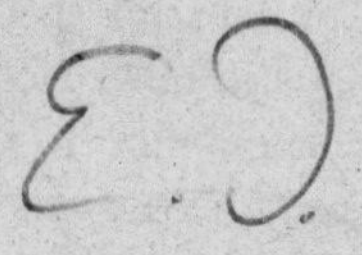